This is Dave Hill's third
Man Alive. He has al
newspapers and magazi
and sport. He lives in Eas
children.

Also by Dave Hill

Dad's Life
Man Alive

SINGLE MEN

DAVE HILL

R
review

Copyright © 2005 Dave Hill

The right of Dave Hill to be identified as the Author of the Work has been asserted by him in accordance with the Copyright, Designs and Patents Act 1988.

First published in 2005
by REVIEW

An imprint of HEADLINE BOOK PUBLISHING

First published in paperback in 2005

1

Apart from any use permitted under UK copyright law, this publication may only be reproduced, stored, or transmitted, in any form, or by any means, with prior permission in writing of the publishers or, in the case of reprographic production, in accordance with the terms of licences issued by the Copyright Licensing Agency.

All characters in this publication are fictitious and any resemblance to real persons, living or dead, is purely coincidental.

ISBN 0 7553 2631 8

Typeset in Baskerville by Avon DataSet Ltd,
Bidford on Avon, Warwickshire

Printed and bound in Great Britain by
Clays Ltd, St Ives plc

Headline's policy is to use papers that are natural, renewable and recyclable products and made from wood grown in sustainable forests. The logging and manufacturing processes are expected to conform to the environmental regulations of the country of origin.

HEADLINE BOOK PUBLISHING
A division of Hodder Headline
338 Euston Road
London NW1 3BH

www.reviewbooks.co.uk
www.hodderheadline.com

For Sheila, Carmel and Moira,
the fabulous Fitzsimons girls.

AUTHOR'S NOTE AND ACKNOWLEDGEMENTS

This novel is mostly set in the adjoining North-west London neighbourhoods of Kensal Rise and Queen's Park. My familiarity with the former comes from living there for a few weeks in a previous life; in the case of the latter it is because my sister-in-law and her children live near the park itself, resulting in my spending many hours there over the past eleven years pushing swings and kicking a ball. Given these connections I should emphasise that all the households I depict in the novel and all their residents are very fictitious indeed – at least, as far as I know. Other chapters are set in the medieval French town of Dol de Bretagne and a nearby campsite. Dol is a real and very charming place and I hope my descriptions of it, which are all from memory, do not deviate too far from the reality. The campsite is based on the one my family and I stayed at in the summer of 2004. Unlike Dol, I have adapted it for the purposes of my story. But if it sounds like your kind of holiday location you will find its most attractive features very similar to those of a true-life Breton one called *Camping Château des Ormes*.

The writing of this novel coincided with a period in my family life during which I have come to appreciate more than ever how special is my wife Sheila and how precious to me are my children Laura, Frankie, Nat, Dolores, Conall and Orla. I am thankful to my editor Martin Fletcher for displaying even more forbearance than last time, his assistant Catherine Cobain, my publicist Lucy Ramsey and everyone else at Headline, who continued to look after me so well. Finally, thanks as ever to my agent Sara Fisher of A.M. Heath Ltd, a distinguished company whose scandalous decision to move to more suitable premises I will probably forgive eventually.

Dave Hill

CHAPTER ONE

Now he was nearly five years old and in Reception class at school, Luke Amiss was discovering more things about his mother and becoming puzzled by his life with her. This didn't spoil the perfect pleasure of resting his head on her breast as she curled round him in his bed. It didn't stop him smiling shyly while she murmured promises about how big and strong he'd be one day. It did, though, mean he had questions for her.

'Mummy?'
'Mummy's asleep.'
'You can't be asleep, Mummy. It's not dark.'
'Yes, it is.'
'It isn't dark outside. I can see through the curtains.'
'It nearly is. And it's too late for little boys to be awake.'
'Mummy?'
'You want to grow up big and strong, don't you?'
'But Mummy?'
' 'Cos if you do, you need your beauty sleep.'
'But Mummy! Isn't it . . . ?'

'Oh Luke, don't you *ever* give in?'

Though Marie hadn't been asleep she could have easily drifted off as Luke's carousel bedside light sent vague animal shapes scrolling round the walls; could have slipped into slumber still folded around her child in spite of knowing she would wake an hour or two later feeling groggy and uncomfortable and down.

'But *Mummy*!'

'Shhh! I can hear Lynda.'

Marie normally heard her sooner. For at least the latter half of her twenty-two years she'd been able to detect her mother sneaking upstairs almost before the ascent began. This time, though, she didn't pick up Lynda's footfall until it had reached the landing and was nearly at Luke's door. For his part, Luke would have quite liked Lynda to join them. He had his best two cuddly toys with him as usual, a couple of floppy puppies called Big Cilla and Little Cilla (conveniently, Big Cilla was the larger of the two). But he held his silence as his mother asked. They waited and kept on waiting until the grandmother's footsteps receded and the bathroom door squeaked open and then closed.

'All right, sit up,' whispered Marie. 'Ten minutes, that's your lot. Is it a deal?'

'It's a deal,' Luke replied, using the brand new moany voice he'd learned from TV or from school. Marie didn't like this voice, but she ignored it. Luke had many voices and she knew he was just trying this one out. His eyes were glassy with a tiredness she'd learned to recognise; the type that fuels urgency in an anxious child.

'Come on, then. It's nearly half-past nine.'

'OK.' Luke continued looking at the roundabout silhouettes, but his mind had fixed on to something else.

'Mummy?'

'Yes?'

'Isn't it I've got a daddy?'

Marie cuddled Luke more closely, but didn't speak.

'Isn't it, though?' he said.

Marie pressed her cheek on to Luke's hair. It was dark brown, unlike hers, which was plain fair-ish at the roots but otherwise pure L'Oreal Champagne. 'Yes, Luke. It is,' she said softly.

'What's his name?'

'Luke, I . . .'

'Isn't it his name is Richard?'

'Yes, it is.'

'Interesting,' said Luke, and pinched his little chin meaningfully. This was a game he'd started playing lately, a ploy for confirming big things he already knew. He knew perfectly well that Richard existed. He also knew that Richard was usually called Rick. He knew the answer to his next question too.

'Are you married, Mummy?'

'No.'

'You have to be married to have babies.'

'No, you don't.'

'Yes, you do.'

'If you have to be married, Luke, how did I have you?'

'Hmmm,' frowned Luke and pursed his lips. 'Funny . . .' He frowned and then he made himself cross-eyed.

Cartoon befuddlement was something else he'd mastered recently.

'Very funny, yes.' Marie did not wish to pursue this topic further. She wanted Luke's weariness to get its way. He yawned and her hopes rose. But then he said, 'Why don't you marry Daniel?'

Marie laughed. 'I can't marry Daniel!'

'Why not?' Luke was re-energised. He liked to hit his mother's funny bone.

'Because I work for Daniel. And he doesn't want a wife anyway.'

'Why not?'

'He just doesn't! Lots of men don't.'

Luke's face turned up to hers. His smile was mischievous but his gaze was intense. Marie returned it and asked, 'Do you wish Elice was your sister?'

'Yes,' said Luke in a 'so what' tone and looked away.

Elice was Daniel's eight year old. It was an Older Woman Thing, according to Daniel, which was the sort of thing Daniel liked to say.

'It really is dark now, Luke,' said Marie, letting her voice go bedtime low. 'Monday tomorrow. School.'

This time the small boy didn't quarrel. His head fell to his pillow. Marie listened to the silence of the street.

'Can you marry Marlon?' Luke asked quietly.

'You never give up, do you?'

'But can you?'

'No!'

'Why not?'

'Because I don't want to marry Marlon.' This was

perfectly true, though Marie constantly wondered whether Marlon would quite like to marry her. Sometimes she imagined him proposing: a bended-knee job, deadly serious. If it ever happened, would she shame herself and laugh?

Marie put her lips to Luke's left ear. 'And I don't want to marry Guy, either.'

'Gabby says you should.'

'Gabby says a lot of things.'

And Gabby did. That afternoon beside the paddling pool in Queen's Park, she'd said she thought her knees were nasty, that she'd pencilled in Thursday for 'jumping on' new boyfriend Pete, and that if she were Marie and did the things she did for three such solvent single men, she'd definitely jump on one of them. Marie had known Gabby for ten years and still couldn't always tell when she was serious. In fact, Gabby quite often didn't seem to know herself.

'So which one should I jump on?' Marie had asked.

'The one with the biggest hands,' Gabby'd replied. 'Isn't it obvious?'

Guy had the biggest hands. He had the biggest hair, too. He was also the oldest and probably the richest. He had gold taps in his bathroom and a red Aston Martin parked outside. Every time Marie mentioned such details to Gabby, Gabby egged her on. It didn't put her off one bit when Marie insisted that no man alive could be less right.

'Give it a go, I say. You'd float his boat, no problem, lovely young lady like you.'

'But Gabs, I don't want to float his boat!'

'You'll end up a sad old spinster. Girl, I'm warning you.'

'I've got enough on my plate, thank you.'

Marie reviewed these conversations as, at last, the shutters came down on Luke's eyes. She switched off the carousel and was halfway to the window when she heard the bathroom door open again. She stopped still and her mind's eye monitored her mother emerging. The picture was so clear she could have framed it: wet hair piled high in a white towel; nails restored to blank pink slates ready to be filled the following day; white silk robe tugged round a body that, as Lynda liked to joke, was hardly any older than Madonna's; powdered feet that left a dusty trail. Then came the low burble of a bedside TV. The glam grandmaternal vision had taken to her boudoir with no plan to re-emerge.

Marie opened Luke's fish-patterned curtains an inch. The streetlights had flickered on, sealing Herbert Gardens in amber. Had she been that way inclined Marie might have characterised this part of Kensal Rise – the interwar-ish, Harlesden-borders part with its outbreaks of pebbledash, occasional bow-frontages and fancied-up porches – as just a little fallen, its once-confident modernity peeling like the paint from a few too many of its windowframes, including those Marie was peering from. But that wouldn't have been fair on the hardworking families who lived there. And it would not have been Marie. She was not a girl to seek out ironies or to savour melancholy. Never mind that her relationship with Rick had crumbled into ruins, she had clambered from them carrying her child. Never mind that the further Rick receded from her life the longer became the shadow he cast, Marie was sure the sun would set on him. And never mind, either, that a few hours earlier, on returning from Queen's Park, she and Luke had walked in to find Lynda sitting weeping, and some old diva croaking from the ageing stereo about the total eclipse of her heart. Marie expected such behaviour from her mother in July. The anniversary was just a week away.

Marie dwelled on these matters for barely a minute before letting the curtain fall back into place. Luke was snoring sweetly. She kissed him lightly on the forehead then stepped quickly from his room into her own next door. She undressed, throwing her jeans, T-shirt and underwear in a heap on the floor, pulled on her England football nightie and sat for a moment on the end of the self-assembly bed her mother had bought for her as a reward for getting good GCSEs. There was no more sound from Lynda's telly. Marie released a soft sigh of relief. Another day had become another yesterday.

And tomorrow?

Tomorrow, she had work to do.

CHAPTER TWO

Weekday mornings in the Amiss household were brittle thumbnail soaps. How might an episode begin? Well, maybe, at nineteen minutes past six with Marie fast asleep and Luke in his pyjamas, bounding in.

'Mummy! I want to wee. Will you come with me?'

'Oh Luke . . .'

'Mummy? I said—'

'I heard you, I heard you. Why don't you go by yourself like a big boy?'

Luke was clutching Big Cilla and Little Cilla. He was also clutching himself. He was hopping and he was leaking in short spurts. 'But Mummy, Lynda's in there,' he went on. 'Will you come downstairs with me?'

Marie groaned. She'd lain awake till after midnight thinking about Luke asking those questions about Rick.

'Quick, Mummy! Quick!'

'OK, OK.'

Marie struggled out of bed. She followed Luke and the two Cilla puppies as they scampered downstairs, grasping the banister and imploring, 'Lift the seat up, lift the seat up, lift the seat up, lift the seat.'

Luke lifted the seat but kept hold of both Cillas under one arm. This left one hand free with which to lower his trousers but the pressure on his bladder had become so great he had no time to re-deploy it to guide his aim. The upturned lid took the worst hit.

'Look where you're pointing it, Luke, *please*.'

Marie sat, defeated, on the bottom stair. Inwardly, she scowled up at Lynda – the queen of the household once again hogging the throne room just when someone else needed it most.

Luke had adjusted his direction. The new sound was like a fire hose blasted at an open drain. The crash of the flush followed, and Luke burst forth, pyjama bottoms tugged above his quivering pink prow but lodged below his buttock line astern. He half-hopped, half-ran to the front room where an electronic burp announced he'd switched on his keyboard. Soon came the lilt, pre-programmed, of 'Rocket Man'.

'Luke! Please! No!'

Marie, needing a wee herself, grabbed her tiny Elton and hoisted him away. Still fuming about Lynda she lugged him into the kitchen, peeled off his pee-damp nightwear and wiped him down with a J-cloth grabbed from the sink. He ran off, naked, moonwalking joyfully. She got hold of him again and hugged him back into the toilet where she closed and locked the door and he did the macarena as she, wielding the J-cloth again, frantically sponged lid, seat, floor and wall.

'Luke, will you be *quiet*!'

'Huh?' he said, bemused.

'Shhh!' she urged him softly. 'Shhh . . .'

She took his cheeks between her palms as she sat astride the porcelain. He stared into her face from underneath his fringe, as if aware of her presence for the first time. She was reminded of when he was first toddling and followed her everywhere, screaming whenever he was left alone.

'You'll have to have a shower,' she whispered.

'Uh-huh.' He nodded dumbly.

'Will that be nice?'

'Uh-huh.'

'Good.'

But he wasn't really listening. In his head he was away with Power Rangers or McFly, and when Marie at last coaxed him back upstairs and ducked into the bathroom her mother had finally vacated in order to dress and groom herself, he wouldn't join her under the water. She pursued him, pinned and sponged him while he begged for mercy and guffawed. And by the time she'd forced his school uniform on, it was seven forty-eight and Scene Two of the Amiss weekday morning drama was already overdue.

It was a set-piece at the kitchen table.

'Eat your Sugar Puffs, Luke, there's a good boy.'

He was stirring and humming and studying the packaging – everything except eating. Marie was in her dressing-gown, sipping a cold cup of Kenko, dimly registering the Radio 1 breakfast show.

SINGLE MEN

Chris Moyles: *Streuth, did I have a skinful on Saturday?*
Sidekick Dave: *I dunno. Did you?*
Chris Moyles: *I dunno either. Got so drunk I can't remember.*

Marie had not had this problem. She'd stayed in on Saturday night. These days she was forever staying in.

'Mummy? Where's the toy? I can't find it!'

Luke was rummaging for the presumed free gift. The box was nearly full, which meant its displaced contents had risen halfway up Luke's arm and begun spattering the table like polystyrene hail.

'Don't do that,' said Marie.

'Why not, Mummy?'

' 'Cos you're making a mess.'

'But Mummy! It says on the packet—'

'Just take your hand out. I'll look in it for you.'

'But *Mum-mee*!'

In walked Lynda, fragrantly, precision-clad in a floral print top and peach jacket-and-trouser combo flagging 'firmly feminine'. Marie, pretending not to see her, reached across the table and gripped the Sugar Puffs box violently.

'Luke, I said stop!'

This was supposed to make a point to Luke, to her mother, to herself – a point about demanding discipline. It seemed entirely lost on Lynda. 'What's the matter, Lukey? Can't you find your little toy? Here, let Lynda help.'

From a shelf she took her largest mixing bowl. Then she took custody of the Sugar Puffs by the neat expedient of lifting the inner bag clean out of the box, leaving her grandson and daughter clutching cardboard. With her back towards them, Lynda poured the contents of the bag into the bowl. When she turned back a toy rested on top, just like in a commercial. 'There you are, Lukey! What did I say?'

Luke grabbed the toy gleefully. It was a neopet: a tenner's worth of electronic twitch and chat. As such, it was no free gift. Lynda had bought it and sneaked it in. 'Thank you, Lynda!' Luke said glutinously, as if Lynda were Barney the dinosaur.

'That's all right, Lukey.' Lynda retuned the radio as she spoke. Terry Wogan was awaiting her.

Terry Wogan: *Now here's an ageing but still toothsome classic number you'll remember. It's that Tina Turner lass!* 'Simply the Best'!

'I'm going to get dressed,' mumbled Marie.

It was a cop-out exit line too. Marie could not tackle Lynda about spoiling Luke while Luke was in the room and she didn't have the heart to anyway. Back in her bedroom she pulled on her oldest jeans and a mauve *faux* rugby shirt and gathered up her gumption for the last mother-daughter cameo of the Amiss a.m. show which, true to routine, took place at eight-fifteen beside the full-length mirror in the hall.

'Do I look all right, Marie?'

SINGLE MEN

'You look lovely, Mum.'

'Do I honestly?'

'Yes. Honestly.'

Marie looked on wearily as Lynda dipped a hip, half-turned to one side and pouted slightly, sucking in her cheeks. 'Oh well,' she said. 'I'll have to do. See you later, babes.'

'Bye, Mum.'

'Bye-bye, Lukey!' called Lynda more loudly towards the open door of the front room where, in Marie's absence, she'd installed Luke before his small screen pal Nick Junior.

'Bye-bye Lynda,' came the reply.

'Kiss kiss!'

'Kiss kiss . . .'

This ritual complete, Lynda left Marie to savour her Chanel vapour trail and wonder, not for the first time, if the reception desk of a car dealership in Cricklewood merited quite such obsessive attention to appearances. Then she hurried back upstairs to change.

It was a cloudless morning, so balmy her anti-perspirant was already besieged. It was also a Monday – Daniel's Day.

Marie sifted quickly through her T-shirt drawer: viscose tropical halter; crochet orange vest; hot pink croptop with the words *Big In Texas* picked out in sequins on the front. Each would delight Daniel in its different way, but each risked inviting unwelcome attention too. Before going to Daniel's she would be taking Luke to school. Revealing the recovered flatness of her tummy in the playground risked attracting certain judgements by other pupils' mothers. These did not bother Marie for her own sake – her self-doubt did not extend to her virtue – but for Luke's. It had not escaped his notice that the Jakes and Ellas among his infant peers had parents who looked older than his gran. His mum, by contrast, could pass for his big sister, and other people's children could be cruel.

With a *frisson* of bold decision Marie picked the *Big In Texas* top and rolled it on. From a hanger in her white wardrobe she took an oversized jean jacket. If she fastened all the buttons, her midriff would be concealed. She threw her wide, white gunslinger belt into her little pink rucksack and slid her silver gypsy earrings into the back pocket of her jeans. In her dressing-table mirror she checked the tumble of her topknot and then, in an act of emulation that would have bugged her had she recognised it as such, dipped a hip, half-turned to one side, pouted and sucked in her cheeks.

'Mummy!'

He was calling up the stairs, suddenly aware he was alone.

'Coming, Luke!'

Marie's bedside clock informed her that it was eight forty-eight. She put the jean jacket on, slung the rucksack over one shoulder and hurried to her child.

'Cupcakes!' he gleamed from his front door.

'Good morning, Daniel!' Marie sang. How she longed to be cool and carefree, but already a blush was on the rise.

'Looking good,' Daniel said. He gave the 'good' the inflexion of a single raised eyebrow and let it lounge on his tongue like a Siamese draped over a *chaise-longue*. 'Bit of hipswing, bit of navel action. What's the T-shirt say?'

During the walk down from Luke's school Marie had drawn the gunslinger belt from her rucksack and lashed it low around her pelvis, bandit-style. The jean jacket had been tightly packed away and the big earrings put in place. In a shop window reflection she'd mascara-ed just a little and lip glossed quite a lot, reminding herself never to let Luke borrow her compact again. As she'd approached Daniel's door she'd felt a little clench of deep-down anticipation even though she knew it was absurd – or maybe because she knew. She'd pulled his door key from her purse feeling excited and exposed. Would he somehow see the sensations bubbling inside her, just as he seemed to see everything else?

'Hey, Cupcakes! I said what's the T-shirt say?'

She walked faster and he followed her down the hall. She was already foraging under his kitchen sink by the time he caught up. 'Just a *minute*, Daniel!' she said.

'What are you looking for?' he asked and squatted next to her.

'I'm looking for the rubber gloves.' She lied. The truth was she was burying her face.

'Kinky,' he teased.

'Oh stop it,' she begged.

'All right, I'll go away.' He chuckled and got up, but didn't leave the room. A few feet to Marie's right, cups clinked in a continental way.

'Coffee, Cupcakes?' Daniel enquired. In the corner, his Gaggia steamed expectantly.

'Yes, please.' Marie felt safer on the ground of gratitude. She emerged from beneath the sink and was relieved to find that Daniel was not looking at her but absorbed at his windowsill, watering the herbs. It was a moment of advantage for Marie. She seized it, secretly surveying her employer from the rear.

Daniel was thirty-seven but he could have been much younger. He had retained something of that string-bean physique common among teenage boys and had the type of haunches Gabby termed 'squeezable'. Daniel's shoes were chunky brown suede brogues. His jeans were crisply laundered and weathered impeccably. His T-shirt was tight-fitting and dark blue. The sunlight streaming through the glass picked out grey flecks in his wavy, dark brown hair.

He set aside his watering can and turned her way. '*Big In Texas*, eh?' He read it brazenly, straight off her chest. 'An' thet ain't no Bible belt you're wurring, Missy-Lou.'

Coming from any other man Marie had ever met, this would have been unnerving lechery. For Daniel, though, she let her hands hang at her sides and, conquering her nerves, stood there very still. 'What do you think?'

Daniel leaned back against his worktop, with his palms flattened against the stained wood surface. He observed her, smirking fondly.

'You're such a *sexy* thing,' he said. 'Why aren't hundreds of boys chasing you?'

'Honestly!' scolded Marie, concealing a massive surge of joy. 'Because I've got a baby, maybe?'

'You don't have to tell them that – not straight away.'

'Because I don't want to be chased?'

'You don't?'

'Not really, no.'

'Cupcakes. Please. *Everyone* wants to be chased.' He leaned towards her, rotating his cod-reproachful eyes.

'*You* might,' she replied. 'Some of us are more willing to wait.'

'Yes, yes, and *miaaow* to you too.'

He looked a little distant then. Like a waitress wiping a table, Marie rushed to sponge the stain of silence away.

'So did you have a nice weekend?'

'Not really, darling, no.'

'Oh dear.'

Daniel did not elaborate. With a twinge of disappointment Marie deduced that his teasing was partly a performance to disguise his dismay. His heart was in its unhappy place. Marie knew not to go there straight away. She would, though, make it known she was willing to pass that way. 'How's Elice?' she asked.

'As brilliant and beautiful as usual. Went off this morning humming "Summertime" with *The Wind in the Willows* under her arm.' As he spoke Daniel moved to the frothing Gaggia and began working the handles and taps. He went on: 'The truth is, Cupcakes, I'm blue.'

'Oh dear.'

Daniel paused while placing cups on the table: wide, clunky white ones on matching saucers.

'It's Miss Valencia,' he said. 'The usual thing.'
'About Elice?'
'Inevitably.'
Marie sat down and enquired, 'What's happened?'
'Bitch only wants to steal her. Take her away to *El Cid* country and turn her into a fellow termagant.'
'That's terrible,' said Marie, wondering what a termagant might be. Something vicious and selfish, presumably.
Daniel sipped his coffee. Marie took this as a cue and did the same. Daniel said, 'I met her on Friday evening in a restaurant near the shop. Not that she *ate* anything, of course. She just went on and on and on . . .'
Marie was starting to feel tiny. Daniel's depressions had a shrinking effect on her, unlike his playfulness, which buoyed her so wonderfully. He switched to his Miss Valencia voice. ' "Hi must be with my *bay-bee*! Hi ham a *mother*, hi ham *forlorn*!" '
Marie had never met Miss Valencia, or heard her speak. She was quite confident, though, that Daniel's impersonation was just like having the real thing in the room. Daniel was good at mimicry; even better than Luke. He dropped the accent and went on, 'She sat there, raging, orbs oozing . . .' He released a low hissing sound, conveying mixed resignation and dismay. 'Whatever was I thinking of, that night?'
There was no answer to this – at any rate, none Marie felt qualified to provide. Daniel seemed to take this as read. Perhaps he assumed that Marie had no answer to the same question when she asked it of herself. Perhaps he would have been right.

SINGLE MEN

'Anyway, Cupcakes,' he said, doing his B-movie sorrow-and-regret. 'This is where I say, "That's enough about me. Let's talk about you instead".'

Marie giggled, because she knew Daniel wanted her to. Then she told him the one or two things that had happened to her lately that she wanted him to hear. She didn't mention Lynda weeping over her LPs or reveal how poor and inadequate she had felt on Friday evening after going with Luke to the birthday party of a classmate whose father was an architect and who so clearly was destined for better things. She mentioned going to the park with Gabby, though. And she told him about taking Luke to have his hair cut on Saturday morning. Daniel teased her, suggesting that the real reason she went there was that the young barber liked to flirt with her, not to mention all his customers. Marie denied this strenuously, even though it was fairly true. Then Daniel rose and said, 'Well, duty calls. But first, a gift for you.'

He rose and sashayed to a cupboard. From it, he produced an unopened bottle of Flash liquid.

'It's brand new and just for you,' he said. 'I know you're going to get on famously.'

'You shouldn't have,' said Marie, who'd learned that such a response was desired.

'You're probably right,' Daniel said. 'But, Cupcakes, I adore you, can't you see?'

Did Daniel adore her? Marie thought he did, in a certain way. As for other ways, well, she'd once dreamed of Daniel, and his tongue was *everywhere*. She'd felt safe inside the dream. She felt safe with Daniel in real life too because she knew the dream would not come true.

She'd found him through a woman who worked at the nursery she used to send Luke to. Once he'd stopped clinging and wailing and refusing to be left and Marie had stopped going home to cry about it, she'd made it known to people there that she was seeking part-time work now that she had free time in the day. The woman, whose name was Christa, had told her she would talk to an old friend. Christa was roughly Lynda's age, but otherwise could not have been more different. She wore monkey boots, no make-up and no bra. 'You'll like Daniel,' she'd said. 'His daughter used to come here. He's sweet.'

Marie had never heard a grown man described as 'sweet' before, unless he was an old-age pensioner. And although Christa had told her that Daniel was in his thirties, when she'd set off to meet him, she'd been unable to shift her expectation that a dear old gentleman, perhaps a widower, would come shuffling to the door.

The appearance of the house did nothing to dispel the misconception. It was on Chevening Road, a short section of which bordered the north side of Queen's Park. There was no car in the front yard but a quaint old bicycle, and ivy cascaded round the door. It was mid-October, and heaps of fallen leaves had gathered undisturbed. Marie had expected things to be different round here, for Queen's Park was much more posh than Kensal Rise. To her, though, richer meant smarter and newer. She was unprepared for affluence embracing a bohemian vision of the past. That vision had a name. It was Elice.

She'd stood there in the doorway looking Marie right between the eyes. 'You're here for Daddy, aren't you? Follow me.'

She'd worn a 1930s flapper frock, a little pillbox hat, a string of beads that dangled right down to her waist and flat silk slippers studded with fake pearls. She'd seemed to Marie to be in fancy dress and yet hadn't behaved as though she were. There'd been no embarrassment at being seen by a stranger togged up in this way and no hint of childish showing off. She'd simply led Marie down a hall with a strip of grey-blue carpet, laterally striped, on its timber floor and old-fashioned paintings of arrows and angular shapes along its walls. Daniel was waiting for her in a book-lined study, perched at a desk with rounded corners and a decorative wood inlay round its edge. At his elbow was a lamp in the shape of a naked lady with wings like a giant butterfly. Elice had offered Marie a large, old armchair that looked to her like it belonged in one of those black-and-white movies she'd half-watched in the afternoons on Channel 4 when she'd been miserable with Rick and Luke was learning how to crawl.

'So you're one of those young single mothers,' Daniel had said, acting aghast.

'Yes, I suppose I am.' Marie had kept smiling, though every instinct was already telling her she ought to run away.

'Always pleased to meet a fellow social outcast,' Daniel had smiled.

'Oh. OK,' replied Marie. How could she work for such a weirdo? But if she bottled it, what would Lynda say? 'Why didn't you go back to your A levels, babes? Do them at college. Do them from home.' And other ways of saying 'told you so'.

Elice had then asked her, 'What's your little boy's name?'

'Luke. He's four.'

'I knew a Luke once,' Daniel had said wistfully.

'Did you, Daddy?'

'Just the once. That was enough.'

Father and daughter had giggled privately, and Marie had felt a pang of jealousy. Then Elice had asked if Luke enjoyed music. Marie had wondered who was running this interview.

'Yes. He loves music. He's always singing.' Was this the right thing to have said? Marie hadn't a clue.

'Does he like books?'

'Not so much. Not really.'

'Oh well. Art?'

'He likes art, yes. He does lots of painting.'

'Which artists does he like?'

'Um, well, he just really likes the painting. Especially boats. He's mad about boats.'

'He sounds enchanting,' Daniel had said.

'That's one word for him,' Marie had replied adoringly, and all of a sudden she'd been doing all the talking, at first edgily and then with intoxicating fluency. 'He's a

SINGLE MEN

little monkey sometimes, but he's got so much energy. He does voices – funny voices – and imitates what he sees on TV.'

'Brilliant,' went Elice.

'*Top of the Pops*, he loves that. And *Stars in their Eyes* . . .'

'Fantastic,' went Elice.

'He's a little actor, really. A proper little show-off, actually.'

'Tell me,' Daniel had intervened. 'Would ten pounds an hour do?'

'Oh. Right. Thank you. Are you sure?' Marie hadn't arrived with any firm figure in mind. But this was more than she'd allowed herself to dream.

'Lovely. Great. Fine,' she said.

'Four hours a week ought to do it. Does that suit?'

'Fine. Great. Lovely.'

'There won't be all that much to do. I'm quite clean for a boy, apparently. Elice's room's a very different story. A seething pit of squalor. The last cleaner who went in there has yet to reappear.'

Elice had winked at Marie. They'd exchanged smiles for the first time.

Marie started the next Monday. She arrived at eleven and spent the first half an hour just looking round. She'd never been anywhere even a bit like this before. Like the table and lamp in the study, the living-room furniture was from another time, one Marie could not quite place except vaguely in relation to expensive retro greetings cards, the sort she never bought. The cutlery was bone-handled and the dinner-plates were square. There were many cookery books, but not one was by Jamie Oliver.

Marie had cleaned the bathroom, with its bevel-edged mirrors and Jazz Age tiles. She'd cleaned the kitchen, top to bottom, though she'd been frightened to touch the Gaggia. She was diligent, meticulous, quite desperate to please, but there hadn't seemed an awful lot to do. She'd peeped into Elice's bedroom, just to see. Not one inch of the floor was visible. She'd returned the Hoover, bucket, mop and cleaning cloths to their places and even then it was barely two o'clock. She'd killed twenty minutes blowing dust off ornaments, until her conscience permitted her to leave.

That evening she had received a phone call.

'Marie? Daniel here. Beautiful job you did today.'

'Oh. Thank you.'

'And Elice agrees. Did you look in her bedroom?'

'No . . .'

'You should have. It's hell in there.'

'Well, maybe next time.'

'Delightful.'

'Um . . .'

'Yes?'

'I'm sorry, but it only took three hours.'

'Don't let that worry you. I'll sort your money out for you next time.'

And so things had proceeded until the end of the year: Marie doing her best to fill up the four hours, Daniel thanking her and leaving an envelope containing forty pounds in cash. Then, in January, Luke started at primary school and Marie began arriving at Daniel's earlier. That was when the coffee chats began. He'd have just got back from delivering Elice to her little private school and insist Marie sat down when she arrived.

The Gaggia bubbled and Daniel told her things: that the framed picture in the kitchen of a red-mouthed woman leaning on a typewriter wearing a tilted, wide-brimmed hat was, in fact, an advert for Olivetti from 1935; that the big, flat-fronted cabinet in the living room was, in fact, a cocktail cabinet and when you opened the front a light came on revealing a mirrored interior and a row of shallow glasses individually housed; that the funny black telephone with a dial instead of buttons was no less than a Bell 300, designed by Henry Dreyfuss and a classic of modern industrial design. 'Modern at the time, of course,' Daniel explained.

He'd also explained that artefacts like this were his business: stuff from the 1920s and 1930s. He had a mail order operation and a shop in West Hampstead. Then, one February morning, he had said, 'Marie, we have a lot in common, you and me.'

'Oh. Do we?'

'Of course we do. We're both bringing up children on our own.'

'Well, yes.'

'We're both between men, as they say.'

'Oh. I see.'

'We share the same Jeyes Fluid genes.'

'But . . .' Marie hesitated. She couldn't turn back now. 'What about Miss Valencia?'

'An aberration. A one-off. I thought she was a TV: that

body hair, that baritone, that high-class hooker look they go in for.'

Marie looked puzzled – a TV?

'Stands for transvestite, Cupcakes. You know: transvestites? Chaps in skirts?'

'Oh. Oh I see.'

'You know how it is. A dark portal beckoned. I was very drunk indeed. The rest is history. So, you and me – we're both living with the price of past mistakes. Speaking of which, where's yours?'

'My mistakes?'

Daniel had emphasised the singular. 'Mistake-*uh*. Little Luke's dear daddy, I mean.'

'I don't really see him any more.'

'Boys – who needs 'em, eh?'

She'd looked at him blankly. He'd smiled warmly. 'We're going to be great friends, you and me.'

It was the first time he'd called her Cupcakes. It was also the occasion when he asked her if she'd mind picking Elice up from school now and again. He'd pay her extra for this service – it went without saying – and for a cab so she could fetch Luke from his school first and then collect Elice. 'Why, they might even become friends.'

At that stage Marie still wasn't sure about Elice, despite the smile they'd shared at the interview. Her bedroom was intimidating – not the clutter but the contents. She seemed to have the tastes and interests of someone at least three times her age. Even so, Marie gladly agreed to become a childminder as well as a cleaner and, more organically, a confidante. The fact was, she was so pleased to perform whatever duties Daniel asked of her that she occasionally stopped and wondered why. But he was so easy to talk to, and seemed so interested in her, that in no time at all she'd told him all about Luke and Lynda and why she didn't want to study A levels just now. The thing was, she trusted him. It even seemed completely natural when she told him that her dad had died when she was just fourteen.

CHAPTER THREE

Memories of Clay – her father, Clayton Amiss RIP – did not exactly haunt Marie. But they did ghost up on her occasionally.

It might happen when she was meeting Luke from school: a boisterous father would hoist a little girl on to his shoulders or invite one to jump into his arms, and Marie would try to remember whether Clay had ever been such a father and she so worshipful a little girl. Or else it might happen at home. Here, the memories were sharper. Yet they were clouded in a different way. Adolescence had transformed her father in Marie's eyes from a man who liked a joke to one who laughed a bit too loudly to be true.

This clashed with the version of Clay that Lynda kept alive. The photos she displayed of him, the camcorder footage she stored and the anecdotes she sometimes told insisted that their marriage had been all sweetness and light. Marie, though, saw many shadows in the past. And when Lynda fussed round Luke too much, or spoiled him

SINGLE MEN

too shamelessly, it hardened her suspicion that Lynda had been Clay's doormat, his servant and his mother hen.

Such speculations didn't darken many of her days. They did, though, sometimes darken her Tuesdays.

Tuesday was Marlon's day.

The first part of the morning went much like the one before. Both Luke and Lynda tried Marie's patience in their distinctive ways: Luke by communicating entirely in lion language, an attention-seeking blend of harassing infant English and bloodcurdling roars; Lynda simply by being the fretful, fragile creature she became every July. Marie's underlying mood, though, was quite different from on Monday. There was no flustered change of clothing after her mother left the house, no flushed anticipation of the fake flirting and flattery provided by Daniel. For Marlon she wore old joggers and a nylon overall because to do for Marlon was to be downbeat and, for the most part, all alone: alone with the strictly non-intimate clothing items he left for her to iron; alone with the ornate Italian furniture that felt so oppressive in a young bachelor's pad; alone with the often tragic contents of his fridge.

Marlon worked as something in the City. Marie did not know what sort of something, but she was starting to know Marlon – enough to grasp that he was a lost soul.

She went through his front door, then a newer internal one, and climbed his stairs. Marlon occupied the upper half of a house on Milman Road, which bordered the western side of Queen's Park and formed a junction with

Chevening Road – Daniel's road – at its top end. Entering the kitchen, Marie sniffed the air. Marlon owned a book called *Household Management for Men*, yet elementary tasks such as opening a window or emptying his bins seemed beyond him.

These failings stirred sorrow in Marie, who saw Marlon's domestic helplessness as evidence of his unhappiness. Her sorrow, though, was also for herself. Being at Marlon's brought home starkly that she would never lead a *Cosmopolitan* lifestyle in a smart flat overlooking a nice park. As she wiped down Marlon's sink top or cleared clutter off his floors she recognised the burdens of motherhood more clearly, disliked her dependence on Lynda more intensely and, rewinding her life story to a point preceding both, found herself pondering her mixed feelings about Clay. Doing for Marlon was more than a menial matter to Marie: it was how she contacted what might have been.

After putting a dying lettuce out of its misery, Marie left the kitchen airing and checked elsewhere. As usual, she had this feeling that Marlon wasn't really living there. Every treasure and trinket in Daniel's house reflected its owner's sharply-defined identity, yet Marlon's interiors seemed to have been imposed by some overwhelming external personality that crushed the daylights out of his own.

The living room was where this mismatch reached a crescendo. Elsewhere the sofa and two armchairs would have looked marvellously palatial. Here, though, they simply seemed too grand. Each piece was puffed-up, tasselled and tufted with gilded inlays and carved wooden frames. There was a bossy sort of coffee-table and footstools swarmed everywhere. The overall effect was of an exclusive salon where powerful men conversed amusingly. Yet Marlon was just one man and there was nothing of the potentate about him. Above a fancy fireplace hung a family portrait: father and mother, daughter and son, their teeth gleaming with prosperity. Marlon was the youngest and the smallest: the photograph was recent, but he looked about thirteen.

Marie went to the bathroom, which had become a little slimy. She did not, though, check the state of his bedroom. She never did. That was because Marlon kept it locked. Marie did not, however, find this strange or insulting. Instead she put it down to boyish embarrassment. At twenty-four Marlon was two years her senior, yet she saw him as a child in grown-up's clothes. She'd never quizzed him about his bedroom and he'd never mentioned it. *Don't ask, don't tell*: the dictum summarised a part of their relationship. It was a diminishing part, though.

Having taken stock of the tasks confronting her, Marie did what she always did next: she headed for the kitchen's utility annexe where Marlon's ironing board and washing machine lived. Marlon was a light touch employer to the point of indifference. Two things, though, mattered urgently to him: one was Marie's regular presence in his home, even though he'd shared it only a few times; the other was his shirts. For a domestic dunce he washed these efficiently but couldn't iron them to save his life and he needed a freshly pressed one for each day of the working week.

It was when Marie went to discharge this latter duty that she first sensed a looming emergency. Normally, a pile of clean but crumpled shirts awaited her. On this particular Tuesday, though, there were none. She'd just made this discovery when she heard the front door close. This perturbed her slightly because her previous – and so memorable – encounters with Marlon had all happened later in the day.

She tiptoed into the kitchen, listening hard. She called, 'Hello!'

There was no reply, only the plod of laboured footsteps on the stairs.

'Hello-oh!' she called again, as falsely casual as could be.

The plodding halted on the landing, at which point Marie broke cover. A slight, tentative figure in a beige suit, white collar and blue tie stood with his forehead pressed hard up against the wall.

'Marlon! You made me jump!'

Without shifting from its peculiar lean-to position the figure spoke. 'Hello, er, Marie.'

He looked forlorn and disconnected – even more than usual.

'Why aren't you at work?' Marie asked.

Marlon eased himself upright. 'Sadly, I didn't get to work.'

'Why not?'

'Shamefully, it seemed more sensible to wander in the park.'

His strained formality was normal, as was his language of perpetual regret. What was different on this day was the impression he gave of talking to somebody else – somebody who, unlike Marie, he expected to give him a hard time.

'You look *dreadful*,' said Marie, recovering her poise. 'You ought to sit down.' She felt oddly as if she were the person who lived in the flat and he was some long-lost eccentric relative who'd walked across a desert to be there.

'Yes. Thank you, er, Marie.'

He wandered into the living room. Marie let the cold tap run and found a glass. When she took the water to him Marlon was sitting, slumped, half-swallowed by an armchair that might have been made for a Roman emperor.

He stared into the distance, absently.

'Here you are,' said Marie over-loudly, concerned that her message would not get through.

'Thank you,' said Marlon. He took the glass without looking her way.

'Are you ill?' asked Marie.

'In a sense I may be.'

Whatever did that mean? There was another too-long silence.

'Why don't you go to bed? I can carry on without disturbing you.'

'I don't think so. Thank you anyway.'

'Actually, Marlon, I think you should.'

'Do you?'

'Yes, I do.' Her gentle insistence concealed a mighty urge to poke him with a stick – or a feather duster at least. Yet she knew that if she did, he would just close up like a sea anemone.

He said, 'I'd like to ask you something, er, Marie.'

Oh my God, she thought. This is it. Would she, er, go out with him? Would she possibly, er, agree to be his wife? And how could she say no? It would be like dumping a puppy beside a road.

'It's quite a personal thing,' Marlon said.

'Oh. Really?'

'It's, ah, a bit difficult, actually.'

'Well, Marlon, if I can help . . .' Even as she said this, Marie heard in her own voice the terrible false lightness of a telesales technique.

'It's . . . It's . . .' Marlon began. He looked at Marie quickly, then away. His body seemed to shrink inside his already over-large clothes. Marie waited nervously. Marlon turned to her with lowered eyes. 'I, ah, need to send some flowers,' he explained. 'I wondered if you'd help me with it, er, Marie.'

'Of course. Of course I will. Don't do that to me, Marlon! I wondered what you were going to say!' Her relieved laugh failed to lift the mood.

'There is a company I'm using,' Marlon uttered miserably. 'There is a catalogue . . .' He flapped a hand towards the door defeatedly. 'I'd like you to look at it with me.'

'I'll get it for you, shall I?' said Marie. She bolted without waiting for a reply. In the kitchen she rooted for the catalogue and wondered what to do. Marlon looked so wrecked and faded. Should she call a doctor? An ambulance, maybe? Even if she did, what could she say? A sad young man's difficulty with sending somebody flowers did not qualify as an emergency, except perhaps in magazines like *Zoo*.

She found the catalogue behind the toaster, half-hidden by an old *Financial Times*. The company was called Worth Waiting. Beneath the bouquet on the cover was the slogan *Purity Blooms*. Marie, though, didn't really take this in. She heard a thud from the living room and rushed back to Marlon. The glass of water she'd brought him had fallen to the floor and Marlon appeared to be asleep. Marie looked at his head – his dark, bewildered head, with its wavelets of ebony hair – resting awkwardly on the arm of the ludicrous armchair and wondered if she should tuck a cushion underneath it. Then, from a small, pointless cabinet in the corner of the room came the click of his ansaphone. Obviously, he'd switched off the ringer. The message being left, though, came through loud and clear.

'Marlon, I must speak with you urgently. I have learned that you're not at work and that this has been happening frequently. It is embarrassing for me personally. Please do not ignore this call. As your father I expect better from you.'

Marlon did not stir.

When Marie secured the job in Milman Road she hadn't known she'd be doing for Marlon. A formal interview was conducted at the flat by a woman in her fifties who looked to have been carved from deep-frozen anti-ageing cream. Marie had assumed, quite reasonably, that the flat was hers and taken from her tart manner, serious suit and expensive-looking scarf that she was a businesswoman of some kind, or possibly a doctor or lawyer. Her face was pale and disapproving, and her helmet of greying hair had ashen tints. She was one of the whitest people Marie had ever seen, yet she said her name was Mrs Alibhai. With an impressive fountain pen poised above an A4 pad she'd asked Marie about GCSEs: 'What grades did you get in which subjects?'

'My GCSEs?' said Marie, startled and yet trying to sound pleased. 'Oooh, now let me see . . .' She'd glanced nervously round the kitchen, which was newly fitted and as sterile as a show home. She saw that there'd be no biscuits or tea.

'I got an A in Food Technology.'

'As they call cookery these days.'

'Do they? Oh yes.'

'And?'

'And an A in Humanities.'

'Go on.'

'Erm. Two Bs, I think. One was in English. I think the other one was in French.'

'You only *think* so, do you?'

This had stung Marie. It was six years since her exams and a lot of things had happened to her since. And how many GCSEs did a bloody cleaner need?

'It *was* French. And I got three Cs: the other English and two Sciences. The others were—'

'I'm not interested in those,' said Mrs Alibhai. 'And A levels?'

'I didn't finish them.'

'Oh? Why not?'

'My dad died of a heart attack. My mum needed my help around the house. That's how I got good at housekeeping.'

'I see.'

Affecting neutrality, Marie had let the bombshell do its work.

'I'm sorry,' offered Mrs Alibhai.

Marie had shrugged – that's life – and savoured her interrogator's momentary unease. Clay's death came in handy now and then. And in prompting Mrs Alibhai to give family matters a wide berth, its mention had ended any prospect of Luke's existence being disclosed. Marie was certain it would be held against her.

'And you already have a cleaning job?'

'Yes, with Mr Darke. He lives on the park as well. He saw the advert you put in the paper and told me about it. He's the one who wrote my reference.'

'So I see.'

That had been it for questions. A short tour of the flat had followed, during which Marie had paid only polite attention to the hours being offered (four a week, as with Daniel) and the starting-rate pay of just above minimum wage (not like Daniel at all). She had been convinced she wouldn't be offered the job and that it would be just as well because Mrs Alibhai would surely be impossible to please. Only when departing had she learned that Mrs

Alibhai was not, in fact, the person she would be doing for. Not that Marlon had been spoken of directly. Mention was simply made of 'the tenant' who was described as 'a pleasant and responsible young man' who would be moving in at the weekend and out at work each day. Nonetheless, Marie was amazed when Mrs Alibhai called that evening to say the job was hers – 'on a trial basis at first. We'll see how we get on.'

Well, it seemed that 'we' had got on fine. A formal letter had been provided, setting out her duties, and a set of keys, together with a clear warning about the consequences should they be misused. For the first month Marie fulfilled all requirements in total solitude and daily anticipated being fired. At the end of it, she received by post a cheque from the account of Mr R. and Mrs C. Alibhai. The bank account address was in Hendon. As for 'the tenant', he remained unknown apart from the fact of his sex and some bits of slobbishness that Marie took as standard among young, single males: snack-food fragments trodden into carpets; damp towels forming musty mounds; dirty saucepans heaped like modern art.

Marie did not complain. The increase in her earnings meant she could force a few pounds on Lynda for her bed and board – a small gesture of independence but worthwhile. The desire for self-sufficiency had always driven her decision to seek work. At first after leaving Rick her sole income had been her child benefit; she'd relied on Lynda for everything else. But having made Luke her fellow refugee from a ruined relationship she was determined to be as single-handed a lone mum as possible – and, increasingly, to be seen to be so by Lynda. That meant taking her skills to market: ironically, skills refined under her mother's tutelage. After Marie had left Rick, Lynda had worked more hours in order to feed the extra mouths. Thus, Marie took on the more mundane household responsibilities. Floor-mopping and furniture-polishing were just the beginning. Soon, no murky sediment dared to malinger round the lining of the washing-machine door and no impertinent spider furnished a cornice or light fitting with her web and got away with it for long. Even Lynda, for whom every ledge and crevice was a germ propagator in a devious disguise, came to respect her rigour.

This was the expertise Marie brought to Marlon's life. Before long, though, she was providing something more.

She'd been cleaning his bath the first time he'd come home.

'Er, hello,' he'd said.

'Oh hello,' she'd replied.

Marlon had then proceeded to say nothing for a while, though his awkwardness was eloquent indeed. Marie had filled the silence by gabbling.

'I'm just cleaning the bath, actually . . .'

Marlon had hovered tentatively.

'I've dusted the living room . . .'

He'd hovered a bit more.

'I hope you don't mind, but I've thrown out some old soup. It was getting a bit furry.'

Further hovering. An eye-contact deficit. An existential social seizure not often found in the Square Mile.

'You *are* the man who lives here, aren't you?' Marie had asked.

'Er, yes.'

She hadn't really doubted it. She'd expected his slight build from the size of his shirt collars – fifteen – although by the look of the one he'd had on, even this was too big for him. He was no more than five feet six inches tall, his eyes were dark brown and his complexion was the colour of strong tea. Everything else about him, though, was weak.

'I'm Marie. I'd shake hands but . . .' She'd turned out her palms, a Marigold overture.

'Er, Marlon. Marlon Alibhai.'

The significance of the surname didn't hit her until she was halfway home.

'He fancies you,' Gabby had trilled when Marie relayed the tale later that day. 'Trust me,' she'd said. 'Next time he'll jump on you.'

Well, Marlon still hadn't jumped on her. Nor did it seem to Marie that he wanted to be near her in that way. He'd backed off from their first encounter almost as soon as it began, sidling from the bathroom then idling in the kitchen and then almost apologising for going out again. He did, though, ask politely: 'And, er, Marie, how is everything?'

'Everything's fine, thank you,' she'd chirruped extra sweetly, believing at that stage that the true motive for Marlon's visit was to check that she was there, earning her pay. 'I'll be finished by one and pop in again on Friday, if that's OK.'

'Well, goodbye then, er, Marie.'

Confirmation that her trial period was over had followed the next Tuesday. Marlon showed up again, this time as Marie was turning the cushions on his sofa. He had a box of cakes with him – luxury confections from a shop Marie had seen but never been in. Two *glacé* tartlets and cups of instant coffee later, she'd learned that Marlon's mother was a part-time company secretary and that his father was 'in property', including the one they were sitting in. And Marlon?

'Oh, it's a banking job. Currency exchange, that sort of thing.' He'd looked a little pained.

'Is it a nice job?' asked Marie, for want of something cleverer to say. She was perched at one end of the sofa by now, a great brocade-upholstered oyster of a thing.

'Not terribly,' said Marlon edgily. He was stealing glances at her secretly. Weakened by the strain of sustaining the conversation, Marie had then dropped the patisserie fork Marlon had provided from a silk-lined presentation box. He'd watched her as she'd bent to pick it up. He'd kept on watching as the tartlet had slipped from her tilted plate and landed beside the fork on the pistachio-coloured shagpile, upside down.

'Oh no!' Marie had cried. 'I'll clear it up.'

'My father wanted me to do it,' Marlon had said, as if explaining some shaming misdemeanour.

'Pardon?' Marie had flustered, already on her knees amid wild strawberries and a fractured pastry case.

'Can I, er, help you with that?' Marlon had asked belatedly.

'No, no, I can manage, honestly.' Marie had been glad of the distraction. But there'd been no hiding from her emotions. She had felt sorry for Marlon. She had been touched by the gesture of the pastries.

Gabby's attitude had been more raucous. 'You'll be nibbling his cream doughnut next. He'll be asking you to hold his macaroons.'

In the event she'd been quite wrong. True, Marlon had produced two passion-fruit meringues, which might have seemed *risqué*, but Marie detected nothing of that kind.

'So, er, Marie,' he'd said and she'd noticed that he had a bloodshot eye. 'Tell me about your family.'

'Well, let me see . . .' began Marie.

Once more they'd shared the bloated sofa. Marie had felt she'd been befriended by a small, leaf-eating mammal that rarely ventured from thick foliage. She'd kept her overall on, not because she doubted Marlon's decency but because prettiness would have seemed out of place. A dainty fragrance would have, too. Marlon, she calculated, would take more comfort from her company because she smelled so powerfully of bleach.

'I'm an only child,' she'd said. 'And my mum's a receptionist.'

'And what about, er . . . ?'

'My dad's dead, actually. Didn't your mum say?'

'No.' Marlon had flinched.

'That's funny, I told her.'

'Did you?' He'd looked away. 'Er, ah, um . . .'

Not for the last time Marie had rushed to his aid.

'It was a long time ago,' she'd reassured him. 'Eight years.'

'You must miss him, though,' Marlon had said, accepting this diminution gratefully.

'Not really.' Marie had been surprised by the starkness of her reply. She'd qualified it quickly. 'Not, like, every day. My mum misses him, though. She still bursts into tears when something reminds her of him.'

'Is she very emotional then?' Marlon had said with more hope than understanding in his voice. He was groping blindly down Empathy Way.

'I think it's time she got over it,' Marie had said. Again, she'd been alarmed at her own candour and yet oddly liberated too. Admitting such a thing to anyone else she knew would have risked appearing cruel. But Marlon, she'd surmised, was too honoured by her company to have judged her in that way. She'd added, 'By the way, I have a little boy.'

'How interesting,' Marlon had said.

'But I'm not living with his dad.'

'How interesting,' Marlon had said again.

'No. We live with my mum, actually.'

'How int—'

'He's four. And he's beautiful.'

'Yes,' Marlon had hastened. 'I'm sure he is.'

Her little speech had made Marie shaky, as if she'd just yelled defiance at the whole world. She'd darted to the bathroom for a piece of tissue. On her return, Marlon, casting about for a consoling observation, had said, 'What is your opinion of these meringues?'

'Perhaps I'll throw mine on the carpet like last time,' Marie had sniffed.

'I wouldn't be offended if you did.'

Marie had drawn a silly kind of strength from this exchange: she being fierce and fragile, Marlon being gallant for all that he was worth. She'd sunk her teeth into the passion fruit then asked, 'So tell me more about *your* family, Marlon.'

'Oh, well . . . Unfortunately, I don't believe there's very much to tell.'

He hadn't opened up, exactly. But each time Marie shook him, something revealing fell out.

'Is your dad Indian?'

'He's from Uganda originally – a refugee. There were quite a few of them, actually. He should have bloody stayed if you ask me.'

Marie was shocked: 'You wouldn't be here if he had!'

'That is true. But that wouldn't concern me.'

'I don't know what you mean.'

'Because I wouldn't be here.'

From most people, this would have been a wisecrack. Not from Marlon, though.

'Well, yes, I suppose,' said Marie. 'Um. Have you got brothers or sisters?'

'I have a sister called Elaine. She's a barrister. I don't see much of her.'

'Hendon's a bit classy, isn't it? Was it nice growing up there?'

'Well, er, Marie. My mother is from there, but I went to a boarding school so I don't know.'

'What was that like, boarding school?'

'It was OK in some ways. Sadly, I wouldn't recommend it.'

'Why not?'

'Hmmm. That is difficult to specify precisely.'

Marie had thought for a minute. Then she'd said, 'Don't you like your dad, then?'

'I'm afraid he is a shit.'

'Oh. I see. What about your mum?'

'The wife of a shit, I fear.'

'But they've given you this lovely flat . . .'

'Only to get rid of me.'

'Oh dear . . .'

On that note Marie'd decided she should leave. But she'd promised to pop back later in that week – just to make sure everything was still OK.

'I, er, regret it if you think I've been outspoken,' Marlon had mumbled as she'd left. His collar gaped at the front, his tie had gone awry and he'd acquired a modest meringue moustache.

'No problem,' Marie had said, resisting an instinct to sit Marlon down in front of *Cartoon Network* with a biscuit and a bottle of Fruit Shoot. 'It was nice talking to you.'

There was more to this than just being polite. The release Marie had experienced from speaking from the heart had made the conversation worth the strain. She'd felt grateful to Marlon and it seemed that he had been grateful to her too. When she'd revisited as promised that Thursday afternoon she'd found a gift-wrapped box lying on the kitchen table and, on a personalised compliments slip, a message written by hand.

I thought Luke might like this.
Yours faithfully,
Marlon

P.S. I'm sorry if he doesn't.

Inside the parcel was a radio-controlled toy motor boat – and yes, Luke had liked it very much. Marie had liked what it signified: that as well as being uptight, needy and a bit weird, Marlon tried to be thoughtful and kind. From then on she had wanted to protect him. But as she stood there in his living room listening to his father's scolding on the phone while Marlon himself slumped defeated in his chair, she knew that she would have to do much more than that.

Through the open external door Marie watched her mother from the kitchen. She was kneeling at a flowerbed using a trowel to plump the earth around the bedding plants she'd just dug in. On the grass the nylon walls of a small one-piece tent the shape of a pyramid bulged under the strain of containing Luke and his best friend Milo as they wrestled playfully inside. Marie was ruminating about Marlon and had been constantly since leaving him. She was so deep inside her thoughts that she jumped when the landline started to ring.

As usual Marie didn't answer it straight away but

SINGLE MEN

instead waited for Lynda. So she was puzzled when her mother didn't move. The boys' giggles were muffled and too intermittent to drown out the ringing and normally Lynda would have been halfway to answering it already. Instead, she kept on digging, studiedly. Marie took the call on the seventh ring.

'Hello?'

There was no reply.

'Hello?' said Marie again. 'Hello?'

She could hear someone was there; hear their uncertainty about what to say or do. Wrong number, probably. Marie waited for a broken English half-apology or a background mutter followed by a click. But then:

'Marie?'

'Yes?'

'It's me.'

'Who?' Her question was genuine. She had forgotten how he sounded on the phone.

'It's Rick.'

'Oh. Right.' She shot another glance down the garden. Outlines of little bums and elbows continued distorting the walls of the tent. Lynda remained engrossed. As Marie searched her head for words, Rick's came tumbling:

'. . . it would be nice to get together. It's been a long time, and everything, obviously, and I was wondering, like, obviously, you know . . .'

She had no prepared response for this frayed-nerves opening, and simply stood there, half-listening, as her shock reflexes went through their routine.

'. . . an' I just wanted to say, like, obviously, it was all my fault, mostly, and it seems a shame we can't be, you know, friends.'

'I don't know,' said Marie inadequately. 'I don't know.'

The boys were out of the tent now and taking turns at diving into it instead. Marie watched Milo stand, laughing, as Luke hurtled headlong. Lynda had shuffled her kneeling pad a bit further away.

'How is he anyway? Marie?'

'He's all right.'

'Is he? Brilliant. It'd be great to see him, obviously.'

This latest use by Rick of his worst verbal tic word snapped Marie out of her daze.

'Obviously for you, maybe.'

He was silent for a moment as a harsh momentum gathered in Marie.

'It's his birthday soon and—'

'No, Rick.'

'I was thinking . . .'

'He doesn't want to see you.'

'Well, obviously, I wouldn't know about that, but maybe—'

'He doesn't want to see you, Rick.'

Rick paused. Then: 'Have you asked him? He's nearly five, he must be wondering who his dad is, mustn't he?'

'No, he isn't wondering. He isn't ready.'

'When will he be?'

'I don't know. We'll have to see.'

'So you think he will be then, eventually?'

'I never said that.'

'I love him, Marie.'

'I've got to go.'

'You've got to understand. I'm sorry about what happened and—'

'I've got to go. I'm sorry.'

'It's not as if—'

Marie placed the handset back on its base. She crossed the kitchen and turned on the oven. Two Hawaiian pizzas lay boxed and cling-wrapped on the table beside the salad she was determined to serve. She wanted to make a good job of preparing the table. There were people to make a point to: Lynda, from whom she rarely wrested control of food, and Milo's mother, a fashion designer, due to arrive for Milo soon. She wasn't a bit snobbish but she was poised and elegant and roughly double Marie's age. The need to demonstrate her competence was pressing and not only to others now that Rick, Rick, Rick . . .

Marie checked the clock, checked the chill of the five quid bottle of white wine in the fridge.

The phone rang again. This time Marie rushed for it. She did *not* want Lynda getting involved.

'Hello.'

'Is this Marie?'

'Yes, this is Marie.' She knew the posh PA's voice only too well; its condescension and its total lack of warmth. It's owner was called Nigella.

'I have a message from Doctor Jelly,' Nigella said.

'Oh good, I was wondering if you'd call.'

'I did try your mobile but you appear not to have it switched on.'

'Sorry about that. I probably didn't hear 'cos I've just been down the garden. So, what does Doctor Jelly need?'

Marie didn't like being ticked off in this way, but at least Nigella wasn't Rick. She listened to her instructions for tomorrow – Wednesday, Guy's day – and went back to pretending that her former life was distant history.

CHAPTER FOUR

'Absolutely no complaints *at all*.'

In fact, the last two words weren't quite 'at all'. The speaker's Surrey drawl flattened the 'at' into 'ad' and morphed it with the front end of an elongated 'all' to form a whole new verbal entity: *adawl*.

'Absolutely no complaints *adawl*.'

The drawl was drawing closer to Marie.

'Wouldn't mind a run out with one or two other models, though. Wouldn't mind *adawl*.'

By the time Marie had pushed shut his heavy front door, Guy Jelly had joined her in the hall. He noted her presence but didn't quite acknowledge her, as if that would be a commitment too far. He wore trainers the size and the design of Formula 1 racing cars and Adidas joggers whose triple-stripe motif up the outside of each leg emphasised their wearer's giddy height. His topmost six inches comprised the type of hairdo worn by stadium rock stars before New Wave swept them away. The light grey of his T-shirt was darkened at the armpits by fresh sweat. Two leather leashes hung loosely from one hand and he spoke into a cordless using a language peculiar to his tribe.

'. . . ye-agh . . . ye-awe . . . yaar . . .'

Marie had been shopping: not for herself but on behalf of this imposing specimen, the third man she did for and a very different creature from the other two. Where Daniel was a cool ironist, a barbed melancholic and an inveterate aesthete, Guy was a bedrock hearty. Where Marlon was a tender mess of troubling misery, Guy was an outgoing force of nature, driven by some impulse from the wild, despite being on the high side of forty-five.

He loped, still talking, back into his front room as if indifferent to Marie being there. She knew not to take this personally. She'd been dealing with Guy for long enough to know that this apparent deep disinterest could be replaced in an instant by an overpowering blast of bonhomie.

She set off down the beige-carpeted hall. In her left hand, bearing the name *Margot's Superior Confectionery* was a glossy, cream-coloured, cord-strung carrier bag. From her right hand bulged a blue plastic one. The latter contained offal: basic supplies for Hamlet and Schmeichel, the two Great Danes who shared Guy's home. Procuring internal organs for these giant canines was but one of the varied duties Marie performed for Guy in return for the wads of banknotes he threw at her now and then saying, 'Speak up, luvvie, if it's not enough.'

Marie walked into Guy's kitchen, where the dogs

sprawled like velvet hillsides across the stone-tiled floor. Each was nearly as long as Marie was tall. In moments of high affection, whether outdoors or in, they would plant their front paws on her shoulders and slobber adoringly until she ordered them, 'NO!' in the firm voice Guy had taught her, and they would wheel away chaotically, tails thrashing, and shove their snouts into the nearest bush or bin. This morning, though, their recognition of Marie and the gift she came bearing was restricted to slow wagging and the beseeching scrutiny of dimwit eyes. Clearly, these two males of the house had burned off their excess energy. Marie wondered whether the third had done so too.

She put the *Margot's* carrier on the table, placed half the offal in the freezer and the other half in the fridge. She took a cursory look around. The floor could do with mopping, the table-top with sponging down, but there was no point in starting anything. Doing for Guy meant forgetting cosy concepts like routines. The one reliable thing about him was his unpredictability.

Maybe the small ad Marie had placed in a local newsagent's window should have been more precisely worded . . .

Cleaner/housekeeper
All duties considered
Call Marie

. . . but she'd done it on impulse, flushed by her

amazement at getting the Milman Road job, and there'd been no indication of Guy's eccentricity when Nigella the Posh PA had made contact the next day. On the contrary, she'd been groomed to expect a man of stern conformity: 'Doctor Jelly is a very distinguished surgeon who expects the highest standards of his employees.'

Snobby cow, Marie had thought. But she'd turned up the next morning with her overall just the same. Kingswood Avenue ran down the eastern edge of Queen's Park, and the prospect of having clients – as she by this time thought of them – on three of its four sides struck Marie as the beckoning of destiny. The clincher was a horoscope egging her on:

New opportunities may seem out of your league but now is not the time for caution. A strange coincidence may be a happy one for you. Seize the moment, girl!

She'd arrived with her hair tied back and all flesh save her hands and face concealed. She'd left four hours later with fifty quid in her pocket, smelling faintly of Great Dane and wondering how a man who hardly seemed to be in charge of his own grey matter had come to be trusted with other folks'.

'Just get stuck in, luvvie. I'm just a crap bloke, yeah? There's a bucket thingy somewhere. And Domestos. That's the right stuff, isn't it? Buggered if I know . . .'

First impressions can be wrong, but not this time. Marie had soon accepted that Dr Jelly's madness was incurably part of the territory.

'Luvvie! Choccies? Yum-yums?' Guy strode into the kitchen, looking everywhere but under his own nose. 'Ah-ha!' he exploded, spotting the *Margot's* bag at last. 'You got them, luvvie! You're my girl guide – have I ever told you that?'

In fact, he'd told her several times. The first had been only a fortnight after he'd taken Marie on. The theory may have been that she'd make his shabby house spotless every Wednesday morning and top him up on Fridays if required. The practice had turned out to be more whimsical. True, she'd soaked a few red-wine stains out of his white carpet, defrosted his freezer and generally purged the worst of the grime. But she'd already been diverted to get shoes repaired for Guy, as the distinguished surgeon had insisted she call him, buy books on shark-fishing for him and get the Harlequins rugby shirt Will Carling had once autographed for him put in a frame. Then, one Wednesday, she'd let herself in and found him waiting.

'Luvvie! Got a prob. Girlie business. Need your help.'

He'd ushered her into his front room and insisted she sit down while he paced against the wide-screen backdrop of Sky Sports.

'Thing is,' he'd continued, 'I need something a bit special for wifey. That's *ex*-wifey, actually, but we're trying to stay chums – for the kiddies' sake, yaar?'

He'd looked at her hopefully, as hapless as he was huge, as clueless as he was keen. Marie had heard people remark on the likeness between dogs and their owners. She was beginning to see what they meant.

'You need a present for her?' she'd asked.

'Yep. Yup. *Ye-agh*. You'll need to be my girl guide,

luvvie. What I mean is, guide to girls. What a girl wants, what a girl needs and all that, right?'

'But—'

'Think about it, luvvie. She's out there in the country with the baa-lambs and the trees. Need to keep her happy. Be a brick and pop to the shops for me, OK?'

She'd stood there, open-mouthed. He'd pulled his wallet out. 'Here you go. There's a ton.' He'd held out a stack of notes. Big hands, thought Marie.

'But—'

'Something nice, luvvie, you know. Little bit of something super.'

'But—'

'Bit of smelly, bit of jewellery, bit of . . . whatever.'

'But I don't know what your wife – your ex-wife – likes . . .'

'I've got total faith in you, Marie – no worries *adawl*.'

'But—'

'Gotta go now. Gotta drill a hole in a chap's head. *Ciao*.'

With that he'd shot out of the door. First, Marie had panicked. Then she'd caught a train to Hampstead and thrown herself on a shopkeeper's mercy.

'What sort of lady is she?' the woman had enquired.

'I've never met her. I didn't even know she existed until today.'

'What about her husband?'

'He's her ex-husband, actually.'

'Interesting!'

SINGLE MEN

'I don't know how to describe him really. Except he's a brain surgeon and he's a bit, well, mad.'

It was a home furnishings boutique: very expensive, very arty, totally un-Marie. The owner, though, had been intrigued by her assignment and together they'd assembled a profile of Guy's ex from the small number of clues available. The shopkeeper had thought elegantly untidy, green wellies, probably called Rosie or Lucy. Marie had left with a pair of amber earrings, a silver picture frame and directions to *Margot's Superior Confectionery*. She'd returned to Kingswood Avenue and left the three gift-wrapped items on the kitchen table, together with the change of £4.73, ignoring Guy's instruction to keep it which just hadn't seemed quite right.

She hadn't heard from him again until the following Monday, when for the first time he'd phoned her personally.

'Terrific pressies! Wifey pretty chuffed. You're my girl guide, luvvie. Savvy?'

That was the beginning of Marie's voyage of retail discovery. She'd lost count now of the times Guy had pounced or called or left a note . . .

'Sweeties needed, pronto!'

'Birthday, luvvie, forgot completely!'

'Something *fun*, Marie! Something young! God only knows, don't ask me!'

. . . forcing her to drop all thoughts of Mr Muscle and instead to make some mercy dash to her new friend in West Hampstead or into the West End for a handbag, bath oils or a fancy little scarf from Liberty, terrified all the while that someone frightfully-frightfully would tap her on the shoulder and demand to know precisely how such a lot of dosh had got into the mitts of a nice, bright, respectable but basically *below stairs* creature like herself.

There were other, less personal errands too. Nigella usually briefed her about these.

'Doctor Jelly wishes you to walk Hamlet and Schmeichel.'

'Doctor Jelly says would you collect his crampons, please.'

'A car is arriving for Doctor Jelly. Take delivery of it, would you, please?'

'Pardon?'

'A car. C.A.R. Take delivery of it, please.'

'Oh. A car. I see.' Snobby cow.

The car in question had been a red Aston Martin. Marie deduced from the part of Guy's phone conversation she'd overheard on the way in – 'Absolutely no complaints *adawl*' – that he'd been pleased with the purchase yet was on the line to this or that dealer, keen to sample rival vehicles –' . . . wouldn't mind a run out with one or two other models, though. Wouldn't mind *adawl*.'

This, she reflected as she checked beneath the sink for Windolene, was Guy all over: however good things got, he couldn't rest until he'd tried out something else and then something else again. Her broad impression was of a man addicted to continual crisis, endlessly revisiting previous decisions, unable to leave well alone for long.

Maybe that explained his failed marriage. From the

SINGLE MEN

random scraps of information he'd let fall, she'd gathered that 'ex-wifey' lived in Sussex on a farm and that she and Guy had had two children, seemingly called Jumbo and Mopsy. Each to their own, thought Marie. Yet she could not but be intrigued by the world these bizarre monikers conjured for her, a world where kilts and jodhpurs were routine leisure garments, where pheasants were nervous, and people really did say, 'Anyone for tennis?' all the time.

Now, Guy peered into the *Margot's Superior Confectionery* bag. He sniffed the contents appreciatively, then looked up at Marie, saying, 'Got a special job for you today.'

'Oh. OK.'

'Boy Racer needs a damned good seeing-to.'

He was standing directly in front of Marie, eyes locked on to her eyes, legs apart, looking down. For a second she was startled. Boy Racer? Was he referring to himself? She'd spotted Guy checking her out from time to time, but never felt that he harboured designs. It wasn't their age difference that would have put him off, simply that they were members of different species.

'Pardon?' she said uncomfortably.

'Boy Racer. Cute little red thing with four wheels.'

Ah-ha! The C.A.R.!

'Oh sorry,' said Marie. 'I see!'

'Needs a proper clear-out for the weekend. Messy boy, that's me. Can you do that for me, luvvie? Dashboard, windows, upholstery?'

'Yes, I'm sure I—'

'But leave the doggie basket and the smelly old jumper.

Don't touch them *adawl*. Those are for Ham and Schmeichs. Ex-wifey put the woolly through the washer once and they both sulked for a week.'

Marie nodded her understanding then almost fainted from relief as Guy's mind leaped off elsewhere, taking with it his Sir Steve Redgrave physique. Marie's mental picture of Mrs Jelly sharpened: she saw pure exasperation and perpetually flushed cheeks.

One of Guy's big hands tugged open the fridge and the other entered it, powerfully. The second hand emerged holding a huge Cornish pastie. Guy took a large bite from it, then tore chunks off and lobbed them into the Great Danes' absurdly grateful jaws. At last, hurling a cheery '*Ciao*' over his shoulder, he departed the house and hailed a waiting taxi, leaving Marie to calm Hamlet and Schmeichel and to locate the Aston Martin keys.

Marie left Guy's just before two and headed home. The inside of the Aston Martin had proved to be a dumping ground for empty drink cans, snack-food wrappers, sundry parking tickets and, for all Marie could tell, a number of undiscovered diseases. On its rear seat the dog basket was chewed and malodorous while the sacred jumper – an ancient tank-top affair – was mustard-coloured beneath a layer of compacted hair. Marie doubted she could have touched it even if she had been asked. It was, perhaps, the single most disgusting clothing item she had ever seen.

In the bathroom she sniffed her hands and armpits, dived under the shower and emerged with less than half an hour remaining before she had to pick up Luke. She re-banded her hair so that her ponytail stood higher on her head. She put on her orange crochet vest and a pair of long-legged shorts. Into her little rucksack she threw crayons, a drawing pad and a change of clothes for Luke, shoved her bare feet into her trainers and rushed off to the school.

She arrived still feeling fraught, yet once in the playground she unwound. Luke was a handful but he anchored her. Shepherded by their teacher Dorothy, the Reception class filed out all big-eyed, like small nocturnal creatures under lights. Marie pressed forward with her fellow parents. Luke saw her, ran to her and hugged her leg. She picked him up. A memory of Clay crept up then went away.

Luke asked, 'Isn't it today we see Elice?'

'Yes.'

'*Ye-ess!*'

He clenched a fist and did a little leap of triumph. Together they headed off. Marie could have arranged a mini-cab and Daniel would have paid her back, but the day was fine, Elice didn't need fetching until French Club finished at five and Marie's energy had flooded back. She was a girl in a feelgood movie or an advert for summer holidays. She walked fast, Luke skipping to keep up, and chattering constantly.

'And Mummy, isn't it birds used to be dinosaurs?'

'Did they, Luke? I don't know.'

'Dorothy says so. And isn't it that bugs come if you don't clean your teeth?'

'Bugs? Toothy bugs?'

'But Mummy, isn't it?'

They stopped at a shop for snacks and drinks. Luke took a Kinder Bueno from the fridge cabinet, where all the chocolate had been placed to stop it melting in the heat. Marie bought sandwiches packed in plastic triangles and two cans of Coke, and a carton of apple juice for Elice, who disapproved of fizzy drinks. With the same moral crusade in mind she bought three Tracker bars as well. She paid, smiling, and she and Luke floated on, cutting east across the main traffic flows until the houses became smarter and they arrived at what Luke called the Noddy School.

Holdean Academy was a small, private primary school installed in a converted townhouse. Daniel had sent Elice there in order to, as he put it, 'preserve her individuality'. When Marie and Luke walked in, insurgents from the philistine conformity beyond, she was sitting on a loveseat in the tiled entrance hall reading a book. The Head's secretary emerged from her office, a tweed-trousered figure with a steely non-haircut and spectacles dangling from a chain around her neck. 'Hell-oh,' she said in her usual way, a way in which Marie heard forbearance just-and-just prevail over censoriousness.

'Hello!' sang Marie and jogged Luke's arm.

'Hello!' he said, and offered a chocolate-coated smile.

'Off you go then,' said the secretary to Elice.

Elice slung her old-fashioned leather satchel over her shoulder and stood up. Her straight, dark hair was cut into a crisp bob and tucked behind her ears. The correctness of her posture was confirmed by her summer frock, which was of lime-green cotton with a white embroidered collar. White ankle socks with rolled-down tops cuddled her ankles above branding-free white canvas lace-up pumps. She was a throwback, a page from some photo collection of classic bygone looks, which her father probably gave her for Christmas. She held up her book. 'I'm already on chapter three,' she said. 'Have you read it, Marie?'

Marie already knew the answer, but inspected the cover anyway. Lewis Carroll: *Through the Looking Glass*. 'No, I haven't,' she admitted.

'It's really *excellent*,' Elice said. 'Are we going to the park?'

'Yes.'

'Oh good! To the bandstand?'

'If you like.'

'I *do* like! Hello, Luke!'

Elice addressed the younger child with her heels pressed together, Mary Poppins-style. She bent towards him stiffly from the waist. Luke stared up her, smitten, but found his voice.

'You're posh,' he said.

Elice smiled indulgently. 'Do you know what "Posh" really means? I do.'

Luke waited deferentially.

'It means "port out, starboard home", which is about having the best view from a ship.'

On foot it was twenty minutes to Queen's Park. By the

time they got there Luke knew his left from his right, the corresponding nautical terms and had grasped the rudiments of social class. After nipping into Daniel's to fetch a picnic rug, and for Luke to change his clothes, the trio settled on their favourite bit of grass. Many children were playing in the vicinity, but the bandstand was unoccupied.

'I'll be the posh lady, and you can be my son,' said Elice. 'Your father can be dead.'

Luke nodded and the bandstand became a cruise ship from the Olden Days. Viscount Darke and his widowed mother surveyed the sceptred isle through telescopes. Handkerchiefs flapped in greeting along the coast. Marie, it was decided, was a mermaid preening on a rock. She delighted in this game but soon dropped out. Her memory was insisting on re-running old reality scenes. She'd been trying not to see them since Rick's surprise phone call, but as Luke and Elice went deeper into their fantasy, she couldn't close her eyes against them any more.

She saw Rick on the night she broke the news to him, hunched over the steering wheel of his Fiesta Popular after she'd asked him not to kiss her any more. It was half-past eleven at night and they were parked round the corner from Marie's. She was sixteen, he was twenty-three. He still lived with his parents but he had a job with an insurance broker. He had a bank account. He could drive. She'd been watching the lights of somebody's Christmas tree, the first one she'd noticed that year. She'd said, 'I'm going to have a baby. I'm sorry.'

SINGLE MEN

They'd been going out for nine weeks: Marie had marked them off in her diary. They'd met in a disco bar in Kilburn, which Marie was too young to be in legally. Gabby had been there too, and some other girls from school, and Rick had offered to buy her a drink. How compliant she had been, how accepting! She'd been there with a girl gang, and the vibe officially was, 'Hello, boys, catch us if you can,' but all that had evaporated in the validating heat of male attention. She'd accepted the drink, a 7Up, being too nervy to risk going to the bar. They'd slow danced at midnight and though he'd pulled her close he hadn't pawed.

He'd called her the next day. Then came the pizza and the pictures and the hot fumbling in the too-tiny-for-it car and the undiscussed assumption that all this was provisional, all preliminary while they waited for an evening when Rick's parents would be out. And when that evening had arrived, and Rick hadn't got a condom, Marie had seized the moment and hoped for the best. She hadn't wanted to remember everything she'd ever been told, in earnest sex-ed sessions at school, by Lynda in her mother mode, by teen magazines where the mixed message was: don't do 'it' until you're ready but here's the way to get the guy, get the guy, get the guy. She wanted to be wanted, needed, held. She'd helped him tug her jeans down because she was a helpful girl. She'd told him she was sorted, it was OK.

'I'd only just had my period,' she'd lied to him in the car. 'It should have been all right.'

'What shall we do then?' he'd asked her. He hadn't seemed like a grown-up any more.

'What shall *I* do, isn't it?'

'Well, obviously, yeah . . .'

Marie felt the gnaw of her remorse: had she always punished him for being kind?

'We could try living together,' he'd ventured. 'You know, give it a go. Whatever's best for the kid.'

'I might not even keep it.' But she already knew she would, even though she'd barely acknowledged it to herself, let alone said so to anybody else.

She'd told Lynda two days before Christmas, feeling unable to fabricate even a thread of seasonal cheer without first unburdening herself. Lynda had wept predictable self-blaming tears and yet she had recovered quickly, grateful perhaps for a fresh family catastrophe to take her mind off surviving Yuletide without Clay. By New Year she was encouraging Marie to have the child and mentally furnishing its nursery. It came as a blow to her, then, when a housing charity offered the expectant pair a basement flat at a manageable rent. Lynda had met Rick before the pregnancy occurred and quite liked him, but now she had to ask if he was good husband material.

'We're not going to get married yet,' Marie had said. She could still picture the confusion on her mother's face: on the one hand co-habitation was heading in the right direction; on the other, hers would become a no-child household when for a few, exciting days she'd imagined there being two.

SINGLE MEN

Marie and Rick had moved into the flat at Easter, by which time Marie had dropped out of school. And now their little boy was on a cruise ship with his girlfriend and wanting to know what was what and who was who.

CHAPTER FIVE

The pub's interior had been refurbished to look like a mangrove swamp. Moulded plastic tree roots snaked up the table legs in an equatorial fashion. Fan-assisted fronds swayed mock-deciduously overhead. Every now and then a small thunderstorm would break above a corner water feature, causing a row of tiny sprinklers to saturate and burst the banks of a model jungle river while mini-forks of neon scarred a likeness of a sub-Saharan sky.

It was an ambitious makeover but, like all previous ones, failed to quite eradicate the pub's firm foundations in some strobe-lit corner of an architect's imagination, circa 1972. Combed Artex scallops still graced the toilet walls, the ceilings were too low and there was simply no concealing the panelled window inserts in the walls. Re-branding the pub as the African Queen had also proved futile. To locals it remained the Larkspur, the equally ill-fitting name it bore at birth.

It was Friday night, well after ten.

SINGLE MEN

Gabby dragged greedily on yet another Royals Kingsize and Marie watched the smouldering ring of paper chase towards the filter like the onset of a forest fire. Gabby took the smoke into deep storage for five seconds before funnelling it out through both nostrils. The visual effect was of a blast furnace during a night of heavy smelting. It was a fitting image. Gabby's skirt was short, her bosom bursting from its balcony; her teak-brown hair was tousled, bed-head style.

'Come *on*,' Gabby said, turning to Marie. 'It'll do you good.'

'Oh I don't think so.'

'Oh I don't think so,' Gabby mimicked testily.

'I haven't got the energy,' Marie complained. 'Not like you.'

Gabby accepted the rebuke as a compliment – her reliable response to any reference to her appetite for love. She'd spent much of the last hour recounting her heavily trailed triumph of the previous night. As a result, and in spite of her better instincts, Marie too was now anticipating the arrival of Pete, a man she'd never met but whose genital specifications, underpants of choice and 'squeezable' behind she already felt familiar with. He had arranged to pick up Gabby from the pub and take her to the West End for the night. He'd have a couple of mates with him. They would be unattached and male.

'If I was as pretty as you I wouldn't wait about,' said Gabby, brushing half-interestedly at the inch of fag ash that had just landed, thigh-high on her patterned tights.

Her outfit emphasised a frankly sexual plumpness that in another time or culture would have been the object of envy. Too often, Gabby loathed her shape. Right now, she was revelling in it. 'Your mum's looking after Luke,' she added. 'And I suppose you've still got *needs* . . .'

The two young women giggled, bonding around an in-joke. The euphemism 'needs' had been employed only once by their life skills teacher at school, but it had entered class folklore instantly.

'Speaking of which,' continued Gabby, 'how are your lovely boys?'

'How come,' Marie retorted, 'that just because I don't fancy a night on the pull you start mentioning them?'

'Just wondering,' Gabby said, arching a defoliated eyebrow.

'They're all as weird as ever in their different ways,' said Marie.

'Who's the one you fancy? I forget.'

'I don't fancy him.'

'You know which one I'm talking about then.'

'I've told you – Daniel's gay.'

'He's the one with the little girl, right?'

'Yes.'

'Must be gay then, mustn't he?'

'Oh shut up!'

'And the little lost Indian boy?' Gabby leaned towards Marie, pouting pretended pity.

'I'm worried about him.'

'Those beautiful brown eyes . . .'

'Seriously, I am.'

'That lovely coffee-coloured skin.'

'You've never even seen him.'

'I can imagine him, can't I? And not forgetting Big Hands.'

'I'm gonna slap you any second now!'

Gabby laughed and checked her watch, glancing once more at the door. Blokes and Gabby, thought Marie. Gabby and blokes. Guaranteed catastrophe. She'd thought that way about her friend for as long as she'd known her. They'd met at secondary school and become close when they were fourteen, drawn together by a shared sense of destiny. With their trainers and their sportswear and preference for R&B, they were derided as 'townies' by those among their peers whose mums and dads were journalists and lawyers. Marie and Gabby were bright and capable but lacked the sense of entitlement to high achievement in life that marked out even the least gifted of the professional-class girls.

Gabby in particular had more academic talent than she knew how to value. She obtained C grades and better in all her GCSEs and, while Marie became what used to be known as a girl 'in trouble', took AS courses in Spanish, English and Psychology, passing all three with Bs. It was shortly after scaling these intellectual peaks that Gabby's lack of self-belief, the hidden faultline running through her upfront personality, took hold of her as never previously. For her second year in sixth form she dropped one subject, changed the other two – perversely to Photography and Philosophy – then bailed out of school completely to get engaged to a plasterer called Craig.

Craig was thirty-two and from Kilmarnock. He had a tattoo of an angel on his arm. Underneath it was the name *Maggie* which was, he explained, in honour of his mum. Three months later Gabby learned that Maggie was, in fact, a hard-faced divorcée who ran a bathroom suite emporium in White City and had been in casual carnal congress with Craig's wiry physique since they'd met on a Harlesden building site in 1998. Gabby had caught them hard at it on Craig's narrow bachelor bed one Thursday afternoon. She'd gasped and, in her shock, let drop from underneath her jumper the copy of *Brides* magazine she'd been poring over for days. It fell open at the page about why your something blue should be a garter. Blue was the colour of the suede stilettos Maggie was wearing as she, otherwise naked, lay clawing and roaring under Craig.

'Gabby! Oh God!' Craig had choked, withdrawing smartly in his shame.

Maggie had been less abashed. 'Who the fuck are *you*?' she'd snarled through knees left defiantly raised.

Gabby had been completely fazed. Yet she'd been drama queen enough to do what any self-respecting wronged heroine should, when cast in such a scene. She'd tugged off her sapphire cluster engagement ring and hurled it at Craig before rushing to Marie to weep and scream. She seemed to recover quickly under her mother's wing but didn't return to her studies. Instead she'd got a job in a tanning studio and blundered from one romantic foray to another, filling the *longueurs* between each failed affair by watching too much telly and dipping chocolate fingers in cans of Irn Bru. It was not quite the Girl Power dream come true.

In the corner of the pub, another bijou storm broke over the model river.

'We're going away, you know,' said Gabby.

'On holiday? That's a bit soon!'

Gabby killed the Kingsize and hugged her knees with glee. 'I know! But we're getting on so well . . .'

'Where are you going?'

'I've seen a special offer for this big campsite in France.'

'You? Camping? Abroad?' Marie laughed. Gabby considered Berkshire a bit distant for her taste.

'Yeah? What's funny?' said Gabby indignantly.

'Nothing. Have you got a tent?'

'I'm borrowing me mum and dad's.'

Marie laughed again. Far from true love blooming under a canopy of continental stars, the vision that came to her mind was of Luke and Milo cavorting on Tuesday. She didn't say so, though. The charm of the tableau might have been lost on her friend. It was a parent thing.

Gabby kicked her on the shin.

'Ouch!' said Marie, still laughing. 'Don't get nasty on me.'

'It's not that,' hissed Gabby. 'Here he is.' Already she was pushing out her chest and switching her headlight smile to full beam. 'Hi, Pete,' she said with a low tremor, looking up from underneath her mascara. 'And how are you today?'

'Yeah, I'm good. And you?'

'All the better for seeing you.'

Pete stood before their table, standing proud, seemingly engaged in a permanent audition for a boy band. He stood rigidly, as if the varnish of his self-image would crack at the merest twitch, swivelling his car keys on the forefinger of his right hand. Gabby got up and edged around the table, looking taller than usual, and Marie's mind flashed back to one of their teenage bedroom evenings reading magazine advice about the way to walk in heels.

Take shorter strides and put your heel down first. That way you won't pull a muscle, and best of all you'll have a wiggle when you walk. Isn't that what heels are for?!?!?!?!?

Gabby hugged up against Pete's arm and said, 'I wish you'd come, Marie.'

Was she admitting she was nervous? Marie thought she might be, but her resolve to go back home was stronger still. The sight of Pete depressed her. He was probably nice enough, but Marie could see that he was more interested in who was looking at him than in looking at Gabby. Her heart sank at the thought of squeezing into the back seat beside his mates waiting outside in the car. She gave Gabby a tight, regretful smile of sympathy. 'I need my beauty sleep,' she said. 'I'll walk out with you, though.'

Pete catwalked off without a word, Gabby, his bauble, clinging on to his arm. Marie trailed behind, ambivalent at best, as they stepped out into the still balmy night. The car hung half-off the kerb. Marie saw a pair of young male heads turn towards her. Then Gabby embraced and kissed her.

'You sure you won't come?'
'No. I'm all right, really.'
'What you doing tomorrow?'
'The graveyard, remember?'
'Shit, yeah, I forgot. Sorry.'
'That's OK. Have a good time.'

Gabby took a last anxious look back at her as she climbed into the car. Marie, seeing it coming, smiled and waved. She kept smiling and waving as the car's rear lights disappeared, and a part of her did wish that she'd been in a party mood. But that was never going to happen. She was far too deep inside a memory.

The memory was of another Larkspur night. She'd been round at Leanne Baker's and that's where the trouble had brewed. Leanne was in Marie's year at school and lived in a parallel street five minutes away. The two girls weren't really friends, but as near neighbours who were too old to be children and too young to be adults they had a use for one another, namely comparing notes on growing up.

Marie had known when she'd gone round there that Leanne would be the senior partner – that was the appeal. She had a TV in her bedroom, a sex manual in a drawer and an older brother, Carl, aged sixteen. To only child Marie, thirteen and 32B, the combination whispered a promise of transgression alluring enough to overcome her insecurities and take up Leanne's invitation to spend the evening in her room and maybe get some lowdown on the two older boys who Leanne had gone out with and dumped.

She'd delayed going round until after Clay had left for the pub. He hadn't known she was going to Leanne's. Only Lynda had. Without quite admitting it, they'd conspired over the timing of her departure, tacitly agreeing that it should take place after his. Clay disapproved of Leanne.

Leanne had shown Marie the sex manual after they'd watched *Friends – The One About . . . Whatever*, lying together on their tummies on the bed. It was American and mostly photographic; thinly disguised porn. The penises, in particular, were surprising to Marie: so darkly anatomical, so big and red, not like the sketches used in school sex ed. Then Leanne told Marie that Carl fancied her. 'He thinks you're a bit young yet. I bet you could pull him, though, if you tried. Him and his mates are hanging round outside.'

Marie detected instantly the true and implicit significance of this test. It was not really about Carl and not exactly about sex. It was, rather, an examination of her daring, her willingness to shed the certain primness that clung to her because Clay had installed a classier front door than any of the neighbours', her credibility in the eyes of Leanne. She'd flushed a little as Leanne looked on. She'd thought of Carl, to whom she'd barely said more than three sentences ever. Unlike Leanne, he

SINGLE MEN

didn't send up sexual flares. He went in for baggy T-shirts and still carried his skateboard everywhere. He spat, though, and he swore.

Leanne offered to lend her a different top: tighter and skimpier than the demure Adidas T-shirt she'd had on. 'Come on,' she'd said, a little flushed herself. 'Let's go to the wall.'

Marie knew where the wall was. She also had a good idea what it was for, but had never been near it before: not after dark when its function changed from a boundary parapet into a meeting place for restless local teens. Leanne clearly knew the wall quite well. They slunk downstairs and past the door to the Bakers' living room where Leanne's parents were watching TV. Then it was out into the warm night, shoulders bare.

For a while neither girl spoke as if the night sky were the ceiling of a temple where a deferential silence was required. Marie hurried at Leanne's side, arms folded under her bosom as were Leanne's beneath her fuller, more exposed one, feeling her apprentice status keenly. The wall was in a twilit cross street. They had to pass the Larkspur to get there. As it hove into view, so patently a relic despite its saloon bar recently losing its plastic canopy and ceasing to be called 'Larks', Marie saw that it was a gauntlet to be walked. Overspill drinkers stood in groups on the chained-in forecourt, the women with their cigarettes perched high in scissored fingers, the men cradling pints bow-legged, as if to emphasise and spread the lager's weight.

'All right, girls?'

'Phoo-aar!'

'All right?' returned Leanne.

Marie kept her head down. It didn't mean she passed unnoticed. On this particular night it was so warm that all the doors had been wedged open, meaning Clay also had the option of looking out into the street: a street whose Friday-night theatre would shortly offer Marie a minor part.

The wall she and Leanne were heading for formed part of the perimeter of the small patrons' car park to its rear. Beyond it was a short street containing local shops: a bookies, a laundry, a convenience store and more, all of them shut up for the night. Through the darkness Marie could see that the wall was already occupied and acting as a magnet for others: an older teenage couple kissing; a bunch of noisy nine year olds on bikes. And on the wall itself sat two boys of round about fifteen.

'All right Mark?' said Leanne to one of them.

'All right Leanne?'

'All right Wigger?' she said to the other.

'All right.'

'This is Marie, by the way.'

The boys nodded, but didn't speak. They observed Marie appraisingly.

Leanne sat on the wall, close to Mark. Marie hung back.

'Come on,' said Leanne, beckoning with her head. 'They don't bite.'

Saying nothing, Marie moved nearer.

SINGLE MEN

'Sit here,' said Leanne, patting the brickwork next to her.

There was nothing for it. She took her place next to Leanne, though not as near to her as Leanne was to Mark. Wigger was perched on Mark's far side. Marie, though, was acutely conscious of his proximity. A certain chain of events had already become irreversible.

There was five minutes of small talk: banter and backbiting about people Marie didn't know. She contributed nothing to the conversation. Instead, she waited, waited, waited for the moment that came soon enough when Leanne wasn't beside her any more.

In fact, she was so self-absorbed she hardly noticed them leaving. She saw that a couple had entered a shop doorway opposite. She saw the stitching on the back of the boy's jeans and how they hung: Mark's jeans. A hand was slipped into each pocket: Leanne's hands. Their mouths were clamped, their heads revolving. They faded further into the shadows.

'Smoke?' asked Wigger. He'd pulled a crushed pack from his jacket and was offering Marie a cigarette. Another wagged at the corner of his mouth.

'No, thanks,' said Marie. She was casting around for an escape route. Trapped by fear, she couldn't simply walk away: fear of Leanne's derision, her own fear, the loss of face.

Wigger produced a disposable lighter. He sparked the flame and gazed at it, a connoisseur. His first drag on the fag was brief, and he seemed more interested in holding it in a streetwise way – between forefinger and thumb, tilted back towards the heel of his hand – than in the satisfactions of nicotine.

'What's your name again?'

'Marie.'

'You live up the road, yeah?'

'Yeah.'

Wigger had answered the question she was too timid to ask. 'Leanne told me,' he said. 'She said you'd like coming out.'

'Oh.'

'No good staying in, is it?'

'I suppose not, no.'

Marie had shrunk back a little as Wigger looked her over, too candidly: tits; tummy; tits; face; tits; tits; tits. Marie looked somewhere else: at the younger boys, huddling and spitting; at the just visible edge of the Larkspur's terrace. Getting away without sustaining dreadful damage seemed hopeless. The next best thing had seemed to be to keep quite still.

'D'you wanna drink?' Wigger had asked.

'Not really.' When is Leanne coming back? she'd thought.

'I can get us one: alcopop, beer. I've got a mate who'll go to the off-licence.'

'Not really. Thanks.'

Wigger sucked his cigarette again. Then, with a millionaire's bravado, he flicked it into the street, half-smoked. He seemed to come to a decision. An arm was around Marie's shoulders before she knew it. A spare hand was fondling her. She backed away from his ashtray mouth. Then a child's voice piped up, right next to her. 'Oi, Marie. Your dad's after you!'

Marie did not know the child, who sat astride a bicycle. But she knew the look of glee on his face. An embarrassment was occurring, an Event. It was about to engulf her and there'd be more hell to pay when she got home.

'Marie! Get in!'

Clay was thirty yards away but even at that distance Marie couldn't look at him.

'Man, he's pissed!' said Wigger helpfully.

Marie, pulling away, got down quickly from the wall as if by doing so it would mean Clay hadn't noticed what was happening. The boy on the bike cheered as she walked away, towards her father, her rescuer.

'See you then,' said Wigger mockingly.

Leanne's voice came out of the doorway: 'Where's she going?'

'Her dad wants her,' announced the boy on the bike.

As she approached Clay, Marie began to close down her senses. She saw nothing, heard nothing, didn't speak. She was aware, though, of the thunder in Clay's face. 'Get in,' he said again, as she'd drawn near. 'Get in and stay in.'

Not much had happened when she'd got home. She'd run upstairs to her room and put her head under her pillow to block out the sound of angry voices below. The following morning, Lynda had cosseted her more than usual and yet been reluctant to meet her eyes. Clay had had a job on and left early. He didn't speak to Marie again for weeks.

*

A soft breeze lifted the tips of Luke's hair as once again he veered off the path towards a tempting headstone, his blue Shark's Tale lunchbox swinging from his hand.

'Luke, get off there!' begged Marie, then cast an anxious glance ahead. Lynda was perhaps a hundred yards in front of them and already close to Clay's grave. For once, Marie was thankful for her mother's preoccupation. It meant she was able to remonstrate with Luke at less risk of being told off herself.

'Luke! I said get off!'

'Why?' he asked, ducking behind a sombre black marble slab and peeping out.

'Because it's someone's grave!'

'Why?'

'Because there's a dead body under there.'

'Why?'

Marie stepped after him, intending to make a grab but he stepped away, restoring the distance between them. He'd quickly cottoned on that the graveyard was one of those places, like restaurants and shops, where grown-ups had inhibitions about losing their rag and he, as a result, could test a few boundaries by playing up.

'Why, Mummy, why?'

'Stop it, Luke, *please*.'

He began to giggle, excited by his raising of the stakes. And yet his attention had been caught.

'Why is there a dead body?'

SINGLE MEN

'Because that's what you do with people when they die.'

Luke weighed this information carefully. 'Isn't it dead people come back as ghosts?'

'No, Luke, they don't. There's no such thing as ghosts.'

'There is in *Scooby-Doo*.'

'Scooby-Doo's not real.'

'Is Power Rangers real?'

'No.'

'Yes, they is.'

'Well, the people in it are real. They aren't cartoons.'

'They *are* real, Mummy!'

'Well, the *actors* are real . . .'

Marie checked on Lynda again. She'd reached her destination and was kneeling down; not praying, but inspecting the condition of the site. The flowers she had bought, her trowel and a small watering can lay on the grass at her side.

'Come on, Luke,' said Marie. 'Let's race!'

Luke took off, stealing a march. Marie chased, relieved that he'd taken the bait. She closed right up to his heels, heightening Luke's sensation of flight. It wasn't reverent behaviour but at least it wasn't close to desecration. Panting, they reached Lynda and Marie turned Luke around, putting a meaningful finger to her lips. The grave needed attention. Lynda had tidied it at Easter but volatile weather had nurtured sturdy weeds. Marie read the headstone name and dedication:

DAVE HILL

CLAYTON AMISS
†
A PERFECT HUSBAND AND DAD

Lynda's mobile rang. She answered it, saying, 'I'm at the grave.'

Marie guessed from the absence of formalities that the caller was her Auntie Barbara. In other years she had joined them for this occasion but not this time. Lynda was mostly listening. Her sister seemed to have a lot to say.

Detecting friction, Marie took Luke's hand and stepped away, but couldn't help but get the drift of Lynda's limited part in the exchange: 'I know how you feel, Barbara, and you know how I feel too . . . No, I'm not gonna do that, you know I'm not . . . It was mean, that thing you said . . . No, Barbara. No. No!'

She switched the mobile off and tugged a tissue from the cuff of her jumper. Marie's mind went back to the day of the funeral: the local church she'd never been in before or since; the hire-car ride to Willesden squashed into the back seat beside Lynda and Clay's almost unknown parents on a rare foray away from Brightlingsea; the spot she stood in now, feeling lost and spotty and surprised to be holding the hand of Auntie Barbara's husband, the normally non-tactile accountant Uncle Phil, while Barbara comforted Lynda. And, just to finish her off, there'd been the – to her mind – bizarre ritual of a buffet meal in the home – her home – of the deceased.

At fourteen, she'd lacked the social understanding to cope with any of this stuff and retreated with Gabby to her room. Together, they'd managed a dialogue of consolation assembled from things they'd heard the grown-ups say:

'No one could have known about his ticker. At least it was all over quickly – that's something.'

'He was a man's man who loved life.'

'Look at the work he put into this house.'

In the graveyard the breeze kicked up again. Marie touched Lynda on the shoulder. She asked, 'What's up with Auntie Barbara?'

'Oh, it's nothing, babes. You know what we're like.'

Breaking away, Lynda bent to gather the cut flowers and began arranging them in the stainless-steel urn positioned in the centre of the white marble chips. She said, 'You do remember him, Marie, don't you?'

'Course I remember him, Mum.'

'But you know what I mean. Do you *really* remember him? You were at an age when it's sometimes easier to block things out.'

Marie knew exactly what she meant. She was doing it at that moment, confounded as so often by her mother's neediness. She was less sure, though, that she'd done so at the time of Clay's death. In the days and weeks that followed the funeral, many had commented on how brave and dignified she'd been, though not always in front of Lynda to avoid highlighting the contrast with her very conspicuous distress. None seemed to suspect that this impressive decorum had been made possible by the emotional distance Marie felt from the whole tragedy.

When she looked back she supposed she must have buried some sort of grief alongside him but, if so, it had yet to become disinterred. What she felt now, as she watched her mother suffer and Luke settled himself at the foot of a tree to unpack his snack, was much the same as she remembered feeling then, indeed from the moment she'd heard the news. She'd been in her room, moping, brushing her hair over and over, rotting from the neck up in *Sugar* magazine. Downstairs, Lynda had been preparing dinner. As the smell of moussaka reached her, Marie succumbed to her customary dread of the family evening meal: a ritual of tensions being denied.

Then there'd been a phone call. Marie, eavesdropping, had heard her mother's reflex words of disbelief: 'When did this happen? . . . Are you sure? . . . There's an ambulance, is there? . . . I don't believe it. I don't believe it . . . Oh my God. Oh no . . .'

He'd pegged out while installing a boiler in a basement. He'd been alone; there had been no warning and nothing anyone could do.

'Mummy?'

'Yes, Luke?'

'Why are we here?'

'To think about your grandad.'

'Why?'

'Because he died.'

'Why?'

Marie gave him a warning look. 'Luke, I don't want to play this game.'

SINGLE MEN

Luke took a single small bite from the middle of the front edge of his ham sandwich. He then rejected it and moved on to his Jaffa Cake.

'He died before you were born,' explained Marie, more softly. 'He was Lynda's husband.'

'What's a husband?'

'The man a lady is married to. So your grandad was Lynda's husband and he died. Lynda is upset because she misses him.'

Luke munched his Jaffa Cake impassively. Marie considered adding that the dead husband and grandfather had also been her dad, but the fate of absent fathers was not a subject she liked exploring in her son's company. She wondered if Luke's reading was yet good enough to understand the headstone inscription. More than that, she wondered what he was thinking. She asked her mother, 'Where did Dad come from again?'

'Up north – the north-east. I can't remember exactly. I never went there, you see.'

'Why did he come to London?'

'For the work. There was a lot of unemployment in those days.'

Lynda's shoulders began shaking and Marie, standing back and to her rear, wondered at the staying power of her mother's misery. It took three years for bereaved people to recover – she'd heard this on a phone-in one evening – and she couldn't help but wonder why her mother was taking so long.

'I'm sorry, babes,' choked Lynda, as if reading

her daughter's mind. 'I sometimes think I'll never get over it.'

CHAPTER SIX

'Cupcakes,' Daniel said. 'You know I'm in love with you, don't you?'

'Yes!' replied Marie with a big smile. She was working extra hard at being sunny. She needed to. The graveyard scene had crept into her dreams.

'In that case, will you do me a favour?'

'I expect so.'

'Shoot Miss Valencia for me.'

'Oh. Well . . .'

Marie was at the sink filling a bucket with hot water. She kept smiling but there was something in Daniel she hadn't seen before – at least not in so fierce a form. He was leaning back on his worktop in his usual way, but he was frowning. His eyes were cast down, focused on a point midway between his forehead and the floor. He said, 'I'll double your wages if you agree. And give you a company car. You can shove the body in the boot.'

'I don't know, Daniel. What does Elice think?'

'Cupcakes, it's funny you should ask, because that's what I want you to find out.'

'Me? I don't think—'

'Why not? After all, she's very fond of you. She says you're her big sister. Has it never occurred to you, Marie, that without you there'd be no sane grown woman in her life outside of school?'

'But Daniel, what exactly do you want me to do?'

'Talk to her – please. I can't decide what's best for her until I know what she really thinks. Yet she refuses to discuss her mother with me any more. With you it might be different.'

'Well, I'll try.'

'I'm depending on you, Cupcakes. Without you, I may be doomed.'

After Daniel had left her to mop over the front doorstep then waft dust particles from his Lalique statuette, Marie laboured with the conflicts triggered in her by his request. She wanted to help Daniel because she was, in truth, a little bit in love with him and because she was a compassionate soul. She wanted to help Elice too, although she was far from certain that so shrewd and opinionated a child would accept it from the likes of her. Moreover, while she could see that Miss Valencia was problematic, Marie was well aware that the account she had been given of her – selfish, unstable and quite unfit to bring up a child, not to mention wholly undeserving – had been constructed solely by Daniel. She had yet to utter the sentence that formed in her mouth when the matter was discussed, but she couldn't silence it inside her head: *'But Daniel, she is Elice's mother, after all . . .'*

One hour of torment later, Marie did something she'd never done before: she took her can of Pledge and instead of pointing it at some panelled cabinet door, sprayed it randomly into the air. She then flopped on to the reconditioned Utility sofa and watched the *pot pourri* mist sink to the floor. It was an old cleaner's skive and Marie took no pride in it but she was in too much turmoil to care.

She was unable to stop thinking about Lynda.

'I sometimes think I'll never get over it.'

She was unable to stop thinking about Luke.

'Isn't it I've got a daddy?'

She was unable to stop thinking about Rick.

'It'd be great to see him, obviously . . .'

Marie and Rick. Rick and Marie. How could they have meant so well yet created such a catastrophe?

She'd walked out on him four Aprils ago one bright and breezy Persil commercial morning with Luke in his buggy and all their clothes in bags hung on the handles. Nothing really terrible had happened. There'd been no fighting or raging, just a small escalation of the customary low-level mutual incomprehension and despair. Rick had gone off to work as usual. Marie had planned nothing in advance. Some unconscious survival impulse suddenly told her she had to go. It numbed her against caring about her CDs, her stereo, the pots and pans she'd bought in thrift stores, the unpaid gas bill, the giant stuffed tiger Rick had won for Luke at a funfair, the mini-album of family photographs Rick had compiled one Sunday afternoon, the big surprise Rick would get when he came home. Only after she'd crash-landed at Auntie Barbara's house had reality started to sink in.

'What happened, darling?' Barbara had asked.

'Nothing really,' sniffed Marie.

'There must have been *something*,' Barbara wheedled tenderly.

'It was nothing. Like, nothing. Honestly.'

In fact, it had been something *and* nothing. Rick had never hit her, withheld money from her, yelled at or cheated on her but she didn't think he'd ever loved her either and she was certain now that she had *definitely* never loved him. She hadn't wanted to admit this: hadn't wanted to confess her own contribution to his sheepish retreat from close companionship, his shamefaced termination of sexual contact, his too-equable acceptance that he'd slipped way down her ladder of affection while Luke, in his nappy and the smart Babygros that Lynda had bought for him, was firmly installed on the top rung.

'I was going mad there, Mum,' was all she'd had to say when she'd returned to Herbert Gardens the next day.

Lynda had been calmer than she'd expected and seemed unoffended that Marie had spent a night at Barbara's first. At the time Marie had put this down to Barbara's smoothing the way, explaining within her earshot over the telephone that Marie would have felt bad turning up out of the blue, but that now she needed her mum badly. With hindsight Marie's judgement had changed. She'd decided that, in fact, nothing could have spoiled Lynda's secret pleasure at her return. Oh, there'd been all the predictable guff – 'Would it have been better if you'd got married? Might it have helped if Rick had moved in here?' – but when Luke had begun to cry Lynda had all but snatched him from Marie, cooing, 'Let Lynda give you a cuddle. Come to Lynda, little man . . .'

Marie had absorbed more than enough problem-page pop psychology to know where Lynda was coming from: Luke was the son she'd always wanted, and the fact that Lynda had never said she'd wanted one only convinced Marie the more. After all, she'd been invading Marie's maternal stage before Luke had even vacated her womb. She could recall the delivery suite scene vividly: Rick holding her right hand apologetically, Lynda pumping and squeezing the other, sobbing, 'Push, darling, push,' like she was a guest star in *Holby City*. The longsuffering midwife had later observed as Marie held Luke to her breast, 'Sometimes, my dear, you can have too much help.'

Marie and Rick had moved into their flat by then. His parents, reticent types, kept their distance as they always had, as if Marie were one of life's inevitable inconveniences. Marie didn't mind this. She'd found she quite liked being left alone and increasingly wished Lynda would do the same. The closeness they had shared in the two years since Clay's death had been the product of Lynda's protectiveness. It began to wear away as her advice became more irksome, her gifts – of bargain baking trays, old curtains she'd 'put away', endless tactile toys from Mothercare – more of an imposition than a help. By the time Luke was sucking rusks it had become a fixed wisdom of Marie's life that Lynda needed emotional support more than she did, and that she really ought to look for it elsewhere.

Marie yawned and heaved herself to her feet. It was time for her to do upstairs. As she ascended she flicked the *art nouveau* wrought-iron banister with the feather duster she held in her left hand while lugging the vacuum cleaner in her right. She came to the landing and debated which room to look in first. There was the guestroom, which she generally ignored unless Daniel told her someone would be staying. The bathroom got a once-over routinely. She liked the bathroom – so ornate – but was more fascinated by the bedrooms.

Daniel's was a chamber of *frisson* and mystery. Like most who hadn't tried it, Marie was intrigued by homosexuality and the processes it entailed. What she'd read or heard about in feverish girl-talk sessions seemed either unappealing or, particularly where the male back passage was concerned, plain unfeasible. She found it hard to imagine Daniel having sex with a man, and his bedroom, though exotic in terms of décor, had never yielded a single specialised accoutrement. It struck Marie that Daniel had given up on sex. That 'Boys, who needs them?' comment might have been heartfelt.

If so, she couldn't quite agree. It was true that finding

one hadn't been a priority for some time. And even before Rick, she'd been ambivalent about them, accommodating their advances rather than welcoming them. She knew boys fancied her for they were always sniffing round, yet she'd never felt ready for them, never been certain she was sexy or pretty. Oh, she'd worked hard at how she looked. She'd posed and accessorised and restyled her hair constantly, been as obsessed with these things as Clay had been about his D.I.Y. But there'd been something futile about it; something secretive and self-denying. The Wigger episode had got her off to a bad start and she had needed rescuing. That was where Rick had come in. He might have turned out to be as naïve as she, but at the time he had seemed steady and mature. He'd played the game of sex and dating. He would look after her.

On Daniel's landing, Marie started to cry. Needing a soft place to sit down she chose Elice's room, which at that moment seemed the most welcoming.

The door stood halfway open. Marie walked through. The room was no longer a bombsite. Marie had made it a priority to tidy it and keep it that way as best she could, though the result sometimes put her in mind of a museum. There was a basket chair and a collectable old dolls' house, complete in every miniature detail. The shelves in the room were massed with china dolls and hats and books, including, alongside the inevitable Jacqueline Wilsons, sun-faded hardback tomes with titles like *Girls Jamboree!* and *How Lottie Saved Her School*. Elice's curtains were made of old brown velvet and her duvet was adorned by a deep green candlewick throw. It was all a world away from Marie's tastes when she had been that age: braids and bangles and luminous cycling shorts and The Spice Girls about to head her way.

As she sat on the bed and tried to compose herself, Marie saw on the bedside table an object that was new to her. It was a bright red fabric-covered binder of some kind, A4 size and tied with a matching ribbon. Marie reached over and picked it up. On the front cover was a photograph. It showed a dark-eyed, raven-haired woman with strong but careworn Mediterranean features. She was holding a tiny baby. Marie undid the ribbon bow and opened the front cover. There was a frontispiece, and on it the same photo was reproduced. This time, there was a caption underneath. Handwritten in blue ink it read: *From Esmerelda de Silva Santana. To Elice, her precious child.*

It was an album of similar images, and Marie, as Elice's carer and cleaner, was confident it was a recent gift. Was it the reason for Daniel's renewed urgency about Miss Valencia? Maria could see why it might be. The poignancy of it, the care with which it was assembled, the message of maternal hunger that it sent ... had she been in Daniel's shoes she might have perceived it as a threat. But while she sympathised with him, she was resentful too. He was asking her to investigate this love, so he might know better how to thwart it. For the first time since she'd known him, she felt that Daniel was misusing her.

*

SINGLE MEN

Marie got home by two and flopped in front of the telly. She saw that Lynda had obtained an A-level prospectus from the local sixth-form college and left it meaningfully on the coffee-table. Marie considered reading it but the booklet failed miserably to leap unaided into her hands so she watched *Homes under the Hammer* instead. She was just drifting, dribbling, gently off to sleep when her mobile rang. She answered it guiltily.

'Hello?'

At first, she could hear only noises off: male noises, joshing and jolly.

'*Jonny Wilkinson . . . top totty . . . Alfa Romeo . . .*' Then the loudest of them spoke to her directly. 'Luvvie? Guy here. Need a girl-guide favour. *Priddy* urgent, actually.'

'Not today, Guy, I—'

'Tomorrow, luvvie. Fit it in for me, yeah? Love you for ever if you do . . .'

'Well, all right.' She'd have to do it after doing for Marlon. But would she have the time? Or energy?

'Need something *beautiful*. A necklace. Posh jewels – on the young side, yeah?'

'How, ah, young do you mean?' Was it for his daughter, maybe?

'Not too middle-aged, know-what-I-mean? Ex-wifey wants to feel more thirty-two than fifty, yah?'

'Anywhere in particular?'

'Henry Lean, New Bond Street. Top notch, luvvie.'

'Well, I'll try.'

'I'll leave some readies on the table – pick it up and spend it all. And get something a bit glam if there's any readies left over. Posh scarf, whatever, something to wear . . .'

'I'll—'

'But *not* knickers, or anything like that. Too risky.'

'I'll—'

'Must go luvvie. Just gotta saw a chap's head off. See you later. *Ciao*.'

CHAPTER SEVEN

Another Tuesday.

Another Marlon day.

Marie let herself into Marlon's flat to find its signature features still in place. Otherwise it seemed as if a poltergeist had called. Half-empty takeaway cartons and soiled plates defaced every corner of the kitchen. Shoes were strewn across the hall, some lying on their sides like cars that had taken a bend too fast. The four Alibhai visages still shone down from the living-room wall but looked even more unreal than before amid a scene of almost surreal disorder. Video and DVD boxes lay scattered like rooftiles the day after a typhoon. A cigar butt had dropped from the lip of an ashtray on to the paper-strewn coffee-table and lay there like some cautionary image in a fire safety ad campaign. There were two empty wine bottles and one half-empty glass. The TV screen had been smashed in. The curtains had been torn down, bringing the rail halfway with them. A fancy light fitting had been wrenched loose from the ceiling and dangled from a tangle of plasterboard and wire.

'Shit!' gasped Marie.

She had an impulse to escape. Some ground-in streak of pessimism warned her that because she had been the one to walk in on this bedlam she'd somehow be held to blame for it. 'Caught in the act!' a passing Constable would cry, and no one would believe a girl like her. She fought to be rational. Had there been a break-in? Then came a more chilling question. *Where was Marlon?*

Marie edged towards the bathroom first. Approaching the door, she worked through a mental flip-chart of clichés: shocked expression and protruding electrical flex; corpse floating, face down, with drugged eyes; blanched visage amid razor blades and blood-spattered tiles.

The door swung back under the pressure of her outstretched toe. She breathed a deep sigh of relief. There was no dead Marlon in the bath. Marie took two steps forward and saw that nothing was out of place apart from one stray toilet roll that had travelled across the floor, unfurling a dozen Luxury Soft sheets. It looked like the failed effort of an ungracious football fan. Marie cleared it up and sat down heavily on the closed seat. Then her relief was trumped by a new wave of nervous anticipation. It was the bedroom that beckoned – that forbidden space – and when Marie approached it she saw that the door was standing half an inch ajar.

'Marlon?' She listened, hoping for snoring. 'Marlon? Are you there?'

She pushed the door, the crack widened and she

looked in. Mental images of corpses flooded her head once more. She entered the bedroom on tiptoe – as if the deceased would care – and unconsciously elected only to notice bland details. As such she saw that the walls were magnolia and that there were few conspicuous trimmings: no posters, no ornaments and no obvious personal effects. In contrast to this sparseness the bed itself was as elaborate as the living-room furniture, its headboard pink and padded with a mock-laurel leaf trim. A patterned double duvet had slipped to the carpet. The mattress was bare except for a white sheet, two fat pillows and a clumped fistful of tissues, which told its own tale of dearth and solitude.

There were four more pieces of furniture: a chest of drawers, a wardrobe, a desk and a chair. On the desk stood a computer sleeping softly, a few books, an unruly spread of paper and several pens. Marie wondered if the desk might hold some sort of clue as to whatever it was Marlon had been up to, but the wardrobe called on her attention first. She tugged its double doors open and, with a little shriek, jumped back. Marlon's corpse did not fall out. Nor did that of anybody else.

As Marie regained her breath, so her sense of decorum re-established itself. She lifted one of the pillows and placed it protectively over the tissue clump. In doing so she uncovered a small brown plastic bottle containing pills. She scanned the typed directions on the white sticky label and squinted at an unfamiliar word, spelling it out slowly in her head. *Ven-lax-a-fine*. Whatever it was, it was new to her. She wondered what ailment it was for.

Then Marie went over to the desk. Before touching anything she engaged in some moral reasoning. Was she about to pry into Marlon's private world out of a pure concern for him, or was a bigger part of it less noble? She was about to shrug and have a dig round anyway when she spotted something that vindicated her. Sticking out from underneath a sheet of scribbled-on A4 were Marlon's keys. She knew they were the set he regularly used because she recognised the fob. She looked at each in turn.

There were five keys in all. One was a car key, which intrigued her because she didn't know that Marlon had a car. Of the other four, three were familiar because she had a duplicate set for getting in. The fifth was surely for the bedroom. The presence of the keys strengthened Marie's fear that it had been Marlon himself who'd smashed up the flat. Unless he had a spare set and had taken it with him when he'd gone out instead of his usual one, he'd then locked himself out of both car and home. She'd noticed on arriving that the front door hadn't been double locked as it usually was. Moreover, it was the first time she'd known him fail to lock his bedroom: Put all that together and a poke around his desktop now seemed completely justified.

Marie drummed two fingers on the keyboard. The screen woke up with a whirr to reveal an indigo screensaver. The model was new to Marie but she soon figured out how to access Marlon's surfing history. She prepared for the worst: Marlon might be a shrinking violet and a gentleman, but was there a man alive who didn't prowl the internet for porn? It was, then, a surprise to find that the top item on his list of recent website hits was called *Waiting For It: How Sexual Abstinence Works*.

Marie dragged the cursor to it and let go. A white man's face formed before her. He wore spectacles, a sweater and a smile. Above his image was the question *Why Not Have Sex Before Marriage?* Beneath it lay the promise: *Because Waiting For It Works* and then in a smaller font, *The Reverend Gary Tibworth Explains How*.

Marie double-clicked on the Reverend Tibworth's nose. Beneath the cheery heading *Save Yourself!* a page of text appeared. Marie set to reading, feeling guilty yet enthralled.

Why is it that society is better fed materially than ever before and yet so spiritually starved? How can it be that in an era when we talk about our emotional needs so freely, the quality of so many people's personal lives is so poor? What is the reason why in a time when the young in particular are given more and more information about sex, fewer and fewer go through life in lasting and fulfilling relationships?

The answer is that we've come to believe what I call the Three Great Sexual Untruths.

Marie was sharply aware that Marlon might turn up at any moment. Even so, the minister had seized her attention. In her experience, sex and dishonesty – albeit mostly with herself – were intimately entwined. She read on.

<u>The First Great Untruth: Sex Brings People Closer</u>
Giving and receiving sexual pleasure is one way we show we're close to someone. It is not the way we get close in the first place! To get close to someone we have to talk to them, get to know them and build a bond of trust. Sometimes people's closeness is such that they fall in love and are sexually attracted to each other. But it is still unwise to actually have sex until that love is formalised in a lifelong commitment to be faithful, honest and true — in other words, in marriage!

Marie remembered Rick's bony body pumping in the dark. She tried to stop remembering and moved on to . . .

<u>The Second Great Untruth: Having Sex Before You're Married Makes For Better Sex In Marriage</u>
In recent decades it has frequently been argued that waiting until you're married before having sex with your partner risks disappointments after you are wed. Surely, the argument goes, it is better to find out if you are sexually compatible with somebody else before *you make your commitment to each other, rather than after. That may sound plausible in theory. In practice, however, people often regret not waiting. One leading psychologist has discovered that many women who have sexual intercourse early in relationships are often unhappy both sexually and emotionally within marriages later.*

Marie paused to ponder this. Did it necessarily follow that the early intercourse caused the later unhappiness, or would those women have been unhappy anyway? Maybe they had always been unhappy. Maybe that was why they had intercourse early in relationships in the first place. Again Marie began thinking about Rick. Again, she hurried back to the Reverend Tibworth's script.

> *<u>The Third Great Untruth: More Casual Sex Means That People Are More Free</u>*
> *This may be the greatest Sexual Untruth of all! And who can be blamed for believing it? All around us, every day, we are urged to 'shop around' in the sexual marketplace as if sex is a commodity, like a car or a TV. In the same way we are encouraged to believe that if we keep on looking until we find the 'right' sex our lives will be transformed in every way. But this is just plain wrong! For one thing, sex isn't everything! And if we simply consume and endlessly change brands, we never find true fulfilment. Sure, there are people who claim that 'variety is the spice of life', and some of them may even believe it. But sex is not something you just pick off the shelf. Sex is a special kind of communication. It is an art. It is a sacred form of creativity that people learn best and go on learning together in the context of a lasting, loving, married relationship . . .*

A sort of lurch passed through Marie as she read this. It was partly a heartstring thing, partly a 'down there' thing like she felt when she dressed up for Daniel. But it was mostly an intellectual epiphany. Sex as an art? Sex as communication? Sex as an activity that you and the other person engaged in creatively for years and years? These were new ideas to her, quite different from the ways sex was talked about among girlfriends, on television or in magazines.

Divorcing the apple-pie image of Reverend Tibworth from his text, Marie recognised in his words an ideal to which she could largely relate. Religion held no interest for her and her attitude to marriage was firmly fixed by her revolt against Lynda's evangelising about what she'd had with Clay. But the underlying principles, the high ambition, the location of sex within a romance within a true love that ran deep . . . this stirred a wellspring of longing and regret that might have overwhelmed Marie, had half her senses not been primed to hear a key in a downstairs lock and a forlorn footfall on the stairs. She felt her life had become tawdry and that Luke had been created and so far raised surrounded by human impurity.

Marie glanced at the clock in the top right-hand corner of the computer screen. It was already 11.43. She switched off the computer and went round the flat turning off the lights that had survived. Her conscientious nature nagged her to start clearing up the mess but she did not know where to start and she did not have all day. At last, she sat amid the ruins, took her phone out of her bag and made a call. Marlon's mobile rang but there was no reply. Marie left a message for him to call her and then she sent a text: *r u ok?*

For five more minutes she sat thinking. Then she went back to Marlon's bedroom for his keys. She locked the bedroom then put the bunch in her rucksack: her duty was to find him and they were his keys, after all. Finally she left for Guy's and the West End. For now, she couldn't think what else to do.

SINGLE MEN

Marie knew that Henry Lean's was a classy jewellery shop because Clay had bought Lynda her watch from there. The Amiss family had never been rich or even truly affluent, but Clay and Lynda had always had more than enough social ambition – and, in Clay's case, enough disposable income when business was good – to aspire to items of quality. Hence the three hundred pounds' worth of bold, gold timepiece that had adorned Lynda's left wrist most days since her tenth wedding anniversary and, in Marie's opinion, with maudlin permanence since Clay's demise.

Despite this jaundiced attitude, the knowledge that Amisses had shopped at Lean's before boosted Marie's fragile sense of having every right to be there as she peered through the glass cabinets in the exclusive store. She was all too aware that she had H. Samuel written all over her and that her own watch was a Swatch.

'Can I help you?' an assistant asked.

'Yes,' said Marie, too quickly. 'I'd like to look at some of these.'

'Certainly. Which in particular?'

'Oh God, I don't know.'

The assistant remained cordial. She was young, almost as young as Marie, but she was groomed to signal cool maturity. She found a key from a collection of them secured to her belt and opened the display case. The watches Marie wanted to see were not the most expensive in the shop. But whichever she purchased would eat up almost all the money zipped inside her jacket pocket – one thousand pounds in cash that she'd disbelievingly collected from Guy's kitchen table as Hamlet and Schmeichel nuzzled her knees.

Marie pointed to the three watches on show that seemed closest to what Guy had in mind. The assistant laid each of them out, pouring them luxuriantly from a white-gloved hand.

'They're lovely, aren't they?' she said.

'Beautiful, yes.'

'Is it for you?'

'I wish,' said Marie. She made eye-contact and detected a welcome trace of female sympathy.

'A present then?'

'Yes. My dad asked me to choose it for my mum – for her wedding anniversary.'

'How romantic!'

'Yes . . .'

Was that part of the lie true or untrue? Had Clay been a loving and generous man or a cruel, controlling one? Who would ever tell her everything? As she stood over the watches, studying their details cluelessly, a clip from an imaginary sentimental movie raced like a passing headlight through Marie's head.

'Which is it to be then, Lynda? We haven't got all day!'

'This one, I think . . . Yes, this one.'

'Are you sure?'

'Yes, definitely.'

'Better wrap it up then! Before she changes her mind!'

'Oh Clay, you are a darling.'

'Too good for you, I reckon!'

SINGLE MEN

Marie picked the watch she judged that Lynda would like least.

'Is cash OK?' she asked.

'Of course.'

It helped that the notes were crisp, straight from the presses virtually. The watch was packed in an elegant box. Eager now to escape before something went skewwhiff, Marie stuffed it into her rucksack and zipped the change away – one hundred and seventy-five quid. She said goodbye and stepped out into the street. Staying deliberately within view of the assistant so as not to give the false impression of making an escape, she called Marlon again.

'Ah, yes. This is Marlon. Regrettably, I cannot take your call . . .'

'Please call me,' said Marie after the beep, then added, 'I'm worried about you.'

With the rucksack strapped on tight, she headed off towards Regent Street. She weaved through meandering shoppers, tourists for the most part, reminding her that, as usual, she and Luke had no summer-holiday plans. For the previous three years she'd depended on the largesse of Lynda for a fortnight knock-down package deal to Cyprus or Spain or Torquay. These hadn't been so bad but there was something about her and her mother pretending to be relaxing and enjoying a nice change that felt so false. Neither had brought up the subject of a break this year. Marie wasn't complaining. Darkly, she had already rehearsed her excuse: '*I'm sorry but I can't take the time off work.*'

She realised she wasn't quite sure where she was. The streets were just about familiar but as she'd brooded on the past – mostly on Lynda before and after Clay – she'd let go of her sense of direction. Flummoxed and suddenly a little overwhelmed by the terrifying value of what she was carrying, she stopped to try and get her bearings. Then her phone rang. She dug it quickly from her pocket. The flashing number wasn't Marlon's, though.

'Hello, Guy.'

'Luvvie! How goes the pressie quest?'

'I've got the watch.' She said it secretively, in case a passing mugger should hear.

'Sorry, luvvie, have you got the watch?'

'Yes.' There was traffic everywhere. It was so loud.

'Terr-ific! And what about the other thing?'

'I'm nearly at Liberty now.' Bloody shop. Where could it be?

'As I said, luvvie, it's for wifey, but it mustn't be too *wifey*. Know-what-I-mean?'

'Yes,' said Marie.

'Not too *wifey* . . .'

'I understand.'

'I mean, no knickers or anything.'

'No, no. You said.'

'Terr-ific. Bring them back this evening, yah?'

'Yes, Guy.'

'Jolly important, actually. OK?'

'OK.'

'By six, eh, luvvie?'

'Oh, definitely.'

'Godda go. *Ciao.*'

The line went dead before she could say goodbye. His manic manner, though, had jolted her awake. Back by six? Believe it! She couldn't wait to get shot of the watch. She checked her own timepiece and saw it was already two o'clock. Problem: there was no way she had time to buy the little something extra from Liberty and be back to collect Luke from school. Shit, she'd have to call on Milo's mum.

Would Luke be cross with her? Maybe. But there was a way to put it right.

Marie remembered where she was. Half an hour later she emerged from Liberty bearing a slender, clam-shaped silver jewellery case: a nice place to keep the watch and it still left Guy with over a hundred quid.

'*Keep the change, luvvie.*' He was always saying it. Well, this time she would take him at his word. After all, Marie reasoned, she wasn't going to spend it on herself. It was Luke's fifth birthday in a few days' time and she was almost literally at the front door of Hamleys, The Most Famous Toy Shop in the World. A little of Guy Jolly's lolly was no more than her darling boy deserved.

CHAPTER EIGHT

'It's for you,' said Lynda.

'Uh?' said Marie.

'A phone call, babes. For you.'

'Who is it?'

'I don't know. It's a man. He keeps telling someone he's not mad.'

Marie's first waking thought had been that the caller must be Rick. He'd got desperate, become aggressive, was dressed as Superman and was hanging off Tower Bridge. Her second waking thought was that if it had been Rick, Lynda would have known. Her third was that it was Marlon. Her fourth was that it was still dark outdoors. What the hell was going on?

Lynda had all the fingers of one hand wedged between her teeth. With the other hand, she passed Marie the cordless from the base beside her bed.

'Hello?'

'Marie? Bit of a strange time to call, yeah?'

'Guy?'

'Problem, luvvie. Locked out. In the shit, actually.'

Marie's mind groped for some bearings. None were there.

'Need a key, you see. *Your* key.'

Marie detected a few sounds in the background: voices shouting, a passing car.

'Yeah, hilarious,' she heard Guy yelling. 'Now bugger off!'

'Guy?'

'Sorry, fucking prats . . .'

'Who? I mean, where are you, Guy?'

'Locked outside – need your key. Getting pretty desperate, yeah?'

'Who is it?' mouthed Lynda, clutching at the drape of her nightie.

Marie turned away from her. She could only deal with one hysteric at a time. 'You need me to come to your house?' she said. 'Is that it? With the key?'

'Got it – on the button! *Ciao.*'

'I'll be there in a few minutes,' said Marie. She switched off the handset woodenly.

'Who was it?' hissed Lynda, pop-eyed.

'It was Doctor Jelly – Guy.'

'Is he mad, ringing at this hour?'

Marie was already out of bed. 'Yes, Mum,' she said. 'In fact, he's mad at all hours. I'll just check on Luke and then I'll go.'

Marie declined to call a cab. Instead, on an impulse, she wheeled her old bicycle out of the garden shed and rode to Kingswood Avenue in a state of surreal elation. The shock of being woken, the rush of adrenaline, the race through nearly empty streets at dawn: these conspired to make Marie feel light-headed and free in a way she hadn't done for a long time.

She passed Daniel's house, swerved to the right, bumped up the kerb and dismounted at speed, just the way she used to as a child. The red Aston Martin loafed at the roadside but there was no immediate sign of Guy. Marie was rather disappointed. Perhaps he'd lost patience and broken in. Perhaps he'd simply found his key. Whatever, she couldn't go home without saying hello.

She went down the short front path, trundling the bike beside her. The clicking of its wheels stippled the morning quiet. She fished for the door key then paused, wondering whether she ought to knock first.

'Quick, luvvie! Top speedy!'

She spun round to see Guy standing behind her. She said, 'Oh my God!' and dropped the key.

'Sorry, luvvie! *Bit* bonkers! Choppy chop!'

He wore nothing but the mustard-coloured tank top from the back of his car, whose welt he held tugged down at the front. His hair was dishevelled, his eyes wild. His voice was hushed and husky, like some plucky Brit escaping from the Germans in a *Boys' Own* adventure tale.

'Key, sweetheart, key!'

He bent to pick it up himself, keeping his foreground portion covered but at the cost of leaving his hindquarters bared. Marie, gawping, backed up hard against

SINGLE MEN

the wall of the porch. Guy fiddled the key into the lock and as he turned it, Marie saw a human figure rapidly approaching from the other side of the frosted glass. It hurled itself against the door and screamed in a female voice, 'Bastard! Fucking bastard! You don't fucking live here any more!'

Marie jumped back as the silhouette threw all her weight against the partly opened door. Braced against it, Guy released the tank-top welt, which catapulted up his torso and came to rest above his navel. Marie's eyes sprang out on stalks as Guy wedged a meaty thigh into the crack and strove to get inside.

'You don't live here, *bastard*!' the woman screamed.
'Don't be silly, Nigella,' panted Guy. 'Let me in!'
Nigella?
'You don't live here, *shit*!'
'Come on now, Nigella! That will do!'
The Posh PA!
In the distance, Hamlet and Schmeichel were barking. Marie flinched as a side-on Guy forced his body between the doorframe and the door and the harpy continued to harangue. Guy's superior body strength began to prevail, so his assailant took a tactical step back. The door cannoned open and Guy plunged through it, measured his length beyond the fitted matting and lay, face down, mooning wanly in the strong light of the hall. Now Marie saw Nigella properly for the first time. She was smallish, mid-thirtyish and raven-haired. Her black cocktail dress was constructed from a number of overlapping layers, her clenched breasts threatened from the top of it. Her heels

were a good three inches high. With one of them she stabbed at Guy's backside.

'Bastard!'

Stab.

'Shit!'

Stab.

'Fuck you, Doctor Jelly!'

Stab.

'Fuck you and your fucking little wife!'

Marie, immobilised, clutched her bicycle for comfort as Nigella's furious assault went on. To her surprise, Guy's response to it was passive. Still appealing to her to, 'Calm down, luvvie, calm down,' he adopted a foetal position and took his privates protectively in one palm.

Big hands, thought Marie.

Nigella's fist, too, held something precious. By contrast, though, she wanted rid of hers.

'And fuck your fucking present too!' she screamed, and flung something at Guy's head. It missed by many feet and Marie recognised it as it smacked against the wall. It was the watch she'd bought at Henry Lean's.

'Sorry, darling,' Guy groaned, but Nigella was already half-flown. She turned and click-clacked towards the door. As she reached the porch, she noticed Marie. At first, she was startled. Then her eyes registered the bicycle, Marie's defensive posture and her general air of youth. 'Who are *you*?' Nigella demanded scornfully, 'the bloody cleaner?' And before Marie could say anything – even, 'Yes, actually' – Nigella had tossed her head and clattered away.

Meanwhile, Guy had begun climbing off the floor. 'Ham-boy! Schmeichers!' he called to the dogs, who Marie could hear snuffling madly from the far side of the closed kitchen door. 'Hang on a minute!' Guy clambered to his feet, and as he turned towards Marie she clapped her hands over her eyes. 'Marie, see to the woofers, will you?' she heard him say. 'Back in a mo.'

Through her slightly fanned fingers Marie saw that Guy had restored his former desperate frontal modesty. She was thankful for this, though not much less embarrassed by the sight of his bare bottom as his long legs bore it upstairs. She had a memory flash of a TV wildlife programme about fleeing wildebeests. Then she was all alone. What should she do now?

It occurred to her to flee, leaving the bare-arsed brain surgeon to the chaos of his personal life and the distress of his Great Danes. There was Luke to get back to, for one thing. Of course, Lynda could be relied on to look after him. Unfortunately, though, she could also be relied on to be pacing round the house in her silk robe, panicking, and that was another good reason for Marie to climb back on her bike and hurry home. Her sense of duty restrained her. She was confirmed in her opinion that Guy Jolly was insane, but helplessly rather than dangerously so. And clearly, he did not want her to go yet.

Marie stepped over the eight-hundred-pound watch and liberated Hamlet and Schmeichel. She shushed and petted them before crossing the floor to where a phone was mounted on a wall. In her haste, Marie had left the house with neither her mobile nor her watch and she checked Guy's mock-nautical kitchen clock before making her call. It was ten to six. She knew she risked disturbing Luke, but figured correctly that Lynda would answer on the first ring.

'Hello?'

Marie recoiled from her mother's breathlessness. She spoke quietly. 'It's me, Mum. I'm at Guy's.'

'Are you all right? What's going on?'

'Yeah, I'm fine. He'd just locked himself out. I'll be home in a bit. He's making me a quick cup of tea.'

'Why are you whispering?'

'I'm not, am I?'

'Yes.'

'It's because it's still so early, I suppose. And the dogs are asleep.'

'The dogs? I see.'

Marie cupped her hand around the mouthpiece as she lied. Hamlet and Schmeichel were, in fact, making large, lurching circuits of the room – their usual way of filling in spare time. Was her mother really taken in or was she indulging Marie in her deceit? Half the problem with Lynda was that you never could be certain who was the more gullible – her or you.

'Is Luke OK?' asked Marie quickly.

'He's still asleep, bless.'

'OK, I'll be back soon.'

Marie finished the conversation even more abruptly than she had intended because she heard Guy's footsteps coming back downstairs. He called out, 'Come and talk to me, Marie. Come on through.'

Marie obeyed despite a rush of apprehension. Guy's summoning seemed to imply an explanation in the offing, maybe a confession or two. Marie wanted to satisfy some of her curiosity, but as the prospect loomed, her subconscious warned her that there are some things it is better not to know.

Passing the rejected wristwatch one more time, she walked into the front room. Guy was sitting in the middle of his sofa, legs apart. He said, 'Luvvie? Have you seen my shoes?'

Marie looked at Guy's feet. They were bare. The tank top had been discarded in favour of a candy-striped towelling bathrobe. 'I found the rest of my dinner rig upstairs,' continued Guy. 'Cut to ribbons, naturally, but *not* the shoes. Black Oxfords – handmade. Rather nice, actually. Sit down, Marie. No, please.'

Marie felt her way into an upright chair, trying and failing badly to keep up. Shoes? Cut to ribbons? Sit down? What ribbons? What shoes?

Guy looked at her and scratched his thigh. 'So you've got a kiddie, right?'

'Yes. His name's Luke.'

Guy knew this already. She'd told him more than once. Was he losing it, or just playing for time?

'Boyfriend?'

'No.'

Guy frowned to show his understanding and made a sternly sympathetic 'I see' sound: 'Hmmmmgh.'

Marie waited. The boyfriend question always made her brittle, except when Daniel was teasing her.

'Luvvie,' began Guy after some thought, 'what do *you* think I should do about my former wife?'

The effects of her rude awakening an hour ago suddenly caught up with Marie. Adrenaline was draining from her and weary impatience was seeping in. At the same time she saw something in Guy's face that told her she wouldn't want to change places with him. His usual madcap insouciance was peeling from him like a face-pack. Marie answered his question firmly: 'Guy, how should *I* know?'

'Cos you're my girl guide, luvvie?' Guy ventured hopefully.

'But!'

'I know, I know, I know. Silly of me. *Not* a thing to ask you. *Not* a thing to ask a little girl *adawl* . . .'

'It's just—'

'Forget it, luvvie, really.'

'But Guy—'

'Bad form. Awfully sorry.'

'Who was that woman, Guy?'

His face fell. Tail no longer wagging. Dimwit eyes. 'Just a sort of girlfriend. Not a serious thing *adawl*.'

'It looked pretty serious to me.'

Guy raised his eyes sharply to hers for a second and Marie wondered if she'd gone too far. Guy's bubble, though, was in no state to reflate. 'Ye-argh,' he conceded ruefully. Perhaps he'd work out later that Marie knew perfectly well who Nigella was. Screwing the snobby secretary, eh? Well, well. Not any more.

As she acclimatised to Guy being a lump of misery, Marie softened slightly. 'If there is some way I can help . . .'

'Shenanigans in the car, you see,' said Guy, breaking in mournfully. 'Got caught out. Should've seen it coming.'

'Maybe,' said Marie, 'we could talk about it later. It's just that I need to get home to my son.'

'Wonderful, kids, aren't they?' said Guy.

'Yes, they are,' confirmed Marie. She felt emotional suddenly. 'I'll be back later, as usual. You could tell me all about it then.'

'Can't do it, luvvie. Gotta saw off someone's head at ten-thirty.'

'Oh.'

'Not literally, luvvie.'

'I . . . didn't think so.'

'Course not, no.'

Marie rose before the conversation died out totally. Guy reached into the pocket of his robe. He pulled out a large red banknote – a fifty. 'Have this,' he said. 'Good of you to come over. Would've died of exposure without you.'

This veiled reference to his earlier nakedness lifted the tension moderately. It meant Marie could refuse the money more easily. 'That's very kind of you, Guy, but I didn't do it to get paid.'

'Take it, come on. Be a good girl.' He flapped the note at her limply.

'I'll come back and tidy up later – and I'll walk the dogs. Is that OK?'

'Right, yeah, definitely.'

Marie completed her slow reversal to the door. 'Goodbye, then,' she said.

'*Ciao* then, luvvie.'

She left him to his dismal contemplation and spotted one of the missing shoes the second after she'd shut the front door. It was jammed, toe first, in a terracotta plant trough on the outside windowsill. Marie tugged it out and left it in the porch. The second shoe had been less artfully abused. Marie spotted it on the soft-top roof of the Aston Martin almost before she spotted the two WPCs peering through its side window and grinning. Feeling light-headed again, Marie slowed the bike and innocently asked them what was wrong.

'Good question,' said the first officer, a short, pugnacious law-enforcer with pink points of excitement on both cheeks.

'We seem to have a clue,' said her companion, whose face Marie couldn't quite see because it was pressed so tightly up against the glass.

Marie said politely, 'What's to see?'

The second officer turned to her. She was dark and petite and was rolling her eyes like marbles. 'Take a peep,' she said.

Marie pieced the story together gradually. Guy and Nigella must have been out for the evening. There had clearly been a major reckoning. Whether Nigella had lost it before or after she'd handcuffed Guy to the steering wheel was impossible to say – as it was to know whether sex had been involved and, if so, whether Guy had wanted it that way. Whatever, even his shirt had been ripped and snipped from him – nail scissors were involved, presumably – and the watch he'd told Marie was for his 'ex-wifey' hadn't appeased his fiery consort at all.

How had he escaped? With the help of a passing workman, seemingly. The giggling WPCs explained that a neighbour had complained about a disturbance, saying that a naked brain surgeon was being sawn out of his car. Once free, Guy had been able to use his mobile phone – which, luckily for him, Nigella hadn't savaged or forced him to eat – to call 'the bloody cleaner' to his aid. Of course, before either Marie or the – frankly sceptical – police had arrived, a few other early risers had spotted him flapping about clad only in a garment he'd probably last worn when he was thirteen, and commented accordingly. Hence the background cries of *'Bugger off!'* Hence his decision to hide in the hedge until Marie rode to the rescue.

'Do you know this brain surgeon fellow?' one of the WPCs had asked.

'I'm afraid not,' Marie had replied. 'I don't come from round here.'

'This is all Daddy's idea,' announced Elice. 'I won't talk to him about it so he's asked you to try to get things out of me.'

'Well, sort of,' admitted Marie.

Things were going badly. She'd picked Elice up after French Club as she had the previous Wednesday, but this time Luke was not with her. Marie had arranged for him to go to Milo's after school so that she and Elice could be alone. This decision hadn't gone down very well. 'I *like* playing with Luke,' Elice had carped indignantly. 'If my usual plans have to be changed for some dubious reason it would at least be nice to have some warning.'

'Oh, la-de-dah,' Marie had countered. She was in no mood to debate the point, especially with Elice in snotbag mode. A day that had begun with such cathartic excitement had subsequently gone steadily downhill. After returning home from the lunacy at Guy's she'd incurred Lynda's displeasure by giving only slippery answers to the many questions her mother had asked, then got annoyed with Luke for imitating Elvis.

Once she had marched The King to school – still hiccuping 'Heartbreak Hotel' – she'd returned to Guy's as promised to walk Hamlet and Schmeichel while he was at work. This was never the combination of romp and pleasant stroll it might otherwise have been because the rule in Queen's Park was that all dogs had to be kept on leads. With a single, docile Dachshund this would have been a piece of cake but keeping both Great Danes to heel for half an hour at a time was a huge physical challenge even when they were calm and the events of the early morning had left them very skittish indeed.

'Down, Hamlet, down!'

'Sit, Schmeichel, sit!'

People were watching.

People were listening.

People were laughing too.

SINGLE MEN

Great Danes, geddit?

Some time ago, thank you.

Back at the Kingswood Avenue house, she'd done a basic tidy, sticking strictly to the rooms downstairs. Let Guy sift through the ruins of his scissored wardrobe. She already had one scene of domestic devastation to worry about – Marlon's – and that struck her as a lot more serious. She still hadn't heard from him, despite sending several more texts and leaving increasingly pleading messages. At this rate she'd have no choice but to go to his parents, no matter how unattractive the prospect. Had he been in touch with them himself? She doubted it. But, if he had, what had he told them? And would they be prepared to share whatever he had said with a no-A-levels person like Marie?

By the time she returned home, Marie was ragged with anxiety and fatigue. Having resolved to give Marlon until nine o'clock that night to get in touch, she'd dropped off for a while in front of the QVC shopping channel but woken feeling much worse than before. She'd showered and she'd changed but nothing had helped. She was still groggy and feeling guilty about Luke to boot when she got to the Academy twenty minutes late, and had been ashamed to meet the Head's secretary's beady eye. It had then taken Elice an age to choose a café to her taste. And now she was throwing a strop.

'What *exactly* does Daddy want to know?'

'I think he thinks that *you* think you don't see your mum enough,' Marie replied.

'You mean he's worried that I might like her too much?'

As she said this Elice rolled her eyes, implying deep disdain for Marie's efforts at finesse. Marie was needled: the eight year old's imputation of lumpen conversation skills put her in mind of the trendy girls at school.

'The thing is, Elice,' she persevered, 'your dad cares about you. He's worried about the whole situation, especially now you're getting quite grown up.'

Elice wrinkled her nose: only *quite* grown up, eh? She said, 'I know all about Daddy, you know.'

'Do you?'

'Yes. I know that he is not as other men.'

'That he's not . . . what?'

'It means he doesn't do girlfriends,' said Elice, describing quotemarks with her fingers around the last two words.

'I know that, yes.'

'Which makes it rather surprising that I'm here.'

'Yes. Well, maybe that's why you're such a surprising girl.'

'I like to think I'm surprising.'

'Yes, I bet you do. What else do you think, Elice?'

'Oh, that families are over-rated.'

Marie paused and sipped her giant coffee. Elice watched her from behind her giant chocolate muffin. It was that sort of café: giant prices too.

Marie said, 'What do you mean?'

'Well, families are supposed to be happy.'

'True.'

'There's even a card game actually *called* Happy Families.'

'Is there? I didn't know.'

'Well, there used to be – with special cards. Daddy has some. Anyway, how many families are truly happy?'

Marie shook her head slowly, to signify that the question was too big. 'Elice, I don't know.'

'Well, my family's not happy.'

Marie pursed her lips. 'What do you mean by your family?'

'My mummy, my daddy and me.' Elice made a display of summoning patience: *I'll explain this ve-ry slow-ly* ... She said, 'My daddy and me love each other, even though I'm cross with him lately – and my mummy and me love each other even though she ran away from me to Spain when I was a baby and even though I only see her now and then, even though she's back in England, because my daddy doesn't like me seeing her at all.'

'Uh huh.'

'And there's the problem, see. My mummy and my daddy do not like each other. Because of that they make each other unhappy. And that makes *me* unhappy! So we are not a happy family! Do you see?'

Marie had to smile. Elice was such a one-off. It was no wonder Luke looked up to her.

'Your daddy died, didn't he?' said Elice.

'Yes, he did.' Marie took this calmly. She'd always assumed Daniel had told her.

'How old were you?'

'Fourteen.'

Elice evaluated this, perhaps detecting for the first time in Marie the cachet of a victim of tragedy.

'Were you very sad?' she asked.

Now Marie had to laugh. Elice's bluntness might have been offensive had her question not been so, so serious.

'I suppose so.'

'You *suppose* so? Don't you know?'

'I've forgotten, you see. It was a long time ago.'

'Your family was happy though, wasn't it? Before he died?'

'Was it?' This, she *hadn't* told Daniel.

'Your daddy and your mummy loved each other, didn't they?'

'How do you know?' asked Marie. The question was genuine.

'They must have.'

'Why?'

'They never split up, did they?'

'How do you know that?'

'Because Luke told me.'

'Oh yeah? What else did he tell you?'

'It was ages ago. He told me that his grandad was very, very funny. He could do lots of funny voices and was always making jokes.'

'Did he now?'

'Yes. And making things.'

'I see.'

'And buying presents for you.'

Well, well, thought Marie. Lynda has been talking a lot lately. She asked Elice, 'Does Luke ever talk about his own daddy?'

Elice nodded, cautiously. She knew this was tricky territory.

'What does he say?'

'That his name is Richard but that he's called Rick.'

'Anything else?'

'Not really. He doesn't know anything else, probably. Or maybe he just doesn't say it. I mean, I think he's *thinking* things, if you see what I mean.'

Marie did know what she meant and she preferred not to discuss it. Instead she went to the counter and bought another coffee and another muffin and a glass of milk for Elice. Happily, Elice had so enjoyed expounding her Unhappy Families theory that her whole attitude was transformed. She spent the next half-hour telling Marie about the play she was writing, the pretend fairies she was friends with and the fashion house she would found when she was eighteen, and all Marie had to contribute was 'Really?' and 'How amazing!' and 'Wow!'

This was just as well because she really wasn't up to any more. It was obvious to her by now that she was falling ill with one of those summer bugs that come at you out of nowhere when you're already tired and stressed and make you feel like re-heated death. At least it meant she experienced some small measure of relief when a text message finally arrived from Marlon:

Hello Marie. I'm afraid I've had to go away for a few days. I have informed my parents. There is no need for you to go to my flat. I will be in touch again on my return. Yours with apologies, Marlon

He wasn't dead. He didn't need her. She could be ill properly. She replied *OK* and left it at that. And now it was time to hurry home.

'So, Elice, please answer me honestly. Would you like to see more of your mummy?'

Elice shrugged. 'Daddy says she's a termagant.'

That word again. Marie sidestepped it. 'But would you like to? If you don't want to tell me, please tell your daddy. He really wants to know how you feel.'

Elice spoke with perfect clarity. 'I think my mummy really needs me. I think she's unhappy. I think she's very, very unhappy indeed.'

CHAPTER NINE

Marie's mobile lay on the carpet close to her, yet its ringtone seemed to reach her from the far side of a foetid bank of fog. She groped for the phone with one hand and pressed the other to her forehead. 'Hello,' she said as brightly as she could. Her brow was clammy, her senses clouded and her temples thumping in complaint. She was anticipating Daniel, hoping it was Marlon, dreading it being Guy. But it was none of the above.

'Whydoesthisalwayshappentome?'

'Gabs? What's happened?' As if she hadn't guessed.

'Hewassoluvleeee . . .'

It was light outside but the curtains had not been drawn. Marie squinted at the mantelpiece clock. To her amazement it was nearly noon. She'd flaked out on the sofa the previous evening and not moved since.

'CanIcomeandseeyouuuu?' mewled Gabby.

'Course you can,' said Marie feebly.

'Whereareyouuuuu?'

'I'm at home,' said Marie.

'Seeyouinaminute . . .'

'OK, Gabby. Bye.'

Marie put her phone down and was just shoving her head underneath the velour sofa cushion she had used as a pillow when the doorbell rang. It rang again as she rolled limply to the floor and yet again, longer and louder, as she made her fevered way along the hall. 'All right, all right, I'm coming,' she groaned beneath her breath, for once not caring a cuss if the Jehovah's Witnesses or parcel postman saw her looking a fright. Opening the door she flinched as the light of day blazed in. Then, through drooping eyelashes, she surveyed the sorry state of her best friend.

Gabby's eyes were red. Her nose was redder. Her hair had gone all ratty and her toenail paint was chipped. Her body language signalled helpless apology, perhaps partly inspired by the realisation that phoning from the porch was pathetic, perhaps partly for still being alive when any worthwhile person in her dreadful condition would by now have hurled herself off a cliff. When she spoke, her words sounded like they'd been wrung from the wad of sodden tissues with which she dabbed her face.

'Can I come in?' she blubbered dismally.

Marie said, 'You can if you want what I've got.'

'Why not?' snuffled Gabby. 'Let's do the job properly.'

'You've been dumped, right?'

'*Huh-owwwwww,*' Gabby hiccuped wretchedly.

'Suppose I'd better make a cup of tea.'

'*Huh-owwwwww.*'

Marie turned and laboured back down the hall, twice

checking that her friend was following. They flumped into the kitchen like disappointed clubbers facing dawn. Marie filled the kettle and switched it on. Gabby perched insecurely on a chair.

'What happened?' asked Marie, poking blindly in the cow-shaped decorative milk jug – a souvenir of Devon – where Lynda stashed a spare pack of paracetamol in case of a nuclear attack.

Gabby sniffed.

The jug was on the highest shelf. Marie's fingers found the packet gratefully. She chased down two capsules with a glass of water and turned to look at Gabby, feeling a fraction more prepared for providing large dollops of sympathy. Gabby was staring out of the window. As Marie's nose caught the acid stench of her own sweat, her eyes saw that a folded slip of paper was protruding from beneath the sugar bowl. It was a note from Lynda.

Hello babes,
Luke is fine, I'll fetch him today. You stay in bed.
Kisses, Mum

Kisses, eh? thought Marie. What have I done right?

She took two mugs from their hooks, threw a tea bag in each, poured boiling water on them and carried both to the table, then a bottle of milk and a teaspoon. 'So come on,' she pressed gently. 'What happened? Was it last night?'

Gabby nodded mutely and pushed out a reinforcing

bottom lip. She drew a deep breath and said, 'He thinks I'm gorgeous, and everything. That's what he said. But not really drop-dead gorgeous.'

'What?' Marie's tone was outraged. 'He said *that*?'

'*Huh-owwww.*'

'Oh Gabby, what a prat.'

'He said . . . *huh-owwww* . . . it wasn't fair on me not to say so. It was better to be honest and end it now.'

'But you're really *beautiful*,' protested Marie. 'What's he want – Britney Spears?'

'Probably,' blurted Gabby. 'And anyway, he's right.'

'Rubbish,' said Marie, with all the force she could muster. This wasn't very much, not for want of sincerity but because her cranium was thudding like a tumble dryer full of bricks.

'It's not rubbish, though, is it?' resumed Gabby bitterly. 'I'm not drop-dead gorgeous. I know it, you know it. I'm fat and I'm useless and I haven't even got a proper job.'

'Gabby, how can you say that? And you *have* got a proper job.'

'It's a shit job.'

'No, it isn't. You're assistant manageress!'

'So what? It's still shit.'

Then they went a bit quiet. The reasons for the impasse were understood by both, though neither wanted to acknowledge them. Gabby wasn't drop-dead gorgeous, at least not in the *FHM* way, and her job didn't represent fulfilment of even a fraction of that 'potential' she and Marie's teachers used to bang on about.

SINGLE MEN

The two friends removed their tea bags, taking it in turns to use the spoon. They each stirred in a splash of milk as if hoping to dilute their failings.

Finally, Gabby said: 'I was an idiot, as usual.'

She scared up a gallows laugh. Marie fashioned a sad smile.

'Why, what did you do?'

'I went and booked us that holiday.'

'Holiday?' It took Marie a second to remember what Gabby had told her in the pub. Then she said, 'Oh my God! That was rash.'

Gabby blushed and reached for her Royals. This was more eloquent than saying, 'Yes.'

'Tell me about it,' Gabby said.

'So he wouldn't go with you?'

'No. It was straight after I told him he ended it. I mean, he was gonna end it anyway. Like, he said he thought it was all getting too intense.'

'Isn't all camping in tents?'

'Ha bloody ha, Marie.'

'Sorry, Gabs.'

' 'S'all right.'

'Oh my God. What are you gonna do now?'

'Dunno. I already paid for it. Like I said, I've been a total idiot.'

Very slowly, Gabby got to her feet. Her whole face was fallen and forlorn. From it came the standby phrase she always used when woeful: 'I'm going for a fag.'

Marie watched her light up and wander down the garden, noticing in passing that smoking lost its glamour when indulged in amid pansies and sweet peas. She felt a tiny bit less wretched than when Gabby had arrived – the tea and paracetamol were working – but still too feeble to make a trip up to the bathroom. Instead, she trudged to the downstairs toilet and when she arrived there, had more than one good reason to sit down. In the too-small mirror, she made a 'yuck' expression at her grey skin and yellowed eyes, and a 'tsk' sound on discovering that one of her earrings had fallen out.

Marie splashed her face with water and was fumbling for the hand towel when for the second time that day her mobile rang. She didn't rush to answer it and by the time she'd flopped down with it on the living-room floor, a message had already been left. It was from Daniel. Marie chewed a fingernail and played it back.

'Cupcakes, thanks for your efforts with La Virago Junior but I'm afraid they haven't done a lot of good. She's still not talking to me. In fact, since she got home last night she hasn't even come out of her room. Ah well. *C'est la vie. Que sera sera.* Please call me a.s.a.p. Bye.'

Marie let the phone fall to the floor. 'Thanks a bundle, Daniel,' she muttered sourly.

'What's happened?' asked Gabby, entering the room.

'Oh nothing.'

'My God, you look ill.'

'And the Pope's a Catholic, I hear.'

'Sorry.'

'Never mind. Nice of you to notice.'

'Sorry, darling, sorry. Honestly.'

SINGLE MEN

Gabby joined Marie at carpet level. Settled, cross-legged, in front of the armchair beside the stereo she seemed a little brighter, partially restored by a good howl. Now it was her turn to offer a shoulder. 'Was that your mum on the phone?' she enquired.

'No. It was a message from Daniel.'

'Oh yeah? Is Luke still in love with his daughter?'

'Good luck to him if he is. She's a little madam, that one.'

'Oh. I thought you liked her.'

'She's still a little madam.'

Marie's mood had darkened too much to elucidate. Gabby soldiered on. 'Still, the thing about your job, at least you care about the people you work for. Not like me.'

'Yeah, well.'

'I mean, shoving sad old slappers under the grill all day.'

'Beats being a slave to three crap blokes.'

Gabby looked surprised. 'I thought only Big Hands was crap.'

'They're all crap,' said Marie, but her heart soon regained the upper hand. 'I mean, they aren't crap *really*, but they've all got problems, believe me.'

'Problems?' said Gabby, now cheering up considerably. 'Like what?'

'I shouldn't really say.'

'I know *that*,' said Gabby gleefully. She jumped back to her feet. 'How about you decide you're going to tell me everything and I'll make us another cup of tea?'

She headed for the kitchen without waiting for a reply.

To some she would have seemed revived, but Marie knew her friend was grabbing at the nearest distraction. Marie herself was too hardened to life's realities to do the same. That was motherhood for you, she supposed. Moreover, Daniel's message had really shaken her. It had brought home brutally her failure to make headway with Elice and stirred again the still unfamiliar feeling of resentment at Daniel for dragging her into his battle with Miss V.

By the time Gabby returned with two mugs and a packet of biscuits on a tray, Marie was smarting with self-pity. Bloody Daniel. Bloody Marlon. Bloody Guy. Bloody Lynda. Bloody everything.

Gabby passed the biscuits. 'Have a Bourbon,' she said with her mouth full. Bourbon biscuits were a favourite vice of Lynda's. She guarded her supply jealously. Marie, unsmilingly, took three. 'OK,' said Gabby, now settling closer to her friend. 'Spill them. Every bean.'

Marie did her best. And yet, in the end, she did so only selectively. She sketched the previous day's strained encounter with Elice but concealed her displeasure with Daniel. 'You're *joking*!' Gabby exclaimed at least a dozen times as Marie told her the tale of Guy and Nigella and the mustard-coloured tank top that the Great Danes moulted on, but kept to herself how pitiful she'd found him, sitting there grieving for his shoes.

She related discovering Marlon's smashed-up flat and that he'd told her he'd gone away, yet wasn't tempted to disclose his cyber communion with the Reverend Gary and his interest in delaying intercourse.

Why the inhibitions? Embarrassment was part of it in

Daniel's case, for Marie felt she looked a mug to get involved. In Guy's she was wary of appearing a pushover and with Marlon it would have been pure cruelty to expose him, even in his absence, to the girl banter of sexual ridicule. With Gabby probing for more details, these qualms made Marie uneasy, fearful of appearing Soft On Men. And underpinning her telling of each of the men's stories a stubborn loyalty endured. All three had changed from being clients into human beings with whom Marie believed she had unfinished business. This time, there could be no running away.

Gabby, of course, saw things differently. 'What a gang of wankers!' she concluded happily. 'So how's everything going with your mum?'

For Marie, this seemed less treacherous territory. 'She's doing my head in, Gabs, seriously.'

'Oh right!'

'She's being such a pain.'

'What's she done exactly?'

'Oh I don't know. Just, well . . .'

And again Marie just, well, couldn't exactly say. There was the bathroom-blocking and the bedroom-door eavesdropping and that business with the Sugar Puffs, but it all sounded a bit petty. There was something else about Lynda lately – like she had a little secret or something.

'Perhaps she's got a bloke,' said Gabby.

'Fat chance,' snorted Marie. 'As far as she's concerned, my dad's still alive and building patios.'

'That's a bit harsh,' said Gabby.

'Yeah, well.'

'She's still good-looking, your mum. She ought to get out more.'

'Like mother, like daughter, eh?'

'You said it, not me.'

The friends became sombre again. Marie talked about the anniversary visit to the grave and Lynda's telephone tiff with Auntie Barbara. She mentioned walking in on Lynda weeping to old records the previous Sunday. 'She's got to get over him sometime, hasn't she? I mean, you're right, Gabs. She's still got a lot to live for. She's the same age as Madonna, isn't she?'

Gabby, intrigued by Marie's mention of pop divas, began thumbing through the stack of old LPs. 'What do you do with these things?' she asked, sliding a vinyl platter from an Electric Light Orchestra sleeve. 'Did Discmans really used to be this big?'

Marie laughed, but her mirth was fragile. Her very bones were aching and her forehead was going hot-and-cold again. She began shivering.

'Elkie Brooks?' Gabby said, wielding another sleeve. 'Who's she when she's at home?'

'Oh yeah. If she plays that "Pearl's A Singer" one more time I'll top myself, you know.'

'Bonnie Tyler?'

'Dunno. Welsh, I think.' Marie was now too woozy even to be disparaging about Lynda's favourite music. 'Gabs, I'm really sorry but I think I should be in bed.'

'Yeah, and it's time I went to work,' said Gabby, putting the empty mugs and Bourbon packet on the tray. 'Trust me, I'm a doctor. Don't go sharing it with someone else.'

They hugged and kissed anyway. After Gabby had gone, Marie took two more paracetamol, got into her England nightie and before falling asleep, telephoned her mum.

'Hello, babes! How's my poorly girl?'

'Pretty ropey, actually.'

'Go to bed properly, darling. I'll get Lukey. You're no use to no one in that state.'

'OK, Mum. I will.'

She felt she ought to have called Marlon. She felt she ought to have called Guy. But she fell into a drugged slumber almost before she got into her bed. At some point, hours later, she stirred at the sound of Luke singing downstairs – 'totally clips of the heart!' – and again when Lynda was coaxing him to brush his teeth. If there'd been an emergency she'd have got up. But she was too glad for the moment to be dead to her messed-up world.

CHAPTER TEN

Lynda continued doting the next morning. Marie woke in time to take Luke to school but her intention to do so, despite still being a sweaty wreck, was thwarted by the appearance of hot tea at her elbow and the promise of buttered toast.

'Luke's bringing it up,' Lynda said.

Marie mumbled a thank you, doubtfully. The approaching sound of china sliding across a metal tray confirmed that breakfast in bed was indeed on its way, though the slow progress of small footsteps suggested its arrival might be subject to delay. Her mother, Marie perceived, was already basking in Luke's reflected glory. It got right up her nose.

'He's dressed, he's had his breakfast, and he's all ready to go,' Lynda beamed.

'Thanks, Mum,' said Marie, keeping her face concealed by covers for fear that her ingratitude was all too plain to see. She couldn't remember when her mother had last seemed so excited. It was as if Marie being sick had somehow liberated Lynda from a distant, barren land where solicitousness was frowned on and the fine art of over-tending had been banned. Now, at last, she had returned to the land of the sick and needy! See that mother hen fly!

'Here's your tablets,' she clucked, plucking a carton from her bag. 'Take two more and go straight back to sleep.'

'But Mum, I need to ring some people – to let them know I'm not well.'

This wasn't really true: Marie had no tasks to perform for her single men that day. Rather, she remained anxious about them.

'I'll ring them for you,' Lynda said.

'No, Mum, no.'

'Why not?'

'I'd just rather it was me, OK?'

'Well, all right, if that's how you feel.'

Umbrage clouded Lynda's cup of joy. She smiled through it quickly, but to Marie the mood switch smacked of some deeper volatility.

'Mum, are you all right?'

'Course I am, babes!'

Marie pondered pursuing the point. She was deflected, though, when, at long last, Luke entered the room.

'Here's some toast, Mummy,' he said. Marie sat up. Luke, hair brushed and skin gleaming, held his tray unsteadily, pride bursting from every pore. The toast gave Marie a cold come-on from its platter.

'Who's a clever boy, then?' said Marie, concealing her

childish resentment of Lynda. 'Did you make it all by yourself?'

'Yes,' said Luke, and Marie saw that few untruths had ever been so well-meant. How he longed to please her. She melted like the butter had, as well as feeling equally congealed.

'And Mummy?' said Luke.

'Yes?'

'You have to stay in bed.'

Lynda nodded in agreement, earnestly maintaining the obvious pretence that she hadn't rehearsed Luke through this line while downstairs.

'All right, Luke,' said Marie. 'I will.' She nibbled on the toast and gulped the tea.

'And now, Mummy,' said Luke, with something close to a bow, 'I'm going to put my shoes on.'

'Very good, Luke,' said Marie, almost shielding her eyes from Lynda, whose cheeks were puckered in ecstasy.

When Luke left the room, Lynda said, 'Are you on the mend, babes?'

'Yes, definitely. I'll have a bath and I'll be fine.'

'Are you sure?'

'Yes, Mum. I'm sure.' Marie tried hard to sound less testy. 'I'll pick him up from school and maybe take him to the swings. Some fresh air won't hurt me.'

'All right, babes. I'll see you later, yeah?'

Lynda walked from the room, floating on scented air. 'Lukey,' she called, 'are you ready down there? Lynda's coming to find you!'

SINGLE MEN

*

It was five-thirty when Marie and Luke came home. The day was hazy and Marie still felt the worse for wear. More paracetamol needed, and more sleep. Luke, in his school uniform, closed the front door. From the living room Marie heard voices lowering. Lynda had company.

Marie joined it, Luke at her side.

She should have seen it coming.

Perhaps she had in some subterranean way.

'Hello, Marie,' said Rick. He held a present in his lap. He wore a suit and tie.

Marie stepped back, taking Luke's hand. She said, 'Mum? What have you done?'

'Marie, sweetheart . . .' Lynda began.

'Oh for God's *sake*,' said Marie.

There were Bourbon biscuits – another packet – and mugs of coffee on the table. Rick was quickly on his feet.

'Marie, I'm sorry if—' he said.

'Mum, for *God's sake*!'

'Marie, sweetheart . . .' Lynda tried again.

Marie placed herself in front of Luke. She didn't want him to see. The suit looked like its hanger had been rudely removed. Its shrinking contents said, 'Marie, I—'

'I don't want to see you, Rick. I *told* you on the phone.'

'I . . .'

'I don't want to see you!'

'I . . .'

'I don't want to see you. I don't, I don't, I DON'T!'

She left the room in a hurry, taking a bewildered Luke with her. Behind her, she left two figures in abject apology, but it was far too late for sorry now. Son in arms, Marie stormed upstairs.

'Marie? Babes?' called Lynda from the hall.

'Go away! Go away! GO AWAY!'

She hurled the words downstairs behind her like heavy furniture and crashed into her bedroom. She lowered Luke to the floor, then slammed the door and sat with her back against it. From some closet of her memory, Clay's disgust rattled her: '*Get in Marie. Get in!*' After his death, she had defied him. And now Rick was quaking downstairs, casting that long shadow, but with the sun rising on him, instead of setting.

'Come here, Luke,' she said. He came and she hugged him. She hugged him for a full minute, listening. Muffled talk floated up to her. After a while, she heard the front door close.

'Mummy?' Luke asked. 'Who was that man?'

'Oh, no one.'

'Why is he here?'

'He's gone now, darling, he's gone.'

'But Mummy . . .'

'Shh!'

Lynda was on the landing. She tapped gently on her daughter's door.

'Let me in, Marie.'

'No.'

Lynda tried the handle. That's how it always used to be: Clay would shout and go away; Lynda would smooth things over even if it took all day.

'Marie, this is silly.'

'No, it isn't.'
'Is Luke in there?'
'Yes.'
'At least let him come out then.'
'What if he wants to stay in here?'

Lynda tried the handle again. Marie leaned back more firmly.

'I'm worried that he's frightened,' Lynda explained.

'He's with me, isn't he?' spat Marie, but checked Luke's face automatically. She saw more puzzlement than fear.

He said, 'Why can't Lynda come in?'

Marie sighed. She got up and opened the door, stepping away. Her mother leaned through it, pitifully.

'Hello Lukey,' she said. 'Guess what's on TV?'

'For God's sake,' hissed Marie.

'Come with Lynda. Let's put *Cartoon Network* on, eh?'

Luke went with his grandmother, his co-operation secured instantly. Marie seethed at her son's disloyalty, but did not intervene. There had to be a showdown. Might as well endure it and move on. Marie, though, underestimated her own fury. And when Lynda returned they both discovered just how little she'd calmed down.

'Please listen to me, Marie,' Lynda began.

'You set that up, didn't you?'

'Just listen . . .'

'You set it up. He didn't just turn up here. You've been sweetening me up for it. All that breakfast in bed shit . . .'

'Marie!'

'Shit, I said. SHIT!'

'I didn't set it up.'

'You *did*!'

'He called me.'

'Yeah! And you invited him round.'

Lynda was bang to rights. 'I had to.'

'Why did you have to? Why?' Marie was on her feet. She seized her pillow from her bed and threw it – threw it at nowhere, anywhere.

'Because,' said Lynda, 'he was going to come here anyway.'

'I didn't *want* him here!'

'He begged me,' Lynda said. 'He wanted to talk to you – about Luke . . .'

Marie flopped on to the bed. She slammed her hand down on it. '*What* about Luke? *What?*'

'He wanted to see him. And see you too.'

'Well, he managed that, didn't he? Thanks to *you*!'

As if by prior agreement, they both paused like boxers between rounds. Over the years their rows had generated rules, though this time there was a risk they'd be ignored.

'He told me he was sorry,' Lynda said. 'He said he's done a lot of growing up. He's got a better job, better money. He says he'd like to give you some for Luke.'

'I don't want his money.'

'He says he doesn't want to argue with you or upset you. But he says . . . he says . . .'

'What?'

'He thinks Luke's got a right to know him – who he is. He says he must be asking. Well, he is, isn't he, Marie?'

'How do you know what he asks for?'

'Because he *tells* me, doesn't he?'

SINGLE MEN

'Only because you ask him!'

'Because he wants to know! And he knows he can't ask you!'

Marie walked up to her mother. She picked her words ruthlessly.

'Don't you talk to me about facing up to the past! Don't you *dare* talk to me about that! Don't you *dare* for as long as you keep moping about Clay and how you won't ever get over him!'

'Marie, I—'

'Well, *get over* him, will you! I'm sick of hearing about him. I'm sick of you going on. You tell me I've got to face up to the past, but *I'm* the one who gets on with it, *I'm* the one who tries to be strong!'

Lynda began to weep.

'Oh stop it, will you, Mum? I don't need Rick and I don't need you. I'm getting out of here, right now! I'm gonna pack my bags and I'm taking Luke with me.'

'Marie, you don't mean it. Please don't say those things.'

'I'm going, Mum. I'm off. I've had enough!'

Gabby was waiting at Kensal Green station. With Luke sitting between them she and Marie travelled together down the Bakerloo line to Waterloo. They didn't talk much, considering, what with Luke to overhear them and the drama of the day speaking so clearly for itself. Gabby stuck to basics.

'Will Lynda be all right, Marie?'

'She'll get over it.'

'Will you?'

Marie was yet to get past seething disbelief.

'What did she think she was doing? Who does she think she is?'

Luke, luckily, had Big and Little Cilla to talk to. He did, though, look up from them as they pulled into the vast South London terminal and say, 'Where are we going?'

'On holiday.'

'Why?'

'Because I'll go mad if we don't.'

'Why?'

'See that?' said Marie sharply. She pointed to a bulging holdall and a hefty backpack mounted on an aluminium frame that Gabby was heaving from the overhead shelf. 'That's what we'll be living in for the next week. And I have got to carry it. Which means I won't be carrying you too. OK?'

Luke looked at her uncertainly. Marie was hardly ever terse with him. Gabby, to move the mood along, said, 'So Luke, you're gonna be a big boy, aren't you? You're gonna help your mum, yeah?'

Luke nodded silently. There was the hint of a quiver in his lip. Marie, relenting, took his hand. 'Come on, let's get off. I'm sorry, Luke. I'm tired and I've had a terrible day.'

Gabby humped the frame and holdall to the platform. Marie then tried to lift them. It took all of her badly diminished strength. They made their shambling way to the mainline platforms. Marie bought the tickets. Gabby saw them into their carriage.

'Hope it stays hot for you,' she said.

'Thanks, Gabs,' said Marie sadly.

'Got your passports?'

'Yeah. I wasn't too wild to forget those.'

Gabby handed over an envelope. 'Here's all your documents. They're in my name but I don't suppose they'll care. Or just lie.'

Marie accepted them and said, 'I'm sorry it didn't work out with you and Pete.'

Gabby shrugged. 'Story of my life.'

'Not for ever,' said Marie.

'Yeah, right,' said Gabby.

'And Gabby?' said Marie as a whistle blew on the platform and Gabby hurried to get off.

'Yeah?'

'Tell my mum I'll be in touch.'

CHAPTER ELEVEN

In the historic town of Dol de Bretagne the Saturday-morning market was in full swing. As Luke peered into wicker cages at huddled ducklings and dusty chicks Marie tried to acclimatise. They'd arrived half an hour earlier, clambering stiffly from the coach they'd taken from Cherbourg. The transition from that sterile, air-conditioned cocoon to this *tableau* of outdoor Frenchness was unnerving.

'Keep hold of my hand, Luke,' said Marie, too nervous for his safety to risk more than brief glances round. She glimpsed aged stone buildings, café sunshades and stalls offering hats and jewellery, toys and lingerie, African art, vegetables, watches, bric-à-brac. Shoppers shuffled with treacle slowness up and down the steady slope of the narrow high street. A bottleneck seemed to be forming at a junction up ahead.

'Look, Mummy!' Luke said. He tugged at her bare arm and she stooped to share his line of vision. Her left hand went to his shoulder, ready to grip his T-shirt if he were

SINGLE MEN

seized by an impulse to skip away. Her right hand gripped the holdall. She moved slowly in order to preserve the fragile balance of her backpack. The object of Luke's interest was one tiny duckling, which had pattered away from its less independent siblings and seemed to be weighing the benefits and drawbacks of escape.

'Can we buy it?' Luke enquired.

'Where would we keep it?'

'In a pond. Isn't it that's where ducks live?'

'We haven't got a pond, though, Luke.'

'We could get one.'

'How?'

Luke shrugged. 'We could dig a hole.'

'We could. But it's more difficult than that.'

'Why is it more difficult?'

At that precise moment Marie lacked the mental resources to explain the harsh realities of water habitat construction to her son. She needed a taxi. She needed a toilet too and appeared not to be alone, judging by Luke's sporadic jogging on the spot.

'Luke,' she said, 'are you thirsty?'

Her son didn't reply. His nose was half-poked through the duckling prison bars. 'Hello ducky!' he chirruped.

The yellow fluffball ignored him, then waddled randomly away.

'Goodbye, ducky!' said Luke. He stared dolefully after its tail as it rejoined the crowd. Then he turned to Marie. 'Mummy,' he said, 'I'm thirsty.'

'Funny you should say that.'

'Why?'

'Because I'm thirsty too.'

Seizing this rare moment of advantage in the 'why' game, Marie struck out towards the nearest sunshade. It was close to the junction ahead where, as she could now see, the bottleneck was due to a crowd collecting. It made the human traffic meander a little less and was therefore easier to thread a path through.

They'd almost made it to the café when a small cheer rose from the crowd and necks began to crane. Still resting a hand on Luke's shoulder, Marie went up on tiptoe and saw that two young people, a woman and a man, had emerged from the front door of a handsome old flat-fronted building. Her view was far from perfect but she could see enough: the man's suited self-consciousness, the woman's posy and blush. Newlyweds.

'This way, poppet,' said Marie. She edged her boy through some more onlookers then in amongst the plastic terrace tables. A few of the café's patrons looked her way. With all her clobber, her infant, her lack of a male companion and all-over foreignness she felt horribly conspicuous deprived of the cover of the throng.

A slender young man in a short green apron slalomed towards her, notepad in hand.

'Good morning!' he said cheerfully and produced a sweet French smile.

'Hello,' said Marie gratefully.

'Zis table maybe?'

He indicated one at the far edge of the terrace, large enough for a party of four. Marie recognised his kindness and, as he helped her shed the backpack she fished, flustered, for some basic vocabulary.

'Oh . . . *merci*.'

'*De rien*.' He lowered the backpack into a space on the far side of the table, where no one would trip over it. Marie humped the holdall over next to it and noticed that the waiter was helping Luke into his seat. '*Monsieur*,' said the waiter, with a short bow. Luke, for once, was lost for words. The waiter placed menus before them, nodded at Marie and spun away. Sitting down, Marie smiled at Luke. He gazed at her, big-eyed.

'Well, we're here,' she said. 'This is France. I wonder where the toilets are?'

'Is France in London?' Luke asked seriously.

'No. France is a country, like England. Remember? We got here by going across the sea.'

Luke seemed puzzled by this but didn't pursue it. It occurred to Marie that he'd forgotten all about the ferry crossing.

Luke said, 'Where's Lynda?'

Marie answered, 'She's at home,' and added in her head, 'going mental probably.'

'When are we going home?' asked Luke.

'Not for a few days,' replied his mother. 'We've only just arrived!'

She laughed. Luke didn't. Marie began to knot up inwardly. For the whole of the journey her anger and adrenaline had kept self-doubt at bay. She'd sailed on indignation, been fuelled by her fury over Lynda's plotting. Bringing Rick into the house like that! Producing him in front of Luke as if the broken pieces of the past would miraculously reassemble. Now, though, with the campsite only a ten-minute drive away and the reality of seven days' unbroken unfamiliarity closing in on every side, Marie was getting wobbly.

The waiter returned. ' 'Ave you chosen?' he enquired, raising both eyebrows and tilting his head sympathetically. He was in his late twenties, Celtic-skinned and dancer-trim. Marie felt foolish. They'd chosen nothing.

'I'm sorry, no.'

'No problem,' he replied, and as the words came out they were half-drowned by a round of applause from the gathering in front of the betrothed. Amid her anxieties Marie had forgotten all about them, but now the whole café was rubbernecking eagerly.

The waiter went out to the front of the terrace to get a better view. Then, as applause gave way to chatter and shoppers began moving again he returned to Marie and Luke, saying, 'Ze flowers, she threw zem to the bridesmaids.' He made a throwaway gesture and captured Marie with a grin. 'Like mad people! Crazy!'

His good humour reassured Marie and his manner did not suggest that he was making unkind judgements about her. She ordered a cappuccino, an apple juice and two croissants and asked where the toilet was without feeling too silly. Later, she enquired about taxis. Before leaving the café she sent three text messages.

Her one to Gabby said: *We r here. It is great. Love m and l*

Her one to Daniel followed: *Have gone away for one week. Sorry about elice. Marie.*

And finally her one to Lynda: *Have arrived in france. Will be in touch. M*

She had considered and rejected using the word 'sorry' before the 'M'. And as the taxi left the town and headed into the country she noticed that her signal was fading. After a while she switched off her phone and sat back next to Luke. She didn't want to be wanted by anybody else.

CHAPTER TWELVE

By the time she got up the following morning, Marie had already learned some basic facts about life on a holiday campsite. One was that bits of the site in question get everywhere: bits of grass on your groundsheet, bits of dirt in your bedding, bits of grit in your socks and underwear. Another was that for all the shared facilities, a social pecking order is very evident, and she and Luke were on the bottom layer.

They'd taken their first walk around the grounds late on the previous afternoon. Luke had found his ease immediately. By teatime he'd sampled the kiddie climbing frames, the test-your-strength machine, cruised the pedalo lake and dragged Marie round the crazy golf course twice. He'd also discovered, as had Marie, that you could pay for on-site goods and services and even drinks in the English pub by using a Bee-wizzy – a piece of smart technology you wore like a wrist-watch and could load with credit at the reception desk so you didn't have to carry cash.

SINGLE MEN

It made a huge adventure out of visiting the Spar shop. Imagine! Buying sweets without having to pay! But to Marie it re-emphasised what an outsider she was in this community of carefree families. She'd have to really watch her Euro cashflow. And her relative poverty was underlined again as Luke and she meandered through the residential sections of the site. Some of her fellow campers seemed to have better accommodation than many families who lived in Kensal Rise: vast complexes of interlocked domes and awnings or wired-up, plumbed-in mobile homes. By contrast, she and Luke were the have-nots of the neighbourhood. Their property assets comprised one slightly mildewed two-person tent, their furnishings a pair of ageing airbeds and two nylon sleeping bags, and their mod cons, a mallet with a loose head.

It had, though, been while wielding this mallet to futile effect that Marie had discovered something more heartening: that even though the locals were wholly transient, a sort of village ethos prevailed. For a full, mortifying hour after being shown to her plot she'd pored over the tent instructions, heaved bits of green fabric about, and begged Luke to stop nagging her, *please*. Then the rescue rangers had arrived.

'Can we give you a hand, love?'

She'd turned to meet the faces of two men of about forty, each clad in shorts that were a bit too baggy and polo-shirts that were a bit too small. Their expressions were too much of something too: too hopeful to say no to.

'Yes,' Marie had confessed. 'I would really like a hand, actually.'

She didn't like admitting she was beaten. But having completed her flight from hearth and home she had run out of rage and with it, energy. It was hard to believe that twenty-four hours earlier she'd hauled herself out of her own bed, still clammy and weak, and now she was in another country – and more than a little outdoors.

The men's names were Neil and Brian. They were from Crewe and were staying in adjacent mobile homes close by.

'You don't mind us interfering, do you?' Brian had asked.

'No, no, I don't mind.'

'It's just you looked like you were struggling,' Neil had added apologetically.

She had decided to be helpless. Let them think of her as a plucky young single mum making the best of her error-strewn past. She handed over the mallet. Her saviours set to work.

'Here's the groundsheet, Neil.'

'Hello – Brian, this must be the fly.'

'Hang on, Neil, this bit fits on to that bit.'

'I think you're right there, Brian.'

On completing their mission, the men had admired their handiwork and furnished Marie with cautionary tips about the need to slacken guy ropes if it rained – 'as it has done, frequently,' they said several times. They urged her not to hesitate to call on them again.

'That's us just over there,' Brian had said, pointing.

'Next to the Laguna and the Mondeo,' Neil had specified.

SINGLE MEN

The car references had been Swahili to Marie. But she'd been able to pick out the luxury dwellings when their custodians drew her attention to a deluxe gas-fuelled cooking range set up under a gazebo, a clutter of sports equipment and a couple of children's bikes. These men were part of proper families; as was everyone here, Marie had thought, apart from her. Still, the sizes of the bikes had encouraged her. Maybe Luke would be allowed to borrow one. Maybe one of their owners would be his friend.

So now it was Sunday morning. The sleeping bags had been cosy and the airbeds hadn't leaked. They had contrived pillows by stuffing clothes into the nylon bags the tent parts had been in. No further comforts had been needed: they'd both been that tired. And now the sun was shining and they'd ventured out for croissants and they were anticipating pony rides and the adventure pool, and Marie had starting thinking maybe it wasn't so bad being herself and Luke and Big and Little Cilla against the world, when an approaching voice called, 'Anyone home?'

This was a distinctively campsite form of greeting: friendly and deeply illogical. It was obvious that the residents were home. She and Luke were sitting on the grass outside looking at the tiny brick barbecue that distinguished their premises.

'Hello!' said the visitor. 'I'm Jo!'

This was evidently so. She had a big badge saying so. She also had a ringbinder and a smile.

'Hello,' said Marie reservedly.

She wanted to be friendly, but couldn't help but be uneasy. Even in this tanned and possibly still teenage form, Jo represented authority. Marie had registered on arrival the previous day simply by showing the confirmation letter Gabby had received. No one had asked her for identification, or queried why 'Pete' had suddenly become so small. This, though, was a more personal visit. All Marie's insecurities returned.

'I'm your Easycamp rep!' Jo said. 'I've come to tell you about the facilities and help you with anything else you need to know!'

'Oh. Good.'

Again, Marie failed to reciprocate the exclamation mark. The more Jo rejoiced in her at-your-service pitch, the more conscious Marie was of the things she and Luke were missing. Nothing serious: a form of transport, a place to sit, their own cooking equipment.

Jo had her ringbinder open. 'Gabrielle Wayman, isn't it?' she asked.

'Uh, no, actually,' said Marie.

Jo looked up from the binder, puzzled.

'I can explain,' said Marie.

'Peter Burgess?' Jo asked, looking at Luke uncertainly.

'No,' said Marie. 'You see . . .'

Jo waited, still smiling, but less easily. She looked into her ringbinder again. She was compèreing a variation on *This Is Your Life* and things were going very wrong.

'Gabby,' Marie explained. 'That's Gabrielle, who you've got there – she had to drop out, and so did Pete, so she gave the holiday to me. Luke and me, that is. Luke's my son, you see.'

Jo pulled a biro from the breast-pocket of her orange polo-shirt. 'Oh, I see.' The biro hovered.

'Is that all right?' asked Marie.

'I think so,' said Jo. She chewed the end of the biro doubtfully. 'So, what is your name?' she asked.

'Marie. Marie Amiss.'

'Welcome to *Camping du Plaisir*, Marie.'

'Thanks.'

'There won't be a problem, I'm sure.'

'Good.'

Marie was reassured. Jo, however, still appeared perturbed. 'Is someone else coming then?' she asked.

'No. It's just us two.'

'Right. I see.'

Marie said, 'We travelled light. It was a last-minute thing.'

'Right. I see.'

'And we haven't ever been camping before.'

'Right. I see.'

In truth, Jo could not have tried harder to be nice. The difficulty was that each of her standard meet-and-greet conversation pieces ended up highlighting the fact that Marie and Luke were members of an irregular species. She was a student, she explained, and this was her summer job before she returned to Watford and 'hopefully' qualified as a primary school teacher. There was a moment when Jo might have said 'And what do you do?' to Marie but she declined to take it. Marie noticed this. Jo noticed that she'd noticed. They both pretended not to notice that the other had noticed. Marie kept smiling, but for her the exchange amounted to yet another of those tiny tickings-off that seemed to spring unintended from the most routine chit-chat all the time.

More followed. Jo asked Luke if he enjoyed school. Luke told her that he was in Reception class but that on Wednesday he was going to be five. Jo asked him what it would be like, having his birthday while he was on holiday. Luke said he didn't know. Marie didn't quite know what to say. Jo then commented enthusiastically that a lot more children would be arriving the next weekend because that was when most schools started their summer holidays. 'My teacher doesn't even know I've gone away!' announced Luke, with a wicked smile. Marie was embarrassed. She was also galled. Lynda would make it her business to explain Luke's absence to his school on Monday. In a way, Marie was grateful: phoning from the site seemed likely to be difficult. What shamed her, though, was that she'd completely forgotten the job needed to be done.

Things went better when Jo explained that part of her job at *du Plaisir* was to supervise activities for children under nine. There were some 'lovely big tents' next to the Astroturf football pitch, where she and her pals organised 'creative play' every day. Yes, Luke liked the sound of that.

'Maybe see you there, then,' said Jo, rising to take her leave. But then another bum note was hit. 'Oh. Will you be OK with the barbecue?'

SINGLE MEN

'Oh yes, I expect so.'

'You have used one before, have you?'

'Yes.'

'It's just that you said you haven't been camping before . . .'

'I'm sure we'll manage, thanks.'

'It's always the matches I forget.'

Marie hadn't bought any yet. 'Oh yes. Matches.'

She bit on a finger. Did she just send out the wrong signals, or was she genuinely out of her depth? Similar intermittent tremors discomfited Marie throughout the day. After Jo had left, she and Luke decided they'd go to the adventure pool, only to discover that Marie hadn't packed any sun cream: another expense which, though small, she didn't need. Then she had a crisis about her bikini. Even when buying it she'd felt vaguely unnerved by its black ultra-brevity but she'd gone home with it anyway. Now the time had come when she would actually wear it, she asked herself the question why? Was it to attract the eyes of men? A little, probably. But even if men did look, they'd be seeing Luke too. And if one should show an interest, what would Marie do? Too late, she faced the truth that a safe, sporty one-piece would have been a better choice for a devoted single mum.

In the end, the pool visit was trauma-free. Marie kept a black T-shirt on over her top and, for every type of safety reason, stuck close to the keen non-swimmer Luke. In the paddling area she quietly encouraged other kids to play with him, but though he took the odd turn on others' inflatables and copied cries of 'Banzai' and 'Geronimo!'

as he came down the mini-slide, no lasting alliances were formed. He never went long without touching base: he wanted to sit on his mother's back and she to pretend to be a whale; he wanted to put on his armbands – which Marie *had* remembered – and fly with her down the flumes. It was, after all, their first holiday alone together. He wanted to cling to her. And in spite of his sharp toenails, she was moved.

They bought lunch, a little late, from the fast-food café. Roast chicken and chips – a Sunday treat. To escape wasps they ate sitting on a wide stretch of grass, with the adventure pool to one side and a small lake stretching out from its far end. Above the lake a heavy steel cable bore a steady stream of passengers across the water from a high bank on one side to a soft earth landing ground on the other. They dangled from a runner supported only by a climbing harness and clips. Some whooped. Some screamed. Some twisted helplessly. Luke looked up in wonder.

'Can I go on that, Mummy?'

Marie looked more nervously. 'We'll see, Luke. We'll see.'

Together, they whiled away the afternoon. On another part of the grass, supervised by reps, youths and tweenies took turns buffeting each other inside large and ludicrous sumo wrestler suits. Luke was too little to take part. He rolled about laughing instead. Further on was a stable, where ponies of every size were available for rides. Luke was desperate – 'Can I do that, Mummy? Pleeeese?' – as

SINGLE MEN

he'd never sat astride a *real* horsey before. But it was expensive and advance booking was required ('We'll see, Luke, we'll see.'). So they gave the test-your-strength machine a few more lusty clouts and played a couple more rounds of crazy golf. Then it was back to the Spar shop to buy something for tea. It had to be a barbecue meal: Luke wouldn't hear of anything else, and if they wanted to cook there was no other option anyway. They bought bacon, rolls, British baked beans and more than enough sausages because, Luke explained, Big and Little Cilla would eat those.

With these supplies plus a miniature saucepan to cook the beans in, matches, and some biscuits for pudding, they set off on the uphill route back to the tent. Curiosity led Marie to take the path leading past the mobile homes of Brian and Neil. She wanted to see the other members of their families, find out if there was a soulmate for Luke among the kids. Her bikini was concealed beneath the T-shirt, now dried, and a long cotton skirt. She believed she'd made a fair job of her first full day and wanted to describe it to someone who might appreciate her achievement.

Under the gazebo, Neil was flipping burgers.

'Hello, Marie, love. How's it been?'

'Not too bad. Quite a long day.'

'Has your tent fallen down yet?'

'No!'

Others made appearances: Brian with a chef's hat on; Neil's wife Carole bearing salad; Brian's wife Lesley, who was also Neil's sister, carrying plates. All were introduced.

Carole asked Luke what was in the Spar carrier bag. At first, he didn't reply so Marie did it for him.

'We're going to have a barbecue too, aren't we, Luke?' She squeezed his hand. He nodded.

'I bet it's sausages,' said Lesley, joining in.

Luke nodded again.

'And bacon, I expect!' said Carole.

'And beans,' added Luke.

'Ah, sweet!' Lesley enthused.

Luke smiled gloriously. He knew how to charm women of that age.

Neil offered them each a burger. Marie declined but allowed Luke to accept and although adamant that they should not be staying long, agreed to sit and sip a glass of white wine. She learned that the two couples had brought three children between them, all boys. Michael, aged eight, and Connor, ten, were Lesley and Brian's. Seven-year-old Jimmy was Carole and Neil's.

All three were short-haired, wiry and endlessly coming and going on their bikes. These were bigger than they'd seemed when Marie had seen them from a distance and none had stabilisers. This placed them beyond Luke, who couldn't yet ride on two wheels. But if this disappointed him it didn't show. He was too busy charming the grown-ups. The macarena could be wearing when performed at breakfast-time in the downstairs loo, but this new audience was all applause.

Marie finished her wine. The drop-in had gone well. She'd been quietly gratified to discover that Brian had a grown-up daughter from a previous relationship. It made her feel better about herself. Not that she was ready to tell her own story yet.

'Time to go, Luke,' she said. 'The puppies will be hungry.'

'What have you got planned for tomorrow?' Brian asked.

'Not sure. Nothing yet.'

'You know there's football coaching every morning. All ours go to it. Would Luke be interested?'

'Yeah, football,' Luke cried, and did an aeroplane celebration on the spot.

'He's a bit young, isn't he?' said Marie.

'Jimmy'll look after him,' said Neil.

'That's nice,' said Marie. 'Maybe we'll see you there.'

In truth she didn't much want Luke to go. He was no good at football. He just dreamed that he was. But then, unlike her own, Luke's dreams could still take him anywhere. And so it proved the next morning when Luke ran on to the plastic grass for the first time. Unlike all the other boys he had no replica kit – no Arsenal or Chelsea or Man U – just a pair of blue cotton shorts, ankle socks, ordinary trainers and a T-shirt with an apple on the front.

From the touchline, Marie watched in agony as Luke tried and failed to trap a ball under his foot or dribble around a cone. Jimmy, as promised, did his best to look after him but Marie now saw for the first time why sport in general and football in particular was such a kudos thing among boys: if you were good, it showed and was admired; if you were rubbish you were helplessly exposed. Her one consolation was an observation by Neil about the two young coaches.

'They're doing a nice job, actually. You haven't heard anyone put anyone else down – that's because it's not allowed. Now, let's see how they go about picking teams.'

It seemed the session always ended with a series of short matches. The coaches, one a slight, fair lad called Dylan who looked about twenty, the other a tall, broader and probably older guy called Glen with short, dark hair and nicely tanned skin, divided the twenty boys carefully into four groups of five.

'See, that's important,' explained Neil, who'd done a bit of junior coaching. 'If you name four captains and let them pick players in turn, the ones who aren't so good get left till last. It's humiliating for them; I can remember it happening at school. This way, no one has to feel unwanted.'

The same fair-play ethos was applied during the games, with the coaches requiring every player in each team to spend an equal share of time in goal. Marie could see that this spared Luke the potentially crushing experience of letting in goal after goal. In fact, he did not concede once during two of his three stints. And although that was due to no opponent getting a shot on target, he didn't let that stop him from leaving the field of play doing his aeroplane celebration again.

'Well done, Luke,' said Marie, cuddling him.

'That was wicked, Mummy,' said Luke, wrestling free.

By now, all the boys were pitchside. The coaches were chatting to the mums and dads. Marie, having seen the

SINGLE MEN

wisdom of Neil's remarks, went over with Luke to thank them. The nearest was the older one, Glen.

'Thanks for looking after Luke here. He enjoyed it.'

'No problem,' said Glen.

He smiled. He had interesting eyes; somewhere between brown and hazel. Before either he or Marie could say more, the other coach, Dylan, had butted in.

'I wouldn't talk to him, madam. He's a Delia man.'

He winked at Marie. Glen laughed and ignored him.

'What did he mean by that?' she asked.

'He means Delia Smith. She owns Norwich City. And I'm a Norwich City fan – for my sins.'

'Oh, I see,' said Marie, fibbing. She knew nothing about football. The England nightie was just a fashion thing.

Glen bent down to Luke, who was watching everything. He ruffled his hair kindly. 'You're a little battler, aintcha?'

Luke did one of his faces: a kind of goofy, duh-yeah sort of thing.

Glen laughed again. He looked warmly at Marie. 'See you both tomorrow, maybe.'

'OK.'

He nodded, and headed back on to the pitch. Marie watched him, and then was joined again by Neil.

'Marie,' he said, 'we were thinking. If you'd like, we'd be happy to look after Luke this evening so you can go out on your own for a while. I mean, it must be hard work for you all alone and you get no time to yourself in the evenings. I'm sure he'd be absolutely fine. The girls would love having him. So would the boys. What do you think?'

Marie was in two minds. She thanked Neil and said she'd see how things went. At first, she'd thought no. It was still early days and although Luke had taken to campsite life with glee, she wasn't sure she'd feel right about, well, abandoning him. In the end, though, after another non-stop day of swimming and talking and crazy golfing, she accepted the offer. She did it because she knew that, deep down, she was scared of going out and really ought to be braver; and because to turn down the babysitting offer might have looked ungrateful, when those people from Crewe had been so good to her.

She left Luke with them at eight, already wowing them with his Spongebob impersonation and looking forward to a supper of potato Smiley Faces and spare ribs.

There was only one place Marie could go. Eating out alone was a non-starter. The restaurant was too expensive, and going solo to the café would look sad. Either option guaranteed depression. That left the pub.

In her white sandals, cleanest jeans and a pink strappy top, she entered it with trepidation and felt more out of place with every minute that she stayed. One side was dominated by a giant television showing highlights of the day's test cricket: its clientèle was almost exclusively male. The other side was full of families. Without Luke, Marie didn't fit in either camp. Without friends, she didn't fit in anywhere.

She bought a Bacardi Breezer and headed for the terrace, where she felt less conspicuous. She sank the drink more quickly than she should have because she had nothing else to do with her hands. And then she left. As nine o'clock approached, the last of the daylight faded and Marie, almost aimlessly, walked in the opposite direction from the adventure pool down a tree-lined avenue to where there was a large field bordered on one side by a river. There, during the day people sat and fished or hired canoes. It was the quietest part of the site, and right now it suited her. The stars were coming out, but a handful of families were still playing on the grass, hurling a Frisbee or kicking a ball. A couple kissed under a tree.

Marie became reflective. She thought about Lynda. She thought about Gabby. She thought about Daniel, and Marlon and Guy. She thought about Miss Valencia and Elice. She thought about what the future held for Luke. She knew things had to change. She knew she had to grow. How to make it happen was less clear.

CHAPTER THIRTEEN

Dol de Bretagne on Tuesday around noon might have been mistaken for a completely different place from the one Marie and Luke had tumbled into from the coach on Saturday. The high street was quiet to the point of sleepiness, with cars parked where the market stalls had been and very few pedestrians around. Trade at the café where the slender waiter worked might best have been described as restful.

Marie's impression was of neat and clean congeniality. With neither the market-day crowd nor the Englishness of the campsite to melt into, she was more alone with the foreignness of France than ever since arriving there. Yet for the first time since leaving England she felt in command of her situation. Having made her decision to take the bus into town and have a different sort of day *and* having won Luke over to the idea rather than having a row, she also felt that she was being a grown-up and a good mother. The sensation worked like balm on the wounds sustained the previous evening.

SINGLE MEN

'Where are we going?' Luke enquired.

'We're just looking around,' answered Marie.

'Why?'

'To see what we can see.'

They were opposite the building the newlyweds had emerged from on Saturday when the market was in full swing and they had just got off the coach from Cherbourg. It was unfussy, flat-fronted and built from sturdy blocks of stone, creating the effect of modest authority. There was an inscription chiselled by the front door and, in front of the building, a sculpture of a man's head with a tribute of some kind. Marie squinted at these features with mild interest, but her French was too rudimentary to help work out their significance. She guessed the building must be the Town Hall and contain the French equivalent of a register office.

'Mummy, where are we going?' Luke asked once more.

'We're going over there,' Marie replied. Luke looked where she was pointing. Across the road was a turning into a climbing, cobbled street that was almost too narrow for a car.

'Why?' he asked.

'There might be an adventure.'

Luke looked over at the turning then up at her. 'How do you know?'

'I don't know. But there might be. We'll have to see, won't we?'

Tugging Luke behind her, Marie struck out with a display of faked excitement such as parents the world over use to trick innocent children – or try to trick them anyway. Luke didn't really fall for it. He indulged his mother, though, calculating that the off-chance of an adventure was worth taking in the absence of a swing park or ice cream. For her part, Marie was sweetly vindicated when an adventure of sorts actually did present itself in the form of several tiny dwellings with miniature doors, oddly-shaped windows and little stone steps that a small boy could run up and then leap from without having to be caught in Mummy's arms. She walked on, enjoying the rare sensation of feeling unhurried while Luke submerged himself in fantasy. Then, at the end of the little side street, she came to a sort of square with a large and obviously ancient church. Or was it a cathedral? Yes: Marie had seen a leaflet about it at the campsite.

Looking back, she called: 'Can you see the castle, Luke?'

He was heading towards her, but forced to navigate through perils on all sides. This was evident from his ducking, his weaving and his staccato humming of backing music to some U-certificate movie action sequence starring himself: '*Nah-nah nah! Du-nah, du-nah-nah!*'

Marie persisted. 'Look, Luke, a big castle!' The little boy scampered up and clamped himself to her leg. He panted theatrically, still half-inhabiting his escape fantasy. 'What do you think it's like inside, Luke? Shall we go and see?'

Her determination to give her son a Higher Culture experience was in keeping with Marie's aspiration to worldly maturity. At the same time, she wrestled with her uncertainty. What was the procedure for visiting such a place? Would someone ask if they were Christians? Did you have to pray or sing a hymn? Was it all right to just walk in?

Luke was unworried by such things. 'Come on, Mummy!' he urged her, and began tugging her by the hand towards the castle, a young prince eager to prove his valour in combat against the steel-suited warriors within.

'I'm coming,' said Marie, restraining him. 'But remember, in very old buildings you have to be very quiet.'

As they drew closer, Marie looked anxiously for clues about the right way to behave. A scattering of people stood around the building's cobbled apron. They were clearly visitors: young backpackers, student types to Marie's eyes; older couples studying guidebooks or information leaflets of some kind. Marie got more of the measure of the cathedral. To her it seemed a bit misshapen, not magnificent or graceful like the ones people raved about on afternoon-TV shows, the sort she'd watched once or twice when Luke was a baby and she'd been a couch potato half the time.

She watched a pair of the backpackers, a young woman and a young man, approach and pass through the weighty wooden front door. Each had a cagoule knotted around their middle and no hat. Marie took it from this that the dress code was relaxed. Grasping Luke's hand in an unconscious gesture of reverence, she followed the backpackers out of the daylight into the dark.

The vastness of the place struck Marie first – that and the silence on the same scale. It felt bigger and grander on the inside, far more so than the only house of God Marie could recall being in before, the one where she had sung 'All Things Bright and Beautiful' on that dreamlike summer's day when she'd thrown rose petals on top of Clay. Luke, too, seemed aware in a new way of his tininess. Marie's fears that he'd misbehave faded away.

Together, they walked forward, listening to their own echoes and those from centuries before. Stone saints looked down, murals unfolded, pillars soared. Marie was taken back to childhood nights lying awake pondering the boundary of the cosmos and the mystery of creation, and she became a little sad, although not painfully so. They passed down the rows of pews and Marie looked, trying not to stare, at an old woman kneeling, head forward, hand to brow. Luke chewed lightly on his thumb. Marie let her hand brush across his hair.

They came to a small room off to the right. As they entered it, Luke spoke for the first time. 'It's a little house,' he said. He and Marie looked around. The room – in fact, a chapel – was barely twelve feet square with a worn flagstone floor. It contained a huge painting of women and children huddling while angels hovered overhead, a rank of six short benches and a tiny altar with a ledge of flickering candles standing in front of it. At first, Marie thought it was empty. Then she spotted a lone figure standing in the shadows of the corner furthest from where she stood. She spotted too that he had already spotted her. He raised a hand in greeting and stepped towards her, smiling slightly, mostly with his eyes.

'Hello, Marie,' he said.

Marie panicked slightly. Was it OK to speak inside this holy space? 'Hello, Glen,' she answered softly in reply. She turned her eyes back towards Luke. The candlelight had captured him.

'He can light his own candle, if he likes,' said Glen.

'Can he?'

'No problem.' Glen raised his voice a little. 'Luke,' he said, and Marie lit up inside with pleasure at his remembering her boy's name.

Luke looked round, pupils dilated in the gloom. It wasn't clear if he recognised Glen. However, once he'd detected confirmation in his mother's eye he allowed Glen to become his teacher again.

'Look here,' Glen said, and beckoned Luke towards a wooden box of unlit candles secured to the edge of the display. He placed a hand on Luke's shoulder. 'Take one, mate, if you like. Anyone can light one.'

Luke was tentative. He checked with Marie again. This time she made an encouraging face. Luke lifted a candle from the stash and inspected it uncertainly. 'That's it!' said Glen. He pointed to a cluster of empty holders. 'Stick it in one of those, and then we can light it. I'll help you.' There was a taper by the candles in the box. Glen took it, lit it from one of the burning candles and invited Luke to help him hold it. Together, they applied it to Luke's candle. A smile crept across the small boy's face as the wick accepted the flame, and it stayed there as Glen snuffed out the taper by pinching it gently between a forefinger and thumb.

Flickering light fell on Luke's face.

'That was nice of you,' said Marie.

'No problem,' Glen replied. He watched Luke with satisfaction, perhaps remembering the same fascination with wax and flame from his own childhood. In the confined space he seemed taller than he had outdoors. Marie caught her breath slightly as he turned to her and said, 'Do you like it here, then?'

'In France? Yes.'

'No, I meant in here.'

'Oh, sorry. Yes, it's lovely. Very peaceful.' She added hastily, 'Not something I often do.' It had been automatic to distance herself from religion. No sooner had she done it than she worried that she might have offended Glen. Had she interrupted him praying? 'Are you religious, then?' she asked, and felt clumsy. Glen, though, appeared unfazed.

'No, but I like a bit of history.'

'Do you?'

Marie was a bit stumped. What do you say to a football coach who tells you he likes history when you bump into him in a French cathedral? Luckily, Glen helped her out.

'This place is full of it,' he said. 'The whole town.'

'Oh.'

'And this chapel is in honour of Saint Darren Huckerby.'

'Is it? Who's he?'

'He plays for Norwich City,' answered Glen earnestly.

It took a second for the penny to drop. Marie was just getting round to looking at him pityingly – a comedian, how sad – when Luke said, 'Mummy, I need a poo.'

'Oh Jesus,' said Marie.

'Be careful,' said Glen, 'He'll hear you.'

'Oh God!' said Marie, mortified by her blasphemy.

'Him too.'

'Oh . . .' She clapped her hand across her mouth.

'Mumm-ee! I need a poo.' Luke was tap-dancing with one hand shoved halfway up his behind.

'Listen,' said Glen in the voice of a man rolling up his sleeves. 'There's no toilet in here. There's a caff round the corner, though. Follow me.'

She was aware that she kept looking at his hands. They were sturdy and the fingernails were neat and clean. He used them precisely, economically, and often fanned out the tips of them on the table-top when he was in the thick of explaining. He refolded a paper napkin, pressing his thumbs along the creases to make them sharper than before. He positioned condiments symmetrically. Luke watched him from the crook of Marie's arm. They were in a café on the high street. The waitress arrived with a tuna salad, a spaghetti bolognese and a *croque monsieur*.

'It's make your mind up time,' said Glen.

There'd been some dithering over the menu. The salad was Marie's but the other two dishes were yet to be assigned. Luke liked spaghetti bolognese but was worried that it wouldn't be like Lynda's – dining establishments had let him down before. His doubt about the *croque monsieur* was that the food would not live up to the promise of its name which made him think of crocodiles and a joke about them that he really liked – 'get me a crocodile sandwich and make it snappy!' He didn't really think it would be two pieces of bread with a scaly tail sticking from one end and a long head full of teeth grinning wickedly from the other, but he liked the idea of it enough to want to find out for sure. And when Glen had suggested ordering both items and volunteered to eat the one Luke didn't want, the little boy agreed enthusiastically. Now he was presented with the choice and made a great display of hunger, rubbing a hand on his tummy and licking his lips. Yum yum!

'Come on, it's getting cold,' urged Marie. He'd behaved beautifully all day. Inwardly she begged him not to let her down now.

Luke did ip dip doo. Then he did ip dip doo again. Each time the bolognese was 'out' and each time Luke wriggled out of the result. He looked up at Glen, not expecting to find Glen looking straight back. 'Try the *croque*, I would,' he said secretively. Luke pushed the pasta dish gently his way. 'Top decision,' said Glen. 'Mind it don't bite.'

Luke said nothing, but he smiled. Marie took his knife and fork and cut the *croque monsieur* into four triangles, the way he liked his cheese on toast at home. Luke picked one up and began eating. Relieved, Marie said to Glen, 'So, how long have you been working here? At the campsite, I mean.'

SINGLE MEN

Glen had twisted himself a forkful of spaghetti that was impressive for its lack of trailing ends. 'Couple of weeks. Season's only just started really. I'm still finding out about the place. How long are you two here for, then?'

'Just a week.'

'Not long then?'

'No, but it's a break.'

'What from?'

'Oh, you know. Everything.' His hazel-brown eyes fixed on her. In them she sensed him weighing up her answer and she felt suddenly transparent. She laughed nervously.

'Well, we all need a break,' Glen said.

'That's true.'

Glen popped the food into his mouth and winked at Luke. Luke winked back with difficulty – it was more of a blink – and kept his eyes on Glen as Marie said, 'So what's the job like?'

'It's OK. It's a laugh. Bit of a holiday, really. It'll keep me going into September.'

'What will you do then?'

'Dunno yet. Got a few maybes back home.'

'Where's that?'

'Great Yarmouth.'

'By the sea.'

'Last time I looked.'

'Very funny.'

'Stupid joke – sorry. You ever been there?'

'No.' She was anticipating now, half-smiling, half on edge.

'Don't bother,' he said. 'It's full of bloody Greeks.'
'Oh really?'
'Perfectly true. I'm one of them, actually.'
'Oh yeah? You don't look it.'
'Half-Greek anyway. On me mum's side. Greek-Cypriot, actually. There's more of us in Yarmouth than anywhere else except Enfield.'
'Or Cyprus,' put in Marie.
'Now who's being funny?' enquired Glen.
'Sorry,' said Marie, surprised by her own cheekiness.
'All the restaurants are Greek-owned, all the hotels. That's what my family does.'
'They own a hotel?'
'The Excelsior. And a caff – the Cosmopolitan.'
'Your dad's English, though, is he?'
'The last Englishman in catering where Yarmouth is concerned.'

Glen paused to take more food on board. Marie forked up some tuna and wondered what she'd say when the conversation turned to her life and background. She knew only too well that being as young as she was with a child of Luke's age and no bloke attached put certain awkward questions into people's minds. How soon might this Glen get round to asking them? She quickly got in another question of her own.

'So what were you doing before this?'
'Army. East Anglia Regiment.' One of those workmanlike hands, the right one, moved to the glass of water beside his plate. His eyes levelled with hers as he drank and for the first time Marie sensed anxiety in him.

He was a soldier, or had been. What would she make of that?'

Marie turned to her son. 'Luke, did you hear that? Glen was in the army.'

Luke spoke through a cheesy glue. 'Did you drive a tank?'

Glen laughed. 'No. 'Fraid not.'

'What did you do?'

'Oh, lots of things.'

'Did you have a gun?'

'Yeah, I had a gun.'

'Did you do any fighting?'

'Not really, no.'

Luke said, 'We're from England, which is in London.'

'Oh right,' said Glen, nodding sagely.

'From Kensal Rise in London actually,' put in Marie.

'That's sort of west side, isn't it?'

'North-west.'

'So . . .' began Glen.

'Mummy isn't married,' announced Luke.

'Luke!' said Marie. 'Do you mind?'

The boy stared at her blankly. Did he mind what?

Marie checked Glen's face. He seemed not to have noticed Luke's *faux pas*. 'We live with my mum,' she resumed, moving the conversation on. 'And I work as a . . . well, a sort of housekeeper really.'

'Oh yeah? Who do you keep house for?'

'Three blokes.'

'Lucky you!' He wrinkled his nose. 'That's a lot of smelly feet all in one place.'

'Oh, they're not in the same house. Actually, they all live by themselves. Except for one. He's got a little girl.'

'Elice,' put in Luke.

'She's your girlfriend, isn't she, Lukey?'

'No,' said Luke defensively.

'She's older than him.'

'I'm five tomorrow, though.'

'Congratulations!' said Glen.

'I look after her sometimes,' Marie added. 'After she's finished school.'

'OK,' said Glen, nodding. 'And who looks after you, Marie? Or maybe you can look after yourself.'

Now there was a good question. And there, too, was the answer she'd have given had he not lifted it so deftly from the tip of her tongue. Instead, she answered his enquiry in a different way – by taking him into her confidence.

'It's a bit of a long story,' she replied and flicked her eyes Luke's way for Glen to see.

'Oh right,' he said. 'Do you know, I'm so full of spaghetti I don't think I've got room for one of those.'

'Well, never mind,' said Marie.

'I've got room for some pudding, though,' said Glen. 'How about you two?'

Luke had plenty of room. With a special long spoon he devoured the best part of a schooner of chocolate ice cream then let Big and Little Cilla share the rest. Marie and Glen sipped coffees and talked. She explained to him that she was new to camping, but said nothing about the chain of events that had brought her there. He talked about his job, Brittany, and how he was rehearsing for the reps' performance of the songs from *Guys and Dolls* on Friday night. Marie watched him and wondered about him. It seemed that he was popular, one of the gang. Yet a part of him was solitary too.

Luke wiped his mouth with the back of his hand and said, 'Mmmmm.' Little Cilla bit Big Cilla on the bum.

'So,' Glen asked, addressing all four of his companions. 'Are you going to the big night out?'

'What's that?' asked Marie.

'To the circus.'

'What circus? Here?'

'Yeah, it's on the site. Didn't you see the sign on the way in?'

'No.' Marie supposed she hadn't been paying attention – too much else on her mind, probably.

'Yeah, well,' said Glen, 'the Big Top isn't exactly big and it's kind of tucked away. And they did only turn up yesterday.'

'Did you hear that, Luke?' said Marie. 'There's a circus on the campsite! Shall we go?'

'Circus! Yeah, baby!' said Luke, karate-chopping the air.

Marie said to Glen, 'What about you? You going?'

'I was thinking about it,' he replied. 'Maybe I'll see you there.'

Would he be there? Was this a date?

Marie stood near the little ticket kiosk, looking round.

There remained ten minutes before the show would begin and – she was not denying it – she wanted to give him every chance to join them. She'd made quite an effort to look nice, much of it expended on trying to figure out exactly what 'nice' meant when you were going to a circus on a French campsite with your nearly five-year-old child and with no clear idea whether or not the man you wanted to look nice for would turn up. She'd opted for white pedal-pushers, blue yachting pumps, a plain yellow T-shirt and a Nike sweat top, which she had knotted round her waist. No make-up, though – it seemed a bit daft outdoors.

Luke, by contrast, had had no wardrobe dilemmas. His Incredible Hulk T-shirt and blue-grey combat trousers were fine by him, thank you, and while Marie stood fretting he enjoyed himself pretending that the candy floss she'd bought him was growing out of his head.

'Eat my hair, Mummy! Eat my hair!'

Marie took a mouthful to appease him. She was just cramming it into her mouth when she looked up and there stood Glen. He wore a fawn linen suit, a midnight blue polo-shirt and brown suede shoes. His hair was neatly combed and his skin glowed with good health. He'd made an effort, and it showed. 'Good evening,' he said. 'Am I too late for candy floss?'

Luke offered him the stick. He tore a piece off with his teeth and chewed it slowly, like a connoisseur.

'It's good,' he said, 'but not as good as at home. So, are we going in?'

SINGLE MEN

He wasn't just passing through, then. He was with them.

'You look very smart,' Marie said, hoping that being bold about his appearance would lessen her fears of inadequacy.

'I wear a suit whenever possible,' he said.

'Why?'

'No special reason. I just like suits.'

'How do you take care of it on a campsite?'

'Military training.' He looked at Luke and winked. Then he was halfway to the kiosk. 'I'll get the tickets, then.'

'No, you won't,' said Marie.

'Too late,' said Glen. 'I've gone deaf.'

It was a wonderful night out, though, as Marie mused later, the feelings it inspired were different for each member of the party of three. For Luke the whole event was pure wonder. For Glen its appeal lay in the pathos, the bravado and the moments of unintended hilarity. Marie saw the performances in much the same way. For her, however, the experience was less about the animals and the acrobats than the chemistry her male company kindled in her.

When she looked down at Luke enraptured by the little girl who could keep five hula-hoops rotating round her waist, the little boy who could hang so far off the side of a cantering pony his fingers dragged along the ground, and the dogs that walked on ramps of scaffolding, her heart ached with love. When she looked across at Glen seated on Luke's far side and knew that he, like she, had noticed how bored the hula-hoop girl seemed, how exultant the boy was and how the dog trainer looked as if he'd dragged his costume out of the same skip in which he'd dumped his smile, her heart did something else: it nagged her, tugged at her, sent out signals of longing she'd almost forgotten how to receive.

They hardly spoke during the show. Yet when it was over, and darkness was closing in, it went without saying that he would walk back to their tent with them. They compared notes, secretively, for fear that Luke would hear and the spell of credulity keeping him in awe would be broken. At first he scampered ahead, but then he tired.

'Carry, Mummy, carry,' he demanded.

Marie harrumphed at him. She was tired too and she disliked him reverting to babyhood. It always worked with Lynda, though. Maybe that's why he was trying it on.

'Come on, I'll carry you,' said Glen.

He heaved Luke up and threw him over his shoulder. The trio moved on more quietly, letting the campfire smells and nightlights shift their mood. Their silences contained no awkwardness until Marie's tent came into view. Glen halted and looked at her.

'I had a great evening,' he said.

'No kidding?'

'No kidding. It was beautiful.'

'Pardon?' said Marie.

'It was beautiful.'

Marie giggled at him.

'What's funny?'
'The way you say it: *bootiful*.'
'Oh right. That's how we talk in Norfolk.'
'What else do you do in Norfolk?'
'Oh, the usual. Ride tractors. Worry sheep.'
'Can't wait to go there.'
'Maybe you will, one day.'
'Maybe. Who knows?'

Luke was bored by the lack of forward motion and decided to recover his lost strength. He wriggled down from Glen and went to practise headstands against a tree.

Glen said to Marie, 'These days, in the army, if a male officer has to touch a female officer, straighten a bit of her uniform or something, he has to tell her what he's going to do first.'

'Really? How strange.' Her sarcasm was gentle. He ignored it and looked at her searchingly.

'It's to avoid misunderstandings. Like, in case she thinks he's trying to touch her up, or something.'

'I see.'

'So I'm saying to you, Private Amiss, that I am now going to peck you on the cheek.'

He bent halfway towards her. She closed both eyes and angled her face. It was softer than a peck and lasted longer – long enough to let her know it had ended reluctantly.

'We'll see you tomorrow then, shall we?' said Marie.
'I don't think you will, actually.'
'Oh?'
'I have to go and help at another camp. They've got a

few people off sick and I've been asked to go and cover. Then in the evening I've got rehearsals for *Guys and Dolls*.'

Marie said, 'That's a pity.'

'But I'll be here again on Thursday.'

'Is that a promise?'

'Yes. And I hope Luke has a brilliant birthday.'

CHAPTER FOURTEEN

Luke's fifth birthday began shortly before dawn. It wasn't his fault, he explained. First, Little Cilla had needed a wee, which had meant Big Cilla had to go with her. Then he'd needed a wee, which meant Marie had to go with him. And that was why he'd had to wake her up.

'What's it like being five, Luke?' Marie mumbled.
'Like being four but bigger.'
'What's it like being bigger?'
'Twenty-two.'
'Pardon?'
'That's how old you are.'
'Clever you.'
'Mummy?'
'Yes.'
'I need a wee.'
'Can't Big Cilla take you?'
'No.'
'Why not?'
'Because Big Cilla isn't real.'

His anarchic mood endured throughout the day. He went to football again, but this time gave up halfway through.

'Where's Glen?' he asked.

'He's away for the day.'

'Can I have my cake yet?'

'Cake is later.'

'Why?'

'Because it's too early for cake.'

'Why?'

'Because it is. Oh Luke, let's not get silly on this special day.'

The truth was, Marie had yet to buy a cake. She'd given him a card and some presents – a campsite souvenir T-shirt and a selection of cheap toys from the Spar shop – and even found some sparkly paper in which to wrap them up, but she'd seen no really nice celebration food. She should have got some yesterday in Dol. But it was hard when Luke was with her and there had been the distraction of the enigmatic Glen.

'The thing is,' she explained, as they left the Astroturf, 'this isn't going to be a normal birthday.'

'Where's Lynda?' he asked.

'At home.'

'Can we go home, Mummy?'

'I'm sorry. Home is too far away. We're going to phone her, though.'

'Why can't we go home?'

He was trying out his moany voice again. Marie ignored it. She didn't want a battle with him and she wanted him to have a lovely day. At the same time – and to her lurking shame – she was struggling to give him her full attention. She was preoccupied and in more than one way.

For one thing, since last night, she'd begun thinking about unfinished business back home. It was ridiculous because she'd run off here to France to get away from all those things – and, of course, from Lynda who was now a particularly pressing issue. The forthcoming phone call was going to be interesting, as they say.

Then there was Glen. Marie was trying not to get excited. Holiday romances were notoriously shallow and short-lived. The trouble was, she liked him. And was intrigued by him. He was such an unusual mixture: sporty, intuitive, blokey, solitary, witty, a bit wacky, gentle and kind. Perhaps that was the chief reason she was out of sorts today: she wanted to solve his mystery but, frustratingly, he wasn't around. Marie became gloomy suddenly. Perhaps he hadn't really had to be away all day; perhaps he was making it up about *Guys and Dolls*; perhaps he'd got scared and had already, as far as she was concerned, run away.

And another thing: she needed to do some laundry soon.

'Come on, Luke,' she said, 'let's ring your granny.'

'She isn't called Granny,' said Luke sulkily.

'Only behind her back,' replied Marie.

In the event, the birthday phone call went surprisingly well. Marie and Luke didn't have to wait too long for one of the few payphone booths and Lynda, who was at work, answered in person straight away. She gushed into Luke's ear in her customary way, as Marie could overhear even standing six feet away. Marie then spoke to her.

'Mum, I'm sorry about what happened.'

'Oh babes.'

'I shouldn't have said what I said.'

'Oh babes.'

'Let's try to sort things out when I get home.'

'OK, babes. That would be nice.'

Marie couldn't help but notice the absence of any apology from her mother's end about the antic that had led to her storming off in the first place – that unpleasant surprise party whose solitary guest was Rick. But she let it pass.

'Has anyone rung for me, Mum?'

'Only Daniel. He wanted to know how you are. He said he can't seem to get you on your phone.'

'That's right, Mum. There's almost no signal here. If he calls again, tell him I'll see him on Monday.'

Monday. It was only five days away.

Still, with the phone-call burden lifted, Marie was better able to make Luke's birthday go with a swing. He had chicken and chips again, followed by a Magnum. Marie booked him a pony ride for Friday, and tried not to think about the state of her bank account. They swam again, went on a pedalo again and played their now regular two rounds of crazy golf. Then, to the delight of both, they discovered that Brian and Lesley had driven in to Dol and found Luke a proper birthday cake. At teatime candles were duly lit and blown out, 'Happy Birthday'

SINGLE MEN

was sung and slices of cake passed around. Then it was agreed that Marie and Luke would go to the circus again, this time with the Crewe crew.

It was a great end to the day, though the walk back from the circus would have been more relaxing had it not been for the onset of rain. Marie had seen it coming, noticed clouds the colour of bruises gathering in the distance and heading heavily their way.

They made it to the tent just before the downpour really got underway. Huddled together in Luke's side of the tent, they talked rubbish for a while about Big and Little Cilla and where rainbows come from and why fish fingers don't grow on trees. Then Luke said, 'Thank you for my lovely birthday, Mummy,' rolled over and fell asleep.

Marie watched over Luke for a while, pleased with the salvage of the day. Then she crawled back to her own compartment where she undressed, wriggled into her England nightie and snuggled down inside her sleeping bag. She listened to the rain. The longer she listened, the more she became absorbed in the downpour's subtleties, the slight dips in intensity raising the hope that it might stop before dashing it as the deluge picked up momentum again. The fly-sheet thrummed, making the tent's interior feel both more of a retreat and more besieged.

Then there was a different sound: a rustling and a squelching from outside. Footsteps? Yes. And they settled by the front entrance to the tent.

'Hello,' called Marie.

She wasn't frightened. It was probably Brian or Neil checking her guy ropes. There was no resumption of the rustling and no call in reply.

'Hello?'

Although she could not see her visitor, Marie picked up the stillness of indecision. Keeping the sleeping bag round her, she scrambled to the tent door, unzipped it and looked out. A stooped, hooded figure clutched a white carrier bag.

'Hello?'

'Hello, Marie.' The small, uncovered section of Glen's face shone wetly back at her.

'What are you doing?'

'Oh shit,' he said. 'You weren't supposed to hear me.' He held up the carrier bag. 'I brought this for Luke. For his birthday.'

'It's a bit late, isn't it?'

'I was gonna leave it.'

'Still a bit late.'

'Well, yeah. I've been at rehearsals and then someone's tent got flooded . . .' He shrugged then laughed uncomfortably. 'Anyway, here it is. I'm sorry. I'll let you get back to sleep.'

He offered her the bag, but Marie wasn't looking.

'What have you got on your face?'

His spare hand went to his cheek. 'Oh that. Make-up, probably. For the rehearsals.'

'Very pretty,' said Marie.

'*Bootiful*, actually,' said Glen.

'Ha ha.'

SINGLE MEN

'Ha ha.'

He offered her the bag again 'Come on, take it, will you? I'm drowning here!'

'Well, in that case,' said Marie, accepting the bag, 'you'd better come in.'

'Well, OK. But I'm soaking.'

'Just come in.'

When they talked about it later, Marie said it was because she believed he'd really meant it when he'd said he should be going. He said he'd wondered why she hadn't used the famous chat-up line: Let Me Help You Out Of Those Wet Clothes. The thing was though – the precious thing – was that neither of them needed much helping.

'He is asleep, is he?' Glen whispered, as he tugged off his boots.

'Yeah. Took him an hour to stop talking.'

'I'll bet. So now he's five.'

'He is.'

'Big lad.'

'Big pain, you mean!'

With scrupulous care Glen removed his waterproof. He found a place for it and his boots under the fly-sheet overhang, then crawled in and refastened the zip behind him. Still in the sleeping bag, Marie located a torch she'd purchased earlier that day and wedged it, pointing upwards, so that its beam hit the tent ceiling and a reflected white twilight leavened the gloom.

'Hello,' she said from her bedding cocoon.

'Hello.'

'Good day?'

'Not too bad.'

She paused and he waited. She said, 'Would you look the other way?'

He swivelled without a word until his back was turned her way. She liked it that he sat so upright, patiently. Marie pushed the sleeping bag down over her knees. Then she laid it out on the groundsheet. She took the hem of her nightie in both hands, and lifted it off, over her head. Glen still looked the other way and she knew he'd give her the time to tuck it into the tent-bag pillow. She lay down and curled up with her back to him, resting on her left side.

'You can turn round now.'

He didn't touch her at first. She listened to him taking off his clothes. From the few sounds he made she pictured him vividly, folding his T-shirt and joggers, balling up his socks, adding his pants to the pile, mentally marking where everything was. Doing the job thoroughly. Taking care.

Above the patter of the rain she heard him make his way over to her. She felt him close, close as could be, but still he didn't touch her. She sensed him looking down from high up on his haunches, weighing his task.

'Are you cold?' she whispered.

'No.'

He was a little, though. Because of it she shivered as his right hand formed a mould around the right half of her ass. She moved her hips so that she pushed against his palm. He said, 'And I'm going to look at every inch of you . . .'

In the pick 'n' mix of sex tips Marie had read over the years there was a Girl Power position about bedroom passivity. You didn't go there, basically. Instead, the word was Go For It – Be In Control; even when you were underneath you were supposed to be a Girl On Top. With Rick, it had perturbed her that she'd rarely taken the initiative: only when she'd felt guilty; only when she could tell that he thought he deserved a treat. Now, here in this canvas air pocket whose fabric walls were a mere membrane between her and gushing rain, the logic of such advice turned inside out.

'Where shall I kiss you?'

'I don't know.'

'You choose for me.'

'No, you.'

Marie took hold of one of her breasts. She felt him shift his balance and his half-open mouth fall on her flank. Then he sat back again, though keeping her curve in the hollow of his hand. Marie felt rich under his gaze; she felt worshipped, without fear.

'How do you feel?' he asked.

'Nice,' she replied.

'Good.'

'Yeah, good.'

She didn't care that these were inadequate words. He kissed her all along her side, and then again. With his left hand he moved her hair back off her neck, reached over and kissed her there and tugged at her earlobe with his lips. There was more of this, and yet he still held back as if too much of him would bury her. She rolled her body towards him, making a space between her thighs. He dipped all four of his fingertips. His left hand sought out her nape and she twisted still more his way until her spine measured its length on the blanket. She edged her feet towards her, lifting both knees. With hooked left-hand fingers she eased herself open, letting him see. With her spare hand she dabbed wetness from Glen's mouth. She came as he half-cradled her; then, as her breathing cooled, got to her knees and faced him.

No words were needed now. They kissed and Marie pinched a nipple and squeezed a hip. She worked him slowly with her thumbball and her fist until, in a while, he tensed and Marie marvelled that he could be so hard and so fragile at the same time. They clung to each other as the storm hammered on and five-year-old Luke murmured sweet nothings in his sleep.

CHAPTER FIFTEEN

In the morning Marie sat on the ridge above the Astroturf, looking down. It was an odd choice of spot for being inconspicuous but to sit by the touchline as on previous days might have felt a little showy now. She didn't want to push herself on him. And on inspecting her emotions she realised she felt no compulsion to. She felt sure of him, and the feeling was golden. Below her, Luke went eagerly and ineptly through Glen's skills regime while she read and reread the note he'd left.

Dear Marie
I thought I should go early. C U at football later?
Glen
x

P.S. You look lovely in your sleep.

Everything about the note felt right. She believed his reason for slipping away and she liked it for confirming what he'd made known the night before: that he took pleasure in caring about her. She liked the question mark, which showed he wasn't taking her for granted. She liked the P.S., which was what a girl might write. She liked the kiss because she'd liked his kisses. What was more, Luke had liked his birthday present: a junior-size France football shirt.

When the session was over Marie walked down. The Astroturf was as sodden as the grass and Luke's feet had got wet. Marie removed his socks and trainers, keeping Glen in the corner of one eye. Deliberately, she'd stationed herself away from all the other parents. It meant that when, at last, Glen made his way across to her she didn't have to share his company.

'He did well today.'

'Did you hear that, Luke? Glen says you did well.'

'A little battler, like I said.'

Luke head-butted his mother's hip.

'Are you a little battler, Luke?' she asked.

He nodded, looked at Glen, then buried his face again. The grown-ups laughed. What little ice there was had been broken.

Marie lowered her voice. 'And how are you today?'

'Magic,' he replied.

She smiled.

'What's funny?'

'Nothing, only you.' She hadn't heard the term 'magic' in a while.

'All right then, *bootiful*,' he said.

'*Bootiful?*'

'Yeah.' He grinned. 'That's how I feel.' His socks were round his ankles. He held his shoulders back and square. How sweet and strong he looked, bare-legged, standing there.

'That makes two of us,' said Marie.

'Shall we meet for lunch?' he asked.

'Yeah.'

'You decide where.'

'OK, let me think.'

Marie thought. She thought about how earlier that morning she'd showered and, with a certain sadness, soaped away the night before. Yet as she'd stood under the jet she'd felt newly acquainted with her body. He had explored her, and she'd liked the things he'd found. And now she wanted to make the day ahead as perfectly romantic as it deserved to be. An idea came to her: 'I'll meet you in the launderette at two.'

Luke spent the intervening hours doing junk modelling and talking the toenails off Easycamp Jo. Glen spent them coaching the over-eights. Marie spent them feeling sexy and sorting out the dirty clothes.

They rendezvoused as planned.

'I want chips!' said Luke.

'I've brought sandwiches,' said Glen, 'and sparkling water and fruit.' He had them packed in a coolbox.

'You're very organised, aren't you?' said Marie, examining the instructions on the front of one of the washing machines.

'Army training,' said Glen.

'They teach you all sorts in the army, don't they?' said Marie.

'I'll say.'

'I want chips!' repeated Luke.

'I'll get you chips,' said Glen. 'After your mum's loaded that machine.'

He looked on as Marie flung in her underwear: red knickers, black knickers, white knickers, blue. She saw him looking and said, 'What are you thinking?'

'I'm thinking pink,' he said.

'Are you now?'

'Yep.'

'As it happens, you're correct.'

'Superman did that once, you know. To Lois Lane. But only in a film.'

'Pass me that powder, will you?'

Glen handed her a sachet. 'Don't forget conditioner,' he said.

'I haven't got conditioner.'

'I have.'

From his pocket he produced a tiny bottle of Lenor. Marie almost shrieked.

'You know how to make a girl happy, don't you?'

'I've got a big sister. She tells me everything.'

'I never know when you're winding me up.'

'Good.'

'I want chips!' said Luke.

'OK,' said Glen. 'Let's go.'

Leaving the washing machine to do its work, they set off for the fast-food café. Marie linked her arm through

SINGLE MEN

Glen's. They bought chips – two portions – and headed on to the spot on the grass beside the lake where Marie and Luke had sat on Sunday. From the coolbox Glen produced a large tea towel to serve as a tablecloth and spread the food out on it. The water was chilled Evian. The fruit was grapes and strawberries. The sandwiches were Brie baguettes.

'When did you make this picnic?' Marie asked.
'This morning, before you were awake.'
'Cheeky.'
'Forward planning, I call it.'
'Army training?'
'You're getting the hang of this.'

They bantered on for a while. Luke ate all the chips. Zipline riders whizzed past overhead.

'Can I go on that, Mummy?' asked Luke.
'We'll see, Luke. We'll see.'
'I'll take him on it,' said Glen.
'Will you?'
'If he wants.'
'What about me?'
'What about you?'
'What will I be doing?'
'Don't worry. You'll be the next one down.'

They finished the picnic and Glen got up. Taking Luke by the hand he marched him up the bank towards the shed where the equipment for the zipline was kept. Marie followed fretfully. A supervisor kitted them out, and soon Glen was on the launch platform with Luke strapped to the front of him. Marie was still on the rope ladder making her way up when Glen pushed off.

'Banzai!' shouted Luke.

'Geronimo!' shouted Glen.

They landed painlessly in the soft earth at the bottom of the line and moved quickly out of Marie's way. She screamed, 'Oh my God!' three times on the way and alighted in an undignified heap.

'Outstanding,' remarked Glen.

'Well done, Mummy!' added Luke.

'I'm going back to the washing machine,' said Marie.

In fact, they all went and sat together, Luke hypnotised by the tumble dryer.

Glen whispered to Marie: 'I want to be with you tonight.'

'I want to be with you. Let's get everything in order.'

'Don't worry. I've thought of that.'

'Forward planning?'

'Army training!'

'After *Guys and Dolls*?'

He had to supervise volleyball all afternoon, then went to his rehearsal as planned. It was gone eleven when he slipped into Marie's tent once again.

'Is Little Battler asleep?'

'Yes, he's sound. Have you really got a big sister?'

'Yeah. She's got two little boys.'

They undressed and embraced. They kissed. Everything was in order. He built a slow, devoted rhythm in her, holding her gaze and pushing deep. In the morning she found another note. *You are so beautiful*, it said.

*

SINGLE MEN

Friday was Marie and Luke's last full day at *Camping du Plaisir*, a day for doing everything they hadn't managed to fit in so far. Then, at bedtime, as a special treat, Luke would be allowed to stay up late and watch the reps doing their thing.

'Can Big Cilla and Little Cilla come?'

'Only if they don't bark at the singing.'

So Luke did football training for the last time and got a medal from Dylan and Glen: for Best Attitude. Then there was last swimming, last test-your-strength machine, last pedalo and double last crazy golf. And he got his ride on a pony, a plump, short-arsed little thing called Bubblegum who kept on stopping to eat grass.

'Gee-up, Bubblegum!'

Nothing.

'Gee-up, Bubblegum!'

Nothing.

'Mummy?'

'Yes, Luke?'

'A horse went into a pub, and the man said to him, "Why the long face?" '

'Who told you that?'

'Glen did.'

'I might have known.'

'Get me a crocodile sandwich and make it snappy!'

'Yes, boom boom. Now let's get this pony moving.'

'Gee-up, Bubblegum!'

Nothing.

'Gee-up, Bubblegum!'

There was one activity Marie wanted to do which Luke

was too young to take part in: paintball. She'd always wanted to try it ever since she'd seen some bunch of businessmen doing it on TV – and here was the perfect opportunity. She arranged to leave Luke with the Crewe crew for a couple of hours at teatime and persuaded Glen to do it with her after he'd finished work for the day, but before he had to get ready for the rep show.

They met at Reception and trudged together up a slope to a camouflaged shed at the outer edge of the site. Glen nodded to the young men behind the trestle table where the paint guns were cleaned and loaded. They warned him in droll French accents against trying to be a hero. He gave them a short grin, took two of the guns, and showed Marie how to use one. 'And don't fire all your pellets too quickly, or you'll be sunk.'

'We're all going to be sunk anyway, by the look of that mud,' replied Marie.

She was peering through the netting, which enclosed a wooded area where the first battle would take place. She was more apprehensive than she'd expected. Apart from her, there were only two women taking part. The others were all adolescent boys and, for the most part, young men, numbering around twenty. They were pulling on the regulation white overalls and protective rubber helmets, and taking it all very seriously: previous enemy engagements and glorious slayings were being discussed enthusiastically.

Before deployment the players were told the rules of engagement: once you're hit, raise your gun and leave the field; no shooting at anyone who's already 'dead'; no shooting at anyone at all from a distance of less than five metres. As this was being said Marie noticed that Glen was discreetly watching some of the larger, louder lads. As it turned out, they were on the same team as himself and Marie: wearing red bibs as opposed to yellow.

Marie had butterflies. Glen handed her a helmet. The lining of foam shock absorbers was dank with previous wearers' sweat. With a grimace, Marie pulled it on. At her elbow, Glen did the same with his. The visors were scratched and murky. There was a shout from one of the game supervisors, and everyone passed through a gap in the netting. The yellow team headed off right, Glen and Marie's red team headed left. The game was 'last man standing'. In the woods, Glen and Marie took cover behind a short length of wooden fencing erected on a mound.

'OK, go!' the supervisor yelled. Would-be warriors in red foraged forward. Within a minute, hostile yellow pellets were pinging into the undergrowth and bursting on the trees.

Glen did nothing for a while. 'Keep your head down,' he told Marie, his voice muffled by the clumsy headgear. Marie wished she could see his face. He seemed withdrawn, subdued. She took his advice, but poked her gun through a crack in the fence and fired a few times at bobbing heads in the distance. 'Shall we advance a bit?' she said. 'I'm getting bored.'

'All right, then,' answered Glen.

The other surviving red team players were well forward. The lads who'd played before knew what they were doing. Already, the yellow team had lost several of their number and the remainder were pinned down in a corner. Glen led Marie forward, scuttling low through a channel concealed by foliage on their left. Sneaking up, they could see how the endgame was proceeding. At the border of the wood, two yellows were hiding behind a log. From the size of them they were only about twelve. Close by, they could make out a plump, middle-aged man behind an upturned tree stump, keeping his head down and hoping.

Marie took some pot shots at the boys behind the log. She missed, but when they lifted their heads in order to fire back, both were picked off by someone else. It wasn't Glen: Marie couldn't remember him firing a single shot.

The two boys raised their guns and climbed out under the netting, leaving the plump man to resist all on his own. From nearby bushes, three red bibs burst into the clearing, firing. The plump man was caught cold. Game over. He raised his gun. But while two of his attackers left it there, the third did not. He advanced on the plump man and plugged him at close range with two more shots. He turned to his mates with his arms raised in triumph. The plump man lay on the ground, humiliated. The trigger-happy lad, showboating, pointed his gun at him again.

By then, Glen, helmet removed, had covered the distance between them. 'OK mate, that's enough.'

The lad turned to look at him. He said, 'Whose side are you on?'

'I said, that's enough.'

SINGLE MEN

Now the lad removed his helmet too. On the ground, the plump man had begun complaining to the game supervisor who'd stepped in to formally declare the end. 'He'd already shot me once. Three times he did it. Three times. And only a few yards away . . .'

The lad said to Glen, 'What's your problem, mate?'

'I said, that's enough. Leave him alone.'

The lad considered his position. Glen was large and resolute. He plainly hadn't liked what he'd just seen. Bravado fought it out with better judgement. The outcome was self-justification, delivered as a jeer.

'It's only a laugh, isn't it. It's just a game.'

'Yeah. A game with rules.'

'Aw, what do you know?'

'You'd be surprised how much I know.'

The lad now took the path of discretion; it was clearer to him by the second that this was valour's better part.

Marie came to Glen's side. 'Are you all right?' she asked.

'Yeah, I'm all right,' he said softly, almost sadly, as the lad and his coterie slouched away.

The *Guys and Dolls* show was a scream. It was not a full performance, only the songs and the key scenes, but the troupers gave it everything. Dylan, the football coach, played Nathan Detroit. Easycamp Jo was Salvation Army stalwart Sarah Brown. Glen was in the chorus, dressed up, card-sharp style. He really did know how to wear a suit.

Afterwards, round midnight, he and Marie sat up

outside her tent, thinking, talking, making plans for the next day and beyond. Eventually, she asked him about the paintball incident and his contretemps with the mouthy lad.

'Oh, it was just silly.'

'No, it wasn't. He was out of order. And you were really upset.'

'It was nothing. I should have ignored it.'

'No, you were right.'

'It was stupid. I should just get over it.'

'Get over what?'

Glen's head dropped for a moment. He seemed to turn something over in his mind. Then he said, 'I was in Afghanistan.'

'Were you?'

'Yep. Part of the British contingent, backing up the Yanks.'

Marie held his arm tightly. 'What was it like?'

Glen gave a snort. 'Not a lot like paintball.'

Now it was Marie's turn to ponder. Finally, she asked him, 'This doesn't *mean* anything, what I want to ask. I'm not asking to be nosy. And I'm not asking because it might make a difference to how I feel about you. I'm asking because I want to really know you.'

'Ask away.'

'Did you kill anyone?'

'No. Didn't need to.'

'Were you scared?'

'Now and then.'

'What scared you?'

'Seeing dead people. Kids.'

Marie pulled him closer. She kissed his cheek. She said, 'This sounds silly, but I saw a dead person once.'

'Oh yeah?'

'Yeah. It was my dad.'

Glen looked shocked. 'I'm so sorry. That's so sad.'

'I saw him in the morgue,' said Marie. 'I went with my mum. She wanted to see him, I didn't. She as good as made me.'

'How old were you?' asked Glen.

'Fourteen.'

'Must have been tough for you.'

'It was. I don't talk about it much.'

'I'm glad you've told me.'

'So am I. It's different with you. Everything's different with you.'

Marie let Brian and Neil take down her tent the next morning. She was almost as embarrassed as when they'd put it up, but at least she could busy herself packing. She thanked them copiously. It was the Crewe crew's final act of kindness to her. Like Marie, Lesley and Carole were stuffing things in bags, preparing to go. Although they were heading south to another campsite, down in the Vendée, they offered her a lift to Dol, assuming she and Luke would be boarding a coach to Cherbourg, returning by the same means as they'd arrived. Marie explained that she'd already made arrangements, though she didn't give details. The makeover of her lovelife was something she still wanted to keep tightly to herself, and she was pleased when it turned out that she and Luke had already waved off the Mondeo and the Laguna when Glen arrived in the little Renault he had hired for the day.

'Your chauffeur at your service, ma'am,' he grinned.

The note of levity set the right tone for all three members of the party. But just below its surface the two grown-ups were cogitating about major matters of love and life. By the time they reached the port, their mood had become determined and sober. They kissed long and slowly, trying to ensure the spell would last. They made a pact to communicate online on a single day and at an agreed time. They wanted to test and deepen their hunger, not assuage it with cyber snacks and, anyway, they both had work to do. Glen would be finishing in about seven weeks: seven weeks during which Marie was resolved to makeover everything else in her life too.

CHAPTER SIXTEEN

Marie was at pains not to switch her mobile on until both her feet and Luke's were in Portsmouth. As soon as she did, it started to ring. The identity of the caller came as no surprise.

'Hello, Mum.'

'Hello! Have you got off yet? I can see the boat. How's Luke?'

'Where are you, Mum?'

Of course, Marie had already worked out that Lynda had driven down to meet them – uninvited, naturally. Still, mustn't be ungrateful.

'I'm just by the arrivals bit. How's Luke?'

'He's fine. We'll be out in a few minutes.'

'I've got the car!'

You don't say, thought Marie: helicopter at the garage, is it? Then she chastised herself once more. Now, now. That'll do.

'Thanks, Mum. This is really nice of you.'

'That's all right, babes! Is Luke OK?'

'I'll see you shortly, Mum. Bye.'

Now text messages were coming through: several old ones from Lynda which Marie deleted without reading; one from Gabby, welcoming her and Luke home; a couple from Daniel, the first asking Marie where she was, the second saying he'd spoken to Lynda and to have a good time. There were none, though, from Marlon and none from Guy.

Lynda was almost fizzing as they emerged into the arrivals area. She embraced them vividly. She wore purple jeans with a thin pink sparkle belt and a mauve top, ruched and plunging at the bust. Her toenails were red and poked hopefully from a pair of floral Birkenstocks. Marie noted her crow's feet and her first signs of sagging at the neck.

'Aren't you brown?' Lynda chirruped to Luke, who wasn't especially, except with dirt.

'Which way, Mum?' asked Marie.

'I'm in the car park over here.'

Lynda took the holdall from Marie. She lugged it along with one hand, and appropriated Luke's paw with the other. It was a relief for Marie to see both holdall and backpack stored in Lynda's Fiat Punto out of sight. Less welcome was the confessional embrace in which her mother locked her as soon as Luke was out of earshot in the back seat.

'I'm so sorry, my darling. I was just trying to help.'

'It's OK, Mum. I know.'

'It was just that Rick . . . He was genuine, I think. He was trying to do the right thing.'

SINGLE MEN

Marie endured her mother's eau de toilette and stoically absorbed the pressure of her breasts. She felt sorrow for Lynda in her remorse but was uncomfortable with her self-abasement. If only in the absence of anyone else's, she needed Marie's constant approval.

'Mum, we'll talk about it later, OK?'

Lynda sobbed softly on to her daughter's neck. Marie patted her and gently prised her off.

'Let's go home now, shall we? I can't wait to have a bath.'

After this torrid start, the journey up to London went quite smoothly. Luke slept for most of the first half of the journey, which meant Lynda was calmer at the wheel. It also meant Marie could establish her preferred account of the holiday rather than Luke dominating with tales of tent trouble and cloudbursts and Glen. Marie majored on the pool, the pony, the circus, the crazy golf and the Crewe crew. By thus setting the agenda for Lynda's inevitable coming cross-questioning of Luke, she hoped that her lover would somehow blur into the background, become a minor character in Luke's campsite narrative. She had no appetite for maternal probing on that theme. She just hoped that Glen had dreamed of her last night.

'So, what have you been up to, Mum?'

'Oh, the usual. Working, pottering, gardening.'

'How's Auntie Barbara?'

'Oh fine,' she said unconvincingly.

This was all deflating for Marie. While she had returned secretly ravenous for change, Lynda, in spite of their row about Rick and Clay, still showed no sign of being ready to move on. Marie realised ruefully that just because her week away had been an epic drama for her, it didn't mean that anything was different at home. This was confirmed on the outskirts of London when Luke woke up.

'I'm hungry, Lynda!' he said immediately. She directed him to a carrier bag full of snacks she had positioned on the floor next to his feet. It was then no surprise to Marie that when they reached Herbert Gardens Luke got out of the car with the carrier full of vomit and his pants full of crisps. And, naturally, the poor, poorly thing could only recover if he was placed horizontally in front of the telly, and fussed over until he went to sleep.

Marie had hoped that her new future would start happening straight away. It looked like she'd have to wait for tomorrow.

Monday.
Daniel's day.
'Cupcakes! Where have you been?' At the sight of her he rubbed his hands with glee.

'France.'

He led the way into the kitchen. 'I know *that*! What I mean is, where have you been all my life?'

'Why? Has something happened?'

'Well, not to me. But *you* . . .'

He appraised her with theatrical suspicion. She waited. He said, 'OK, what's his name?'

'Whose name?'

'Whose name?' he mocked. 'You know whose name! There's something different about you, Cupcakes. Something boy-shaped. Come on now! Details!'

'Daniel, I—'

'You're cornered, aren't you? How could I tell? Let me see: you're just a *little bit* Plain Jane today, compared with your usual flamboyance. And yet you have a certain glow. Someone has been whispering to the Earth Woman within. Come on, now. What's his name?'

'I'm not saying anything.'

'What's he like? Is he my type? Can we share?'

'Daniel!'

'What's the matter, Cupcakes? Doesn't friendship mean anything?'

This went on a little longer while the Gaggia did its steamy thing. They were at the kitchen table, continental cups waiting ready. Luke was upstairs with Elice in her bedroom. The school summer holidays had started officially for Luke now, and there'd been no time to make a childcare plan. Not that it mattered. It was quite clear to Marie that little if any cleaning was going to get done. Daniel had other matters on his mind.

'Anyway,' he said once he'd calmed down, 'let me give you the latest on Miss V.'

'Yes, I have been wondering.'

'The spitfire.'

'Yes.'

'The virago.'

'Yes.'

'The termagant.'

'OK.'

Daniel stepped back into his shadows. 'I know you did your best for me, Cupcakes, before your holiday, with Elice.'

'I did try.'

'I know. But she's still being difficult with me.'

Marie had been thinking back. She said, 'Did Elice tell you anything about her conversation with me?'

'Nothing. She was too cross with me for making it happen at all.'

Marie resisted a small urge to say she knew how Elice felt. Instead, she said, 'Because you and me, we never actually discussed it, did we? I was ill that night, and ill all the next day. Next thing I knew, I was on my way to Portsmouth with a tent. We never managed to speak.'

'True,' nodded Daniel. 'Quite true. So, what did she say?'

'She said a lot of things about families, actually: families in general, not just her own. But what she said, yeah, is that her family's not happy even though she loves both her parents and they both love her. And that makes *her* unhappy. And because you and – it's Esmerelda, isn't it? – because you two don't get on, you are both unhappy too. So there's all this love, but everyone's miserable.' Marie shrugged. 'So what she's saying, really, is that it doesn't make sense.'

Daniel scratched his handsome head. It was hard to comprehend that he was almost the same age as Neil and Brian, who both seemed far older in most ways. 'Marie,' he said, 'answer me honestly.' He looked at her directly.

'Did I misuse you over this?'

Marie looked straight back at him. 'It was a big thing to ask a cleaner.'

Daniel laughed. 'Good answer,' he said. 'So first, I'd like to apologise to you. You are one of my favourite people. I mean that, I really do. Because of that, I depend on you. But I understand I overstepped the mark.'

'Forget about it, Daniel,' said Marie. 'You know, I'm very fond of Elice. Luke is too.'

'Even though she's a little madam sometimes?'

'I never said that.'

'Only because you're too polite.'

'Maybe.'

'I think you mean "definitely", don't you? The big question, though, is what am I going to do?'

'Do you want my opinion?' said Marie. She saw Daniel's surprise, even though he covered it up well.

'I do, Cupcakes, yes, please.'

'I think Elice feels responsible for her mother, just like she feels responsible for you. I think she wants to make Esmerelda happy, and the only way that can happen is by getting to see more of her. And the only way *that* can happen, is by you and her mother getting on a bit better. Stop hating each other. Try and co-operate a bit more.'

'Go on,' said Daniel.

'And since the two of you can't stand talking to each other, you need someone else to do the talking for you. A go-between, if you like – a peacemaker.'

'Any suggestions?' said Daniel wearily.

'Yes, Daniel. Me.'

His eyebrows went up slightly. 'Have you any idea what a monster she can be?'

'Only what I've heard from you.'

'Well, yes, that's true.'

'So why don't you set up a meeting? Or ask Elice to ask Esmerelda if she'd mind me visiting? I don't know the best way to go about it and I don't know if it would do any good. But I think Elice might like it. And I think it's worth a try.'

Daniel considered carefully. Something was different between Marie and himself, and he was adjusting to it, little by little. 'OK,' he said quietly. 'I'll see what I can do. And thank you for your thoughts. Now tell me, Cupcakes, is there anything *I* can do to make *you* happy?'

'Yes, there is, actually.'

'Name it.'

'Would you stop calling me Cupcakes?'

He eyed her archly, as if to say, 'It's amazing what a good man can do for a girl.' He said, 'Of course I'll stop it, Sweetbuns. Why didn't you ask me before?'

After leaving Daniel's house, Marie made several attempts to reach Marlon. She'd texted him the previous evening, but no joy. Now she decided to pursue him remorselessly. At last he returned a call.

'Marlon? Thank goodness! Where are you? Are you OK?'

'Sadly, Marie, I haven't been well.'

'Oh no. Are you better?'

'Not entirely, I'm afraid to say. But I think I am improving.'

'Where are you?'

'I'll tell you, if you promise absolutely faithfully not to tell anyone else, especially members of my family.'

'Of course, Marlon.'

'Only I'd like you to come and see me. I haven't had any visitors yet. I feel you are someone I can trust.'

He gave her the address of a small private clinic in the vicinity of Harley Street. She promised she would be there as soon as possible in the morning.

CHAPTER SEVENTEEN

Tuesday.

Marlon's day.

Marie, Luke and Lynda travelled together into town. Marie would be separating from the others soon but, even so, the day's arrangements settled her conscience. She was being nice to Lynda both by sharing her company and by letting her take Luke out for a treat – a visit to London Zoo. She was being nice to Luke too – the zoo trip had been promised way back. Also, she was being nice to herself. By making the journey with him and promising to catch up with him and Lynda later she felt less as if she was farming him out. And, of course, insofar as she *was* farming him out, it was in order to be good to someone else. Naturally, she lied to Lynda about the details.

'Marlon's a diabetic, Mum,' she said offhandedly. 'Sometimes he doesn't look after himself properly and has to pay the price. You know what these City types are like.'

SINGLE MEN

'But babes, you're not his nursemaid,' Lynda probed from behind a firewall of foundation.

'I know that, Mum,' replied Marie, firmly maintaining her own false face. 'I just thought I'd pop in and cheer him up.'

'I see.'

'Mummy,' commented Luke. 'I need a wee.'

This emergency provided the distraction Marie needed and Lynda let the Marlon matter drop. Luke promised faithfully to 'hold it' and Marie left them at Regents Park station with any last traces of guilt smothered by a small wave of relief. On the fringe of Marylebone she was struck by how quiet the streets seemed: the effect of the congestion charge, presumably. From her rucksack she took her *A–Z*, turned to the page she'd marked and set off.

She reached the street she was seeking in a few minutes but it took her quite a while to find the right establishment. The only indication that a rehab clinic was there was a small brass plaque beside a smart but anonymous door. In the absence of a handle Marie pushed at it and found that it gave way. She advanced into a carpeted foyer where a manicured receptionist greeted her quizzically. Marie carried no gift or flowers. She knew that she looked out of place.

'I'm here to see Marlon,' she said, then quickly corrected herself. 'Mr Alibhai, that is. He's a . . . young man . . .'

The receptionist cut in briskly. 'Mr Alibhai, yes. Is he expecting you?'

'Yes.'

'Please wait a moment.'

A whispered phone exchange ensued and then Marie was directed to a lift. She rode up to the first floor and buttoned her cardigan before knocking on the relevant room door. A soft voice called, 'Come in,' and Marie entered. Marlon was in bed, propped on a small mountain of white pillows. He looked smaller than ever – a broken little boy.

'Hello, Marlon,' said Marie.

'Hello, er, Marie.'

She hesitated, then walked up to him. A barrier had come down. The setting and his situation laid bare to both of them Marlon's parlous condition, and this freed Marie to place a nurturing kiss upon his cheek. She then seated herself in an upright chair.

'Marlon,' she asked, 'what *have* you been up to?'

From under weary eyelids he gazed out at her. 'Oh well, er, Marie. I'm in a bit of a mess really.'

'You've certainly made a mess of your flat.'

'Sadly, that is true.'

'Do your parents know about it?'

'Unfortunately, I have yet to tell them.'

'Will they have looked for you there?'

'I don't think so. I told them I was going away.'

'I'm afraid I haven't had time to clear it up.'

She felt bad about this. She felt worse about it because of what she'd found out on the day she had stumbled on his scene of destruction: the Reverend Gary Tibworth and the Three Great Sexual Untruths.

'You've been away too, I think,' Marlon said. 'I have noticed your tan.'

'Yes. I'm sorry.'

'Why are you sorry?'

'I don't know. I ought to pay your parents back some money. You're very kind.'

'And you, Marie, have always been extremely kind to me.'

'Oh Marlon,' she said, and now she had worked out why she was sorry. Marlon said nothing, eloquently. Some things, they seemed to understand, weren't meant to be.

Marie thought of Glen. Then she said, 'What about your job? What have you told them?'

'Nothing.'

'Nothing?'

'I'm afraid not.'

'What will happen?'

'I don't know.'

Delicately, Marie then said, 'And what about your dad? Didn't he . . . ?'

Marlon's features formed a thundercloud. 'There's no point thinking about him.'

'But surely he'll be wondering about you. And your mum too!'

'I doubt it, frankly.' Marlon sank deeper into his cloud of duck down. Seemingly absorbing a little of its softness he resumed, 'The difficulty, Marie, is that I've never suited that kind of work.'

'Haven't you?'

'No.'

'But you're good with numbers and everything.'

'Yes, I am.'

She waited for an explanation. Instead, he provided a digression.

'I did have a different job once – with my Uncle Lance. He's my mother's brother.'

'What sort of job?'

'Well, it was nothing much – a summer holiday job when I was at school. Uncle Lance is in property, but not like my father is – it's just one of the things he invests in. Uncle Lance was much more hands-on. At that time he was buying up old houses, doing them up, and selling them on for a nice profit. He said to me one day, in front of my parents, that he could do with some help labouring. It was supposed to be a joke, I think. I was so small and weedy. I must have been about fifteen. But I said I'd have a go – just to surprise people, really. Nobody thought I'd do it, but I did. And it was great!'

Marlon was smiling. Marie nearly pinched herself.

'A lot of it was just demolition work,' he went on. 'Knocking down walls and wheeling rubble out to a skip. It was good, though. By the end of the day I'd be so dirty and so tired!' He smiled even more.

'Dirty and tired?' said Marie. 'Doesn't sound like much fun to me.' She added boldly, 'A bit like cleaning, actually.'

'Yes, but satisfying!' Marlon enthused. 'And then it became more interesting. There was a bricklayer called Monty. Very experienced, a genuine craftsman. I carried a hod for him and some of the time I'd watch him work.

It was fascinating. Bricklaying is highly skilled, you know.'

He spoke of Monty wistfully, as if of a lost world. Marie thought he sounded very old, though that was nothing new.

'Perhaps you should have stuck with it,' she ventured.

'Oh, I don't think so.'

'Why not?'

'Well . . .' Marlon frowned. 'I was lined up for higher things. A levels, university, a career in the City . . .' He looked incredibly dismissive and bored – far better to be dirty and tired.

'Do you know about trading floors?' he said to Marie. 'All that crazy business with screens and rows of numbers and young men in their shirt-sleeves barking into telephones?'

'Well, yes. I mean, I've seen them on TV.'

'The job I got – my father got me really – was doing that. But it wasn't for me. I couldn't cope with it. It got to a stage where I was living every day with a sort of heavy weight pressing on the inside of my head. It was killing me.'

'What happened?'

'They moved me to a different department: more administration, less stress. It was easier. But . . . but you see, Marie . . .'

His mouth began to quiver. A tear ran abruptly down his cheek. Marie reached over and took hold of one of his hands, which felt fragile, almost elderly. 'What is it, Marlon?' she asked gently. 'I'm your friend. You can tell me. I mean, you really can trust me.'

'Marie,' he began, and she could see in his eyes that he'd decided to take a giant leap. 'There's something here I'd quite like you to read.'

From underneath his covers he pulled a laptop. He opened it and handed it to her. A page of bare text was displayed. Marie's first thought was that it must be connected with the Reverend Gary, so she would have to feign first-time acquaintance. In fact, it was something quite different.

Dear Fellow Uncels
I am a young, single male who has sometimes been described as quite good-looking. Also I have a good job with a decent salary. So how can it be that I have these advantages yet I have never even been out with a woman let alone had an intimate relationship with one? I would be interested to know what other people think because I don't really understand it myself. I am certainly attracted to women and I cherish their company when I get it. I don't think I come across as sleazy or creepy, just extremely nervous and awkward. I know I could be a loyal and loving partner for someone and the 'other thing' would take care of itself – all the equipment, so to speak, is working properly. One's only conclusion is that there is something off-putting about me. I am afraid it may be that I communicate how desperate I sometimes feel and the more I do that, the worse it gets.

Let me tell you a few things about myself. I was born in England and grew up in a rather cold and formal family, which put a great deal of emphasis on personal achievement and high social status. I must be vague about the details in case someone reading this guesses who I am. When I tell you that I am almost as worried about what my parents would think of me if they knew I'd written this as I am about other people I know – at work for example – you may begin to understand the influence they still hold over me. I believe they may be the biggest reason I've never had any success with girls.

As a little boy my mother kept me away from other children because she thought they were 'too rough'. Then my father made some money and we moved to a smarter neighbourhood. I went to a prep school there and then I was sent away for my education. By this time I had had my first crush on a girl. To protect her privacy I will pretend her name was Jane. She was little and sweet with straight brown hair, a fringe and big blue eyes. She lived a few doors away from me and I used to see her playing out with other kids. I thought of her as perfect, kind and pure but I don't know if she was because I never had the nerve to speak to her.

Then, from age eleven, I was educated only with other boys. At first I quite liked this because I was away from my parents and I made some new friends. But all that changed when we got a little older and some of the boys began talking about sex. I don't know why it was but I hated them doing it. I especially hated the way they discussed girls. It was filthy and disgusting and when pornography started being passed around I couldn't stand to look at it. For some reason I had a much more romantic view of women than the other boys did but I didn't dare to show it because I'd be laughed at. Sometimes I went to parties where there were girls and alcohol and no grown-ups around and I tried to talk to girls, but none of them seemed interested in me.

There was one thing in particular I couldn't understand about the way girls behaved. From reading books and magazines I had got the idea that girls were more interested than boys in talking about their feelings and that they didn't like boys who were 'only after one thing'. Well, no one could have been more willing to be caring and sensitive with a girl than me and although I had powerful sexual feelings I was perfectly happy to wait. So why didn't it do me any good? Why did all the girls who I found attractive seem to hang round with the boys who only ever said filthy things about girls when they were with other boys? Why did even the 'nice' girls seem uninterested in me? I couldn't understand this and I still don't. Instead, the cruel kids started asking me if I was gay. It didn't help that I was small for my age and didn't have much body hair. I felt lonely and ashamed every day.

My solution was to go into my shell. I didn't mix much or go out. I played computer games and concentrated on my studies, especially science and maths which I was very good at. Eventually I left school and went to university where I carried on pretty much the same. By this time I felt completely isolated. Everybody else had boyfriends or girlfriends or seemed to be having fun just sleeping around. I was so embarrassed by my lack of experience that I avoided company except when computers or complicated equations were guaranteed to be the only topic of conversation. Every other sort of social interaction seemed to end up with jokes and stories about 'shagging' or 'bonking' and your 'first time' and I would become very uncomfortable.

I dropped out of university after a year, suffering from depression. I didn't have any choice except to go back home and

SINGLE MEN

be a failure in my parents' eyes. For six months I did nothing until my mother found me a job at the firm she works for. I suppose she was doing her best to help me but I believed I was an embarrassment. After a lot more drifting round my father pulled some strings and found what he called 'a real job' for me. I hate it, though. I hate the way I'm expected to be.

Meanwhile, my problem seems no nearer being solved. I've often thought of going to prostitutes to 'get it over with' but I don't believe I'd be lucky enough to find a 'tart with a heart' and, anyway, it doesn't match with my ideals. Then I've gone to the other extreme. I have recently been visiting websites promoting sexual abstinence before marriage. My hope is that through these I might meet a girl who is a virgin like me and doesn't want to have sex until we're married. For me that would take off lots of the pressure and when we married it would all work out OK. One of the websites provides an online dating service so that people all over the world who don't want to have sex before they are married can get to know each other through the web. You can even send flowers to the ones you find attractive through a special company called Purity Blooms. I did this once. I haven't heard anything from the girl, though.

So there is my sad story. Even though it's been going on for a long time it hasn't really changed. One of the things that causes me most pain is that I still often have crushes on girls but they never, ever lead to anything. In fact, they make me feel more hopeless than ever. I suppose one day my luck may change. Regrettably, though, I can't believe it ever will.
Thank you, fellow Uncels.

Marie passed the laptop back to Marlon. She took a paper tissue from a box beside his bed and wiped her eyes. Marlon stared out of his window looking as though he had been turned to stone. Marie sniffed and asked him, 'What's an Uncel?'

'Unhappily celibate,' Marlon replied. 'Unfortunately, we are not the most glamorous of minorities.'

'No, I can see that.'

He kept on staring out of the window. She said, 'Marlon, if I'd known . . .'

'No, Marie, no.'

'Marlon, it's difficult. Were you hoping, like, now or ever . . .'

'I really do like you, Marie,' he said, 'but I couldn't ask . . .'

'Of course you couldn't. You're much too nice.'

Marlon seemed to be watching a very distant bird. 'Where has being nice ever got me?'

Marie had no answer to this. And the great irony was that because of her newfound happiness, she could no longer be the one to answer Marlon's prayers. If it hadn't been for Glen she would have climbed into bed with Marlon there and then and very kindly soothed his shame away. If she'd known earlier, she'd have done the same. It would not have made her fall in love with Marlon and she would never have wanted to marry him. But it might have made his company more relaxing, and she might have made less mess with the passion-fruit meringues.

None of this could be said. It did, though, put iron force behind Marie's determination to do something to help Marlon at least get back on his feet. She told him she was glad he had shown her the website letter and repeated that he could trust her completely. She told him that she would go and clear up his ruined flat as soon as she could, keep an eye on his car, and that she would come to see him again soon. By the time she'd finished speaking, he'd found the strength to look at her again. She got to her feet and, had she not been so preoccupied with how to take her leave, would have remembered to give him his set of keys.

In the end she just waved sweetly from the door. She'd have preferred to kiss him again but was afraid that if she did so, he might break.

CHAPTER EIGHTEEN

'I don't like Guy, Mummy,' said Luke.

'Why don't you like him, Luke?'

'He's scary.'

'He doesn't scare me.'

'He's too big.'

'He can't help being big.'

'He's a big poo.'

'Luke, you've never even met him! How can you say he's a big poo?'

'He just is.'

'Isn't.'

'Is.'

They were approaching Guy's house. If anything, Marie was more on edge than her son. She'd still heard nothing from Guy since the morning of madness with the tank top and Nigella, and she was worried about what he might have done. High-powered men of action such as the distinguished Dr Jelly were supposed to be resilient and always in command, but the last time she'd seen Guy

SINGLE MEN

he'd seemed to be on the verge of curling up into a ball and sucking his thumb.

'I don't *like* Guy,' insisted Luke.

'Why not?' asked Marie, exasperated.

'Because he got you out of bed in the night.'

'Aaah,' said Marie. 'Now I understand.'

Lynda had been talking to him about that early-morning phone call. In his child's mind he must have put this evidence of instability together with the few other fragments of knowledge he had about Guy, and come up with a veritable monster! A huge man with big hair who cut bits of people's heads off and did things to their brains. And he had two giant dogs too!

Luke continued to resist, his little bottom lip almost dragging along the ground.

'Listen,' said Marie. 'Guy isn't the only one who gets me out of bed in the night. You do it too.'

'He's a big poo!' said Luke.

'Come on, you're gonna love these dogs.'

'He's a big poo.'

'They're even bigger than Big Cilla!'

Marie led the way through Guy's front gate, coaxing Luke with stick-on cheeriness and hoping nothing weird or wild was in store. She turned the key in the door, pushed it open and stepped in. Luke did his slumped shoulders extra-slow forward creep, which meant covering an inch every three hours.

In a display of thinning patience Marie folded her arms and leaned against the wall, having first checked that the eight-hundred-pound watch was not still lying, discarded, in the hall.

'Hi,' said a female voice.

Marie had anticipated oven scrubbing. For that reason she was wearing her tattiest old trainers, baggiest old shorts and floppiest old shirt. So when she saw who the female voice belonged to, she felt spectacularly underdressed.

She clocked the hairdo first: a great blue-blonde plume held in place by a selection of thick bands. Then, item by item, she took in the rest of the ensemble: a plunging grey-green cotton vest that was struggling to contain an intimidating chest; a pair of wide-flared candy-striped low-slung hipsters adorned by a massive belt which did more to lower the jeans than hold them up. Consequently, the top inch of a pair of tigerskin-print knickers was boldly on display. Her shoes had platform soles down which her father could have abseiled. For Marie had no doubts about who this creature was before she chose to introduce herself.

'Hi. I'm Mopsy, Guy's daughter. And you must be Marie.'

'I'm Marie, yes.'

'And who are you, little dude?'

'This is Luke,' said Marie.

'Hey! Isn't he cute?'

Luke looked surprised. He wasn't doing cute at all!

Mopsy aimed a yell over her shoulder. 'Jumbo! Hey, Jum! Come and see this cute little kid!'

Marie was stunned by the resemblance between Guy

SINGLE MEN

and this, his eldest child. Facially, she resembled him so closely she might have been a cardboard cut-out of him that had been hung, fashion dolly-style, with the wrong clothes for a joke – Hearty Male turned into an It Girl. She resembled him verbally too.

'Jum! Come on! You've just gotta see him. I wouldn't mind *eating* him. Wouldn't mind *adawl*!'

Mopsy's assignment to Luke of the status of exhibit rankled slightly with Marie. She was about to lie that 'actually, he's quite shy,' when from the kitchen a Greek god appeared. Jumbo Jelly – for it was he – must have been at least six feet and six inches tall. His hair was a wiry, unruly yellow mop. His short-sleeved rugby shirt shrink-wrapped a torso so classically heroic as to make Mr Gay Universe look straight. From its neck sprang sprigs of white-gold body hair, each one capable of strangling a bus. Yet the vibe emanating from Jumbo was anything but dominant. Like the cartoon Hercules he seemed more bewildered than butch, sublimely unaware that the heavens had designated him *deus*.

'Om. Hi,' he offered, half-raising an arm, then turned and shuffled off.

'Sorry about him,' said Mopsy. 'He's right in the middle of his cow pie.' She snorted horsily. 'Anyway. Come in.'

Marie looked down at Luke whose eyes were wider than the Arizona Desert. Mopsy went into the front room. Marie followed and Luke followed her.

'Sit down, yeah?' Mopsy said, indicating the same

chair that Guy had pointed to when bemoaning the fate of his shoes. Marie accepted. Luke climbed on her lap. Mopsy sat on the sofa like a carnival queen on a float.

'As you've probably noticed, Doc Jolly isn't here.'
'Yes. Where is he?'
'Gone off.'
'Gone where?'
'Lake Michigan, that's where.'
'What! In America?'
'That's the place.'
'Why?'
'To shoot things, I think. Elks, or something. Whatever they have there. And saw people's heads off, as he puts it. Basically he's run away.'
'Run away?'
'Yeah. Men do it, apparently, when they can't cope.'
'Guy's run away?'
'Sounds to me, Marie, like you're a bit out of the loop . . .'

In fact, in the end, it was hard for Marie to know which of them, she or Mopsy, was the less well-informed about Guy's recent past. Of course, it was news to her that he'd jetted out of the country five days earlier without telling a soul until he'd landed in Detroit. Once Mopsy and Jumbo knew, they'd dashed here to rescue Hamlet and Schmeichel who, it was feared, had been left in the kitchen to overheat and expire. Happily, the fright proved unfounded. Not only had Guy left the back door open so they could trample the garden at will, he had also defrosted all the offal Marie had stored in the freezer, together with all the chops, steaks and mince he had hoarded for himself. For fluid, he'd filled a child's paddling pool with water, locating it on the kitchen floor. It had been, perhaps, the best twenty-four hours of the dogs' lives.

What, though, did Mopsy know about Nigella the Posh PA? It seemed she'd had the general picture for some time. So too had Guy's ex-wife. It might not have mattered that Guy was involved with her, had his divorce from Mrs Jelly – whose first name turned out to be Jayne, not Rosie or Lucy as the Hampstead shopkeeper had thought – been of the usual kind.

The difficulty was that Guy had kept wanting to go back. As Mopsy put it, 'Daddy is basically a baby. He wants to be married to Mummy, then he doesn't want to be married to Mummy; he wants to be married to Mummy, he doesn't want to be married to Mummy. He gets his big old knickers in a twist. Mummy kept letting him come back, because she felt sorry for him, because she liked him really, because she hadn't got anyone else.

'Meanwhile, he's carrying on with the secretary at work – a classic town wife-country wife scene. Not surprisingly, both of them ended up getting pissed off. Daddy couldn't make his mind up. So off he popped. The sod.'

Marie wasn't sure what to add to all that. She decided, on balance, not much. When she thought of Guy as spoiled, puerile and dependent on others to prop his life up, it embarrassed her slightly because in her role as his 'girl guide' she'd let him use her in that way too. When she saw him more kindly, as a man who couldn't pin happiness down, she was reluctant to rubbish him.

'By the way,' said Mopsy, 'there's some story going about that he was caught outside with his trousers down the other week. Something about being sawn out of his car around dawn. Have you heard that one?'

'No,' said Marie, and squeezed Luke's hand for quiet. 'Nothing like that.'

Mopsy got to her feet, hair wobbling voluptuously. 'Anyway, Jum and me, we're not moving in. We're just sorting through some stuff. He's asked us to look after his valuables until he comes back – *if* he comes back. God knows, he's been spending some money. There was a pretty amazing ladies' watch up there – I'm borrowing that! And Jum will have the Aston Martin, when he's old enough to drive it!'

'Where are the dogs now?' Marie asked, as she and Luke prepared to leave.

'Down on the farm with our mother. Having a *faa-bulous* time.'

'Oh good,' said Marie.

Mopsy summoned Jumbo from the kitchen: 'Jum! Come and be polite, there's a good boy!'

Giant footsteps moved their way. Marie went to hand Mopsy Guy's keys. Mopsy slapped her forehead as Jumbo manifested at the living-room door.

'Oh *God*, silly me. Nearly *forgot*. Daddy says would you mind still keeping an eye on the place? With no one living here, there won't be much to do but he says he'd be very grateful. In fact, he says he doesn't know where he'd have been without you. That's right, isn't it, Jum?'

'Om. *Ye-agh*,' Jumbo agreed.

CHAPTER NINETEEN

Free Makeover Advice, it said in the window and on an impulse Marie had gone in.

'Mummy,' Luke asked as she thumbed through a portfolio of laminated photos. 'Why are we here?' He looked round the salon, which had no other customers except a young woman of about Marie's age holding a sleeping baby.

'I'm thinking about something,' said Marie, not looking up.

'What?' asked Luke.

'A new hairstyle,' said Elice, whose thoughts were elsewhere too. She couldn't take her eyes off the teenage girl who was finishing off the other customer. Elice had never seen such glorious Goldilocks hair. Her name was unusual too: Boudica. She'd seen it on her necklace when she'd brought the portfolio over to Marie.

'Why is she having a new hairstyle?' asked Luke.

'Because that's what ladies do,' said Elice.

'Boring,' announced Luke, letting his moany voice out

to play. The tactic had a limited effect. Marie had just taken him and Elice to a children's show at the Tricycle Theatre up the Kilburn Road. They had loved every minute. It wouldn't do him any harm to spend ten minutes being bored.

'I'm just going to talk to the lady when she's finished,' said Marie. 'Then we're going to the internet café.'

'Boring,' said Luke again.

'Here she comes,' said Elice. 'Have you made a decision?'

'Not really,' said Marie, chewing a nail. It had taken her by surprise, this urge to reconsider how she looked. She was, of course, attentive to her appearance – though not obsessed with it like Lynda, she hoped – yet her basic style hadn't changed since she was fifteen. Now that the possibility of a new look had been put before her, she felt all at sea.

'Well, hi,' said Boudica, rejoining them. 'How are we doing here?' The accent was American, the tone was caressing, the golden locks compelling. Elice gazed at Boudica in awe.

'Can you make her look like you?' she asked.

'Uh-huh?' stammered Boudica, sitting down. She looked at Elice with what Marie recognised as the same startled reaction she'd had on first encountering the girl.

'Dazzling, isn't she?' said another female voice. It was the woman with the baby. 'And it's all natural – whatever "natural" means.'

'Oh stop it, Charlotte,' begged Boudica, colouring.

'I can't help it,' Charlotte replied. 'It's in my genes.'

One chair remained free around the smoked-glass table where Marie and the children sat. Hoisting her child a little higher on her hip, the young woman called Charlotte planted herself in it and liberated a bosom, expertly. 'You don't mind, do you?' she asked of no one in particular, jabbing her nipple at her infant's lip. 'After all, this *is* a makeover premises. So this hair salon is now made over into a creche.'

Charlotte giggled and rearranged her top so that the baby's sucking, which had begun in earnest, could no longer be seen. 'Sorry, Bou,' she said. 'Don't mind me.'

Boudica cleared her throat and asked Marie if any of the styles had caught her eye. Marie sighed. 'Oh, I don't know. I'd like something different, but I just can't decide.'

She flipped a few pages, haplessly. Half of her was advising caution, half was urging her to be bold. 'Come on, everyone,' she said despairingly. 'What would you all do if you were me?'

Charlotte volunteered the first opinion. 'Go short,' she said. 'A smart boy cut would suit you. And of course it's intrinsically subversive on a girl.'

Marie wasn't sure what she thought of Charlotte. She was opinionated but she had a winning touch of mischief in her too. She had a question for her. 'So why haven't you gone short?'

'Because even I have a conservative streak,' Charlotte replied smartly. 'I blame my dad.'

Elice too was getting interested in Charlotte: a kindred

spirit, maybe? 'What's your baby's name?' she asked.

'Aeshna,' Charlotte replied. 'He's named after a dragonfly, isn't he, Bou?'

'Only you could have thought of it,' said Boudica.

Charlotte fluttered her lashes ironically. 'Go short,' she said to Marie.

'Any more opinions?' asked Boudica sweetly.

'Medium,' said Elice. 'Like me.'

'You could stay long and have it roughed up a little, put a bit more body in,' said Bou.

'Boring,' said Luke.

Marie shrugged helplessly. 'We have to go now anyway. I'll have to think about it. Boudica, can I take your card?'

She chivvied Luke and Elice on to the street. It was after two-fifteen. Time to swap girl talk for something else.

She sat at the keyboard and faced the screen. It was exactly half-past two. She'd have to keep it simple, she supposed.

Hello, Glen. Are you there?

She waited. A return message came through.

Hello, Marie. How are you?

Her heart lurched deliciously.

I am fine. How are you?

Fine too. But missing you.

'Who are you emailing, exactly?' asked Elice. She'd got bored with her fruit juice, which wasn't even pure. Luke had made his way over too.

'A friend of mine,' said Marie.

'What sort of a friend?'

'A friend I met in France.'

'Male or female?'

Marie hesitated, fatally. It was too easy to underestimate Elice.

'It's male,' said Elice. 'I can tell because you didn't answer straight away.'

'Well, it might be,' said Marie. 'Or it might not. It's one of the two, I expect.'

'It could be a transsexual, of course,' said Elice. 'That's someone who's changing their agenda.'

'I suppose it could be, Elice.'

'Or a hermaphrodite. That's someone with no agenda at all.'

'Your daddy tells you everything, doesn't he?'

'Yes. He doesn't call you "Cupcakes" any more, does he? Did you have a row?'

'No, Elice. We did not.'

'Would you like to marry Daddy?'

'Suddenly, young lady, I've gone deaf. Now both of you, please go away.'

They skulked off reluctantly, but contented themselves with drawing on napkins. Marie typed again.

And I am missing you . . . She checked over her shoulder and continued: *You are the nicest man I've ever known. I can't wait till you come home.*

Glen, at the other end, maintained the theme. *I know a special woman when I meet one. Army training.*

Marie's turn: *Don't start that again.*

SINGLE MEN

Glen: *Been to the circus lately? How is Luke?*
Marie: *No circuses. Luke is well.*
Glen: *Are you sorting out your other boys?*
Marie: *I'm working on it. Then I'm gonna begin working on you.*
Glen: *Can't wait.*
Marie: *Don't be rude.*

They batted nonsense back and forth for about ten minutes more until the patience of the children was too frayed. Glen was the first to write: *I love you.*

Marie replied: *I love it that you love me. And I love you too.*

That night, Marie was unable to sleep. The day had been a good one but it had also snagged her and left her sore. Some of her pain was over Glen. The ache she had for him was like a living thing within: precious and to be nurtured and yet also endured. Marlon was giving her discomfort in another form, because she couldn't work out what to do for him: fixing his flat would be nice, but wouldn't save him. The love wars of Daniel, Elice and Miss V remained unresolved. Rick kept wandering into her thoughts and she knew he tiptoed into Luke's too. Cyclically, she replayed the hairdresser scene: should she go short or stay long? Should she have learned a skill like the striking Boudica? Could she have acquired the cool cleverness of Charlotte – and still had a child as well?

Meanwhile, across the landing slept Lynda. The nighttime silence of the house crystallised for Marie the secretive quality of so much that went on there, so much that was thought. She didn't understand her mother. She loved her, but found her maddening and unreal. Marie was all restlessness and Lynda too often seemed to be the source.

Marie gave up on sleeping and got up. She went down to the front room, switched on the light and dimmed it to half-strength. The time was three-fifteen. What to do? Not the telly or she would soon have company. No book she wanted to read, no magazine. She padded over to the stereo and, like Gabby when she'd visited on that dismal day, began flipping through the albums underneath. As a young child she'd done this often, losing herself in cover artwork in the same way as she had in picture books. Later, she'd despised them for being old and then, after Clay's death, begun to think of them as forbidden, a private musical shrine that her mother maintained in the cause of prolonging her misery.

Sifting through them now was a bit like breaking a spell: Berlin; Elkie Brooks; Dean Friedman; T'Pau. She enjoyed the weight of them as one by one she tipped them against the bulwark of her hand.

Then one felt heavier than the rest.

Bonnie Tyler: *Faster Than the Speed of Night*.

Marie reached into the sleeve. Beside the vinyl record in its paper inner bag was a slim brown envelope. Marie removed it and slid the contents out. Within ten minutes she had discovered something terrible but true. Replacing the sheaf of papers, she took a last look at the cover sheet.

SINGLE MEN

FAMILY DATA RESEARCH
MISSING HISTORY SERVICE
Client: Stephanie Anne Daines

CHAPTER TWENTY

'Barbara here. Leave a message and I'll call you back. Bye.'

The tone followed and Marie spoke carefully.

'Hello, Auntie. It's Marie. There's something I want to talk to you about. Can you call me on my mobile, please?'

Turning to Auntie Barbara was a safe course in one way, yet risky in another. Marie could usually depend on her sympathy, especially when her problem was with Lynda. Yet Barbara's relationship with her sister was close as well as competitive. Marie had her fingers crossed that by specifying her mobile number in the message Barbara would appreciate that she should keep the approach to herself for the time being. How Barbara would react to the matter she wished to raise, Marie had absolutely no idea.

For now she left this in the lap of Fate. She had resolved to make two other journeys into the unknown and these she must begin immediately. She was alone beside Luke's wardrobe, looking up. A nylon overnight bag sat on top of it. Marie reached up, tugged it down and then retrieved the two halves of her son's discarded pyjamas from opposite ends of his bed. She sniffed the bottom half doubtfully but decided they would do. This was his favourite pair and there was no time to wash them now. She folded the pyjamas into the case then added a clean T-shirt, socks, pants, a pair of shorts and a toothbrush in a sealable plastic bag. On top of these she placed Big Cilla and Little Cilla. She waved to them before zipping the bag up. This would be Luke's first sleepover ever. Already, Marie was fighting inner fires of anxiety.

The packing task complete, Marie went to her own room carrying her mobile with her. She paused to listen before opening her dressing-table drawer. This next bit of business needed to be completed before Luke lost interest in his bath toys and either yelled for a towel or came scampering, wet and soapy, into the room. The prognosis appeared fairly promising.

'You shall have a fishy, fishy wishy, wishy,
You shall have a fishy when the boot comes in . . .'

Luke was practising his Geordie accent: his late grandfather could have helped him with that. Marie slid the drawer open and pulled from it a typewritten letter. Reading from the top of it, she punched an unfamiliar number into her phone. The tension she'd been feeling since waking two hours earlier became focused on her gut and magnified. A connection was made and Marie mentally rehearsed her opening lines: 'Hello. This is Marie Amiss, Marlon's cleaner. I have some news about him that I think you ought to hear . . .'

There were two rings, three rings, four. Luke turned up the volume for the chorus.

'DANCE TO YOUR LADDY, MY LITTLE DADDY!'

Overriding a basic instinct, Marie dashed to close her door: she always stayed within earshot when Luke was in the bath. A tense, expectant voice spoke in her ear: 'Hello? *Hello?*'

'Is that Mrs Alibhai?' said Marie.

'Who is it? Yes?'

'Um. It's Marie Amiss, Marlon's cleaner. I—'

'Who?'

'Marie Amiss – your son's cleaner. I clean his flat. You interviewed me.'

All that practising and she'd dried up, though Mrs Alibhai seemed short of words too until she said glacially: 'If it's about money, I'm afraid—'

'It isn't about money,' Marie broke in. As in their previous encounter, the other woman's loftiness hardened her. She recalled the stalled expression on Mrs Alibhai's face when confronted with the stark fact of Clay's death.

'So what is it about?' Marlon's mother said.

'I've seen him and I'm calling you to tell you,' said Marie.

'You've seen him?' Hope. Marie heard hope.

'Yes. On Tuesday.'

'I see. Wherever is he?' Mrs Alibhai's voice was suddenly strained. A supplicant manner did not come to her easily, but there were other things there too: worry; heartache; pain.

'He asked me not to tell you,' Marie said firmly. 'But there are some things I think you ought to know.'

'What sort of things?'

'I'd really like to come and see you. I can get there this afternoon.'

'Well . . .'

'It's not something to discuss over the phone.'

Marie took Luke to Daniel's just after midday, having indulged him in a supersize brunch of fish fingers, oven chips and baked beans. Daniel had promised dietary concessions over breakfast cereal but Marie remained concerned that an alien dinner might prompt a hunger strike in Luke and ruin his resolve to stay the night. What if Daniel had only been half-joking when he'd spoken of couscous, aubergines and squid?

'Elice's favourites,' he'd said, with gravity. 'She'll want him to try them, Cupcakes.'

'Stop calling me Cupcakes,' she'd responded uncertainly.

All the same, as agreed, she dropped Luke off without ceremony and as she walked away, told herself it was a good thing he hadn't waved from the window rather than a sign that he didn't care. It was important not to get all wobbly. That was why she was wearing her smart black skirt, some serious black tights, her best pink top with the collar and the buttons up the front and her best pink, pointy-toed shoes.

She was still worried they'd think her common – to use a Lynda word – but at least she'd be common with attitude. She'd taken strength from Daniel's only comment, which had been, 'You're looking very smart today.' For once there had been no joke innuendo or amused undertow. Perhaps it was because he'd wanted to convey that he knew it was A Big Thing having Luke to stay. Perhaps it was just something about her; something steely he was still getting used to. Either way, she was pleased to have been taken seriously. The trick now was to have the same effect on Marlon's family.

She arrived at the Alibhais' house an hour later. It was a squared-off mini-mansion with its wide porch supported by a Greek-style colonnade. It was set back a self-important distance from the road. Its doorbell was a white ceramic button in a circular brass housing. Marie pressed it and hoped her armpits didn't smell.

At first, Mrs Alibhai appeared not to know who she was. As she'd stared at her suspiciously through the half-open doorway Marie had thought at first that she really *must* look different if Mrs Alibhai hadn't recognised her. On later reflection she'd concluded that she simply hadn't mattered enough to be worth remembering. At any rate, up to that point.

'Oh yes, come in,' said Mrs Alibhai austerely.

'Thank you,' said Marie. She could hear noises coming from inside the house: footsteps on a hard floor at ground level; a door closing upstairs. Mrs Alibhai led her into a large reception room off to the right of a wide, blue-carpeted hall in which a family photograph enjoyed pride of place. It was exactly the same one as in Marlon's flat, except much larger. The same difference of proportion was repeated in the reception room. It was bigger than Marlon's living room, but everything else about it was the same: the carpet, the furniture, the light-fitting, the walls.

At first Marie and Mrs Alibhai simply stood in the room, rather awkwardly. Then Marlon's barrister sister Elaine came in. She was small like Marlon and rather pretty. She wore dark-blue trousers, a light-blue cardigan and a serious expression. She stood there awkwardly too. At last, in came the man who – it now become clear – they were all waiting for: Marlon's father. He was also small: smaller than his wife. He wore fawn casual trousers and a lightweight green Pringle sweater with a stiff-collared white shirt underneath. The collar sat neatly proud of the neck of the jumper, suburban-casual style. His hair was slicked into something close to a quiff. His whole head gleamed with self-esteem, just like in the family photo. The world would stop revolving until Mr Alibhai spoke.

'Please be seated,' he said to Marie, crisply.

He indicated an armchair. It was exactly the same as the one Marlon had fallen asleep in, the last time Marie had seen him at his flat; the time Mr Alibhai had left his irritated message on the ansaphone. Marie reversed herself on to it as if she were in primary school and had been sent to the naughty chair.

Each of the Alibhais now took up their positions: Mrs

Alibhai and Elaine on the sofa that was just like Marlon's sofa; Mr Alibhai on another armchair that was exactly like Marlon's other armchair. The only difference in the furniture arrangements was the distance between the pieces. Here, they might have been configured to minimise the risk of social contamination.

Mr Alibhai leaned towards Marie and said, 'Very well, Miss Amiss. Where is my son?'

Involuntarily, Marie's bottom gripped the seat of the chair. She was on a rocky ledge overlooking a precipice. *Don't look down, don't look down. Don't look down . . .*

She cleared her throat and said, 'I'm very sorry, Mr Alibhai, but I really can't tell you that.'

'Why not?' His tone was all strained patience, rather ostentatiously so.

'Because I promised him I wouldn't. I explained this to Mrs Alibhai on the phone this morning. He says he'll re-establish contact when he's ready, but I'm afraid I don't know when that will be. And neither does he.'

She looked at Mrs Alibhai for confirmation of what they'd said. Given their chilly history she was amazed that she now saw Marlon's mother as a possible ally.

'I know what you said to my wife,' said Mr Alibhai. 'But now I, *Mr* Alibhai, am asking you. So once again, Miss Amiss, where is my son Marlon?'

He was staring right into her. Even though his chair stood ten paces away, his intensity drove needles into her. And yet, she didn't flinch. She had travelled a long way lately and much of the journey had tested her. She had learned to know her mind and stand her ground. She'd found new love and was seeking a new future. She wasn't going to buckle easily.

'Mr Alibhai,' she said. 'Mrs Alibhai, Elaine. There are some things I really do want to tell you. But before I can do that you *have* to accept that I'm not going to give Marlon's whereabouts away. He doesn't know I've come here and he probably wouldn't thank me for saying the things that I want to say. So I already feel I'm being disloyal to him. So please don't try to make me say things he has asked me not to. If you do, I'm afraid I'll have to go.'

She tugged the front of her skirt down to cover more of her knees. It was her only outward sign of nerves. The effect of her words was like someone dropping a rock into a pool that had never before been disturbed. The ripple effect was almost palpable. How would her hosts respond?

'Well, it's . . .' Mr Alibhai shifted his body. He realigned his gaze. 'Well, it's clear that you feel strongly about this.'

'I'm afraid I do, Mr Alibhai,' said Marie.

Mr Alibhai stood up. He shoved a hand into each of his trouser pockets. From one of them he produced a large white cotton handkerchief, the sort you don't see so much any more. He blew his nose loudly, poked about a bit and then sat down again.

This single action had a significant effect. The agitation of the nostrils, the comic trumpeting, seemed to bleed some of the tension from the scene. And it was funny the way he'd suddenly stood up. If Gabby had been there she'd have said, 'Has the Queen walked in?'

Mr Alibhai cleared his throat. He said, 'How do I know that what you want to tell me is worth hearing?'

Marie was puzzled. 'Well, you don't know, do you, I suppose. Unless you want to take my word for it.'

Mr Alibhai laughed – a superior laugh. He made a steeple with his fingers and contemplated his nails. 'I need to press you on this,' he said, 'because if you tell me nothing that I consider to be of value, you will have wasted my time.'

'In your opinion,' said Marie. She glanced in the direction of the silent women on the sofa. Were they thinking what she was thinking? That Mr Alibhai was a pompous, puffed-up, self-important twit?

'Very well,' said Mr Alibhai. 'What do the ladies think?'

'Let's listen to her,' said Mrs Alibhai.

'Yes,' said Elaine.

'Hmmm,' said Mr Alibhai. 'Very well.' He checked his watch. Busy man, busy man. 'Off you go,' he said.

Having been deeply apprehensive only a few minutes earlier, Marie was now beginning to feel rebellious. How could anyone take Mr Alibhai seriously? Yet somehow he was running the show – and badly. She thought about poor Marlon, staring through the window from his sickbed. She took a breath and off she went.

'The first thing you've got to understand is that I'm not just Marlon's cleaner. I am also his friend. And, believe it or not, I'm probably his best friend.'

She paused to let the Alibhais take this in.

'I am not his girlfriend – he hasn't got one of those. I'm

just his friend. I am the only person he knows who he's allowed to see him since he became ill.'

'Ill?' Marie jumped. Mrs Alibhai had spoken again.

'Yes, ill. The reason he's moved out of his flat and left his job is that he's ill.'

'What's wrong with him?' asked Mrs Alibhai.

'Well . . .' Marie thought about this one. 'He's been suffering from stress and depression.'

'Pah!' said Mr Alibhai.

Marie looked at him.

'Pah!' he said again.

'What do you mean?' asked Marie.

'I don't believe in it,' said Mr Alibhai. 'Depression. Stress. Never heard of it! Pah!'

'Well, you haven't seen him lately, have you?' Marie said, as gently as she could.

'Well, obviously,' Mr Alibhai said.

'You haven't seen how *unhappy* he is,' said Marie.

'Why is he unhappy?' asked Mrs Alibhai.

'Because he hates his job and because he hates his life!'

Mr Alibhai shrugged. 'So why doesn't he change it?'

'Because he doesn't know how to,' said Marie. 'And because he thinks he'll upset you.'

'Oh well,' said Mr Alibhai, spluttering. 'He's already upset me! He has *already* upset me! I found him a top-of-the-range job in the City of London and he has made a mess of it!'

'Yes, I heard your message.'

'My what?'

'Your ansaphone message, when you rang him up. I

was there, trying to help him, when he was rattling with anti-depressants that were doing him no good, and you rang him up to tell him off!'

A row. It was a row. Marie saw that she was standing up and heard that she was shouting at Mr Alibhai. She was in these people's home trying to help Marlon and maybe help them too, and she was having a row instead.

'I'm sorry,' Marie said, and sat back down.

Mr Alibhai had not stood up. Instead, he'd begun quivering. To steady himself he was hanging on to the edge of his seat as if it were about to take off.

'I'm sorry,' said Marie again. 'I'd better go.'

She stood up, tugged her skirt down once more, and started towards the door. As she walked past the sofa where the two women sat, Mrs Alibhai said, 'Why don't you shut up?'

Marie stopped in her tracks. She looked at Mrs Alibhai and said, 'Pardon?'

'Not *you*,' said Mrs Alibhai. 'I mean *him*.'

'Oh,' said Marie. Her exit had been disrupted. She was now in a state of limbo. Something else would have to happen before she could leave.

'You and your big mouth,' said Mrs Alibhai.

'What?' said Mr Alibhai. He was quivering again.

'Your great big gob,' said Mrs Alibhai. 'It's all Ramjan Alibhai this, and Ramjan Alibhai that. Who do you think you are? God?'

'What? What are you talking about, Celia?' said Mr Alibhai. Now a second woman was shouting at him. It was all too confusing.

SINGLE MEN

'This girl,' Mrs Alibhai said. 'This rather *brave* girl has come all the way out here to tell us what a terrible state our son is in, and how it seems he cannot bear to see us, and all you can say is how upset *you* are because he didn't like working at some bloody merchant bank!'

'Celia!' exploded Mr Alibhai.

'Don't shout at me, Ramjan!'

'Damn it, I'll shout if I want to!'

'We're talking about our *son*!'

Marie was now in a state of some dismay. She'd arrived with a sense of mission, a belief that she should and could convince the assembled Alibhais of the need to understand their son. She'd envisioned heads nodding sagely and a rational argument won. Mrs Alibhai, after all, had seemed totally in control of her emotions when she'd interviewed Marie for the cleaning job. But now look at the mess. Marie had been unable to properly make her points about Marlon's need for a different type of employment, perhaps with his Uncle Lance; about his need for love and approval from his mother and, in particular, his father. Instead, her intervention looked in danger of sending the Alibhai parents down the fast track to divorce.

But still: Mrs Alibhai seemed to be getting at least part of the message. And Elaine? Elaine was showing her out of the reception room and back into the hall. She'd been inscrutable throughout the fractious meeting. Did she have any feelings at all about Marlon's plight?

'So,' said Marie, determined to get something out of her before she left. 'What do you think about all this?'

Elaine seemed to be wincing. The set-to in the reception room was broadening its scope.

'I came to this country with nothing in my pocket, only the shoes on my feet, and I never fussed about stress!'

'You know very well that the boy's not cut out for it! This is all about Ramjan Alibhai wanting to look big!'

Marie headed for the front door. Elaine caught her before she opened it. 'Give me your numbers,' she said. 'I'll be in touch.'

CHAPTER TWENTY-ONE

'Mum, if something had gone wrong, Daniel would have called me straight away. He's obviously fine, OK?'

'If you say so.' Lynda shrugged and made too big a performance of being flustered because she was leaving late. And she wasn't meeting Marie's eye.

Marie, though, did not bite. Instead she said, 'He's a big boy now. We have to learn to let go, don't we?'

Now Lynda shot her a look. Marie held it and Lynda turned away to the hall mirror, shaking down her outfit and sucking at each of her lips in turn. She didn't ask Marie how she looked. She didn't speak at all. The front door closed behind her with a rattle of rejection. Marie let a full minute elapse. Only when she was quite sure Lynda had gone did she call Daniel.

'Cupcakes!'

'I told you not to—'

'Sorry. Hello, Marie.'

'How is he?'

'He's very, very happy. Slept beautifully, lovely

manners, he's eating his Sugar Puffs now – revolting things.'

Marie's laughter covered her relief. 'They are, aren't they? When shall I fetch him?'

'No hurry. In fact, he seems to have moved in. I thought I'd let them make it up as they go on and see how they're doing by lunchtime. Is that all right with you?'

'Thanks, Daniel. I'm going out for a bit. Let's speak later on.'

'Fine. And I'll brief you about tomorrow when you come round.'

Daniel's tone became grave with this remark. After much umming and aahing on his part, Marie's first ever encounter with Miss Valencia had been arranged for the following day at her London base in Kensington. Elice would be there too.

Marie's hopes were high. It would be another big day; and hopefully with a calmer outcome than the excursion to *chez* Alibhai. At that precise moment, though, it seemed a long way off. Marie had a more immediate matter to attend to and its potential implications were absolutely vast.

She said goodbye to Daniel and went into the living room. The brown envelope fell readily from the Bonnie Tyler album sleeve and Marie checked its contents, not because she thought Lynda would have moved them but because it still seemed possible that she herself had dreamed the whole thing. Then she slipped the envelope into her rucksack. She took a deep breath, put her shoulders back and set off for Auntie Barbara's, hastened by the pull of destiny.

Above the kitchen range was a ceramic plaque containing important information.

RULES OF THIS HOUSE
Rule One: The Boss Is Always Right
Rule Two: If The Boss Is Wrong, See Rule One

This message had been conveyed from the same prominent position for about a dozen years, yet its true import had never been quite clear. Who was the boss, exactly? Uncle Phil said it was Auntie Barbara. Auntie Barbara said it was Uncle Phil. Both seemed to relish the dispute. For Marie the plaque had a further significance: it had been a gift from her. It was the first proper present she had bought for anyone other than Lynda or Clay, and she could still recall the praise she received for choosing so wisely. There was something very relaxed about Barbara and Phil which Lynda and Clay could never quite replicate. Their sons, Steven and Kevin, were both at university, the former studying maths, the latter biology. Marie liked them both but couldn't help but feel a failure by comparison. The talent of Auntie Barbara had always been to help her feel a success.

'So, darling, what can I do you for?' Barbara said.

With mugs of filter coffee they had organised themselves in the little summerhouse which looked out on to the garden of Barbara and Phil's big, cosy and untidy house in Southgate. Barbara raised both eyebrows at Marie but she held the rest of her face still. Marie experienced a loss of confidence. She had looked through the papers in the envelope three times: on the night she'd found them, on the following morning and again during the journey today. She believed she'd grasped exactly what they meant. Yet she still couldn't believe it. She needed Barbara's authority to prove to her that it was true.

Marie's rucksack was on the floor between her feet. She pulled out the envelope. She said, 'I found something in the house the other night. It's about Dad. I'm worried about it and I didn't want Mum . . .'

Here she faltered. She was going behind her mother's back. And suppose Auntie Barbara knew nothing about Stephanie Anne Daines? Would she welcome being enlightened now?

'I'm sorry, Auntie.' Marie drew the documents out from the envelope. 'I just need to know what this stuff means.'

At first, Barbara didn't speak. To compensate for her long sight she raised her glasses like a visor and wedged them on the top of her head. She scanned the covering letter, then fanned quickly but attentively through the papers underneath. With a soft sigh, she lowered her glasses again. 'I know what this is,' she said quietly. 'I've seen it before. And I know exactly what it means.'

'When did Mum find out?' asked Marie.

'Oh, not for a long time.'

SINGLE MEN

'What, years ago or . . . ?'

'A few years ago. Not long after Clay died. The girl tracked him down.'

'Tracked him down where? To our house?'

'Yeah. Literally to your front door. I was there when she arrived.'

'She actually turned up at our house!'

'You were out somewhere,' Barbara said. 'At your friend Gabby's, I think. There was this knock at the door and there she was. Didn't have a clue who she was.'

'So you've *met* her?' Marie said.

'Yeah, I've met her.'

'And Mum's met her too?'

'Your mum's met her too. But just the once.' Placing the papers in her lap, Barbara looked at Marie regretfully. 'Once was enough for her, I'm sad to say.'

After learning from Daniel that Elice and Luke were very, very busy writing and filming a fantasy adventure called *The Diva and the Flea*, Marie had arranged to meet Gabby. In the heat of the first half-hour after leaving Barbara's house she'd wandered in aimless turmoil round the Southgate streets, trying to grasp the scale of what she'd learned. Then she'd realised she was lost. 'Meet me in the park, Gabs,' she'd pleaded. 'I'm all over the place.'

Her intention had been to tell Gabby everything and then try to work out what to do. But by the time she'd relocated the big, round Southgate station and made her way dazedly to the Queen's Park café, she'd changed her mind. It wasn't that she didn't trust Gabby, not in a real emergency. It was more that the import of the story Barbara had told her had become more and more immense and now it seemed too sacred to share straight away. And it was dawning on Marie that she was uncertain about her loyalties. What did she owe Lynda because of this? What did Lynda need?

From a selfish point of view then, it was lucky that Gabby appeared subdued. She'd said the café was too crowded and she didn't fancy it. This made it easier for Marie to be vague about what troubled her and to create a diversion: a visit to the dwelling of Big Hands.

'Moved in with him then, have you?' Gabby asked, reviving briefly.

'Not exactly.'

Because her men had begun calling on her unpredictably, Marie had taken to keeping their keys with her constantly. She led the way from the café, through a tree canopy and then the gate in the railings. They crossed Kingswood Avenue and went into Guy's house. It felt half-abandoned already.

Gabby made her way to the front room. 'Classy,' she opined, looking around. 'So he's just buggered off, has he?'

'That's what his daughter told me.'

'So is she living here now?'

'No. She's with Mummy in the country.'

'La-de-dah.'

'Still, she's the one paying me now – on his behalf.'

'For what?'

'Looking after this place while he's away.'

'How long will that be?'

'Years, for all I know.'

'Has he cracked up then?'

'Only completely.'

'Oh-kay . . . how do you mean?'

Marie told her the story of the tank top and Nigella, Posh PA. She led the way back to the park and struck out for the opposite side. It was strange to be there without Luke or Elice, especially with so many children playing. Everything about the day confirmed the bond of parenthood. Each time a little voice cried, 'Mummy,' Marie looked round. It was almost two-thirty. She decided to call Daniel again soon.

'I presume madam knows where she is going,' said Gabby.

'You'll have to wait and see,' answered Marie.

Gabby left it there. So did Marie. Their introspection was the heart of their companionship now, and they maintained it as, together, they crossed the park. Neither spoke until they were at Marlon's door.

'So this is the sad-eyed Asian boy's place, yeah?'

'Marlon's place, yeah. And I'm warning you – it's in a right state.'

Whatever else Elaine Alibhai had done about Marlon since yesterday, she hadn't popped round to clear up his flat. It was precisely the same scene of hopeless devastation that Marie had stumbled on the Tuesday before she went on holiday. Gabby was first gobsmacked – '*Far canal!* What happened here?' – then was drawn all too easily to the tale of despair the ruins told. As Marie made token efforts to clear some of the mess, Gabby stood in the middle of it, thinking. Then she made an announcement.

'I'd love to have a baby.'

'What?' said Marie.

'I'd love a baby,' she repeated, her voice rising to a nearly comic squeak. She smeared her tears with the back of her hand.

'Gabs!' said Marie and rushed to her protectively.

'I'm so pathetic,' said Gabby, tucking her arms under her breasts.

'No, you're not!' said Marie. She hugged Gabby urgently.

'Yes, I am.'

'No, you're not!'

'For Chrissakes, Marie, listen to me!'

Marie let go and stepped away. 'OK. I'm listening.'

'Sorry,' said Gabby.

'It's OK,' said Marie. She was feeling bluesy too, remembering glacé tartlets and over-egged gallantry.

Gabby stared out at the park, sniffing loudly.

'Have a tissue,' said Marie, who had a Luke supply in her pockets routinely. She checked that her phone was in her pocket. The time was now getting on for three.

'The thing is,' said Gabby, having blasted a clearance in her nasal passages, 'when you had Luke it was, like, what a disaster, she's pregnant and she's only sixteen. And, be honest, well, you know what they mean. It's so young and whatever and you haven't even left school and then it doesn't work out right with the bloke and everything . . .'

'Yes,' said Marie, 'so I've heard.'

'But I look at you now and I think you're brilliant, you know. All the shit that's happened to you, all the struggling you've had to do. But nothing would make you want to change what happened. Nothing has ever made you wish you hadn't had Luke. I suppose that's what's so special about kids. When you've got one and you love it nothing beats it. Ever.'

Marie thought about it. She said, 'I agree with you, Gabs. If only everybody felt that way.'

CHAPTER TWENTY-TWO

Miss Valencia lived in a square in a handsome garden flat owned by some spare part of the aristocracy. She was tall, dark, longhaired and restless, and she had tremendous thighs, which her little black skirt showed off lustrously. Her top was a low-slung lemon lace cascade of frills and bows. She reminded Marie of a wilful mare who hadn't noticed she was no more a pony.

'Daniel, he is a funny man,' she snorted with a great shake of her mane. 'He is a good man, *hi* suppose, in many ways, but funny too. He doesn't make sense, is what *hi* mean. He doesn't *hunderstand* I need my little baby. *Heh*?'

Every sentence came with a challenge. Marie said quietly, 'I think he understands a little better now.'

'OK Marie, is it?' said Miss Valencia, confirming her guest's name for the third time. 'What has he told you about us, *heh*? I am meaning about him and me.'

'Well, Esmerelda,' began Marie. This was difficult. She remembered Daniel's account from long ago: *she had to be a tranny, a dark portal lay open, I was very drunk indeed.* Listening interestedly was Elice.

'*Hi* am sure you can tell me anything,' Miss Valencia assured her. 'We are mothers, we are women. I know we can speak freely.'

'Well,' Marie began again. 'Maybe he was a bit out of his depth.'

Miss Valencia thought about this while Marie crossed her fingers, legs and feet. Her hostess raised her head and whinnied thoughtfully, 'He-yes. That *hi* think is how *hi* would put it too.'

Elice had her hand over her mouth. Miss Valencia, without warning, leaped suddenly to her feet and cantered, clippy-cloppy, across the parquet kitchen floor in her unnervingly high-heeled shoes. From the stove she seized an iron sauté pan and put it on the wooden table with a bang.

'Help yourself, please,' she said, flapping both her hands. 'Is paella: Spanish food you English understand. Not to be rude, or anything.'

Diplomatically, Marie reached for a prawn. There were no plates or cutlery. Meekly, she began picking at the shell. 'The thing is, you see, I don't think he'd ever, you know . . .'

'Had sex with a woman,' said Elice.

'I wasn't going to say that!' quailed Marie.

'This is true,' said Miss Valencia matter-of-factly. 'He had not.' She sighed heavily. '*Hi* was a fool, of course. *Hi* thought *hi* could change him. Women in love believe these things.'

'Were you in love?' asked Elice.

'*Hi* was in love with him. Or so *hi* thought! He, though, was not in love with me.' Miss Valencia fixed her daughter with her innocent brown eyes. 'This is my tragedy, Elice. *Hi* am a woman spurned. And yet *Hi* know, deep down, that *Hi* can only blame myself. Daniel and *Hi* were never to be. He put his pinky thing in me, *heh*? We make a baby! But it was not our destiny.'

'What do you mean by destiny?' asked Elice.

'In the stars, darling. It was not written in the stars.'

'Ah,' said Elice, 'I see.'

Marie looked at her closely and it was clear that she did see. Elice had already grasped the cruel concept of Fate – assisted by her father, undoubtedly – and all its payload of delicious tragedy.

'For a while it destroyed me,' Miss Valencia went on. 'That is why *hi* went away.'

'Where did you go?' asked Elice.

'Oh, to a place *hi* can't describe. A place inside myself where all was darkness and despair. That was when *hi* lost you, my Elice, my sweet. *Hi* couldn't take you there with me. It was a journey *hi* had to endure alone.'

'You poor thing,' said Marie.

Miss Valencia shrugged. Then she tugged a paper tissue from the brown cleft of her bosom and proceeded to weep. She wept for seven minutes unbrokenly – Marie knew this because she watched the clock – sometimes howling at the ceiling, sometimes cradling her face in shaking fingers. And while Miss Valencia wept, Elice comforted her with pats and strokes and kisses and promises that they would be together always, and Daniel would be made to understand.

Miss Valencia recovered. She ate two bananas and she sneezed. Then she said to Marie, 'We are women, *heh*?'

'Yes, we are women.'

'We have to stick together, *heh*?'

'Well, yes. The problem is, Esmerelda, that I have to put Daniel's side to you.'

'Daniel's side?' Miss Valencia bared her teeth. Marie was impressed. Maybe that's what all termagants did. 'What is Daniel's side?'

'I suppose he feels that he's been Elice's number one parent for a long time now and that he doesn't want to risk losing her.'

'Hmmm, yes,' said Miss Valencia. 'He is afraid of me, yes?'

'Well, yes, a bit. But mostly he's afraid of what might happen. What if Elice decides she would much sooner be with you? How will Daniel feel then?'

'Ha! Like shit, *hi* think!'

'Yes.' Marie turned to Elice. 'Elice, would you want Daniel to feel like that?'

'No.'

'Esmerelda? Would you?'

'Maybe, *heh*?' Miss Valencia bared her teeth again. Then she looked at Elice, who had a very firm expression on her face. She was looking at Marie.

'You say these things, Marie,' she said, 'but what about Luke's daddy?'

'What about him?'

'He wants to see Luke, doesn't he?'
'Well, yes. So he says.'
'But you don't want him to, do you?'
'Well . . .'
'But Luke would like to see him.'
'Would he?'
'Yes.'
'How do you know?'
'Because he told me.'

Marie was suspicious. Was this Elice being a little madam again?

'When did he tell you?'

'Yesterday. When I was being the Diva and he was being the Flea. I've got it on video if you'd like to see.'

Marie fell silent. Miss Valencia laughed. Then she burst into tears and howled for four more minutes, while Elice gave her kisses and offered to buy her sweets. After that Miss Valencia recovered and took Elice through to the next room where she put on some Latin music and the pair of them raised a merry clatter attempting the *paso doble*.

Marie thought of Luke doing the macarena.

Then it was her turn to cry.

Elice embraced her father when she returned home. Love and forgiveness ran like honey. Daniel was so moved at the dark spell being broken that he could hardly speak. Marie had never seen him so melting. Eventually, he told her: 'Marie, what would I do without you? And you look *so* beautiful too. Why aren't *loads* of handsome young men chasing you?'

'Because I don't want to be chased?' replied Marie, enjoying the shared reprise.

'Darling,' he scolded softly. '*Everyone* wants to be chased.'

She left them waving from the step. Elice would give him the outline of the deal: Miss Valencia would find a flat somewhere much nearer; Elice would spend time with her once a week and, if all went well, at weekends too. The details would be arranged with the help of a professional mediator. Their daughter wanted them to learn to get along. *Heh?*

Marie's plan at this point was to go home. She'd left Luke with Lynda, which made both of them happy, but she felt she'd hardly seen him all weekend. Yet as she walked she knew she wasn't quite ready.

A taxi with its light on rumbled by. Marie hailed it without fretting about the fare, as if the wealth of her emotions would somehow take care of it. Twenty minutes later, and down to her last two pounds, she was sitting once again by Clayton's grave.

'What kind of man were you?' she asked the headstone quietly.

It said what it always said:

CLAYTON AMISS

†

A PERFECT HUSBAND AND DAD

'It's all right, I forgive you,' said Marie.

She thought for a few minutes, enjoying the stillness, feeling pleasantly invisible. Then she took out her mobile. First, she rang Boudica the hairdresser. Then she rang home.

'Hello?'

'Hello Mum.'

'Oh babes, how did it go?'

'Fine.'

'Where are you now?'

'Not far away.'

'Where's that exactly?'

'It's OK, I'll be back soon. I've got some things to tell you actually.'

CHAPTER TWENTY-THREE

Three weeks later . . .

From the bandstand balustrade a miniature mariner surveyed the verdant waves. He was on the lookout for someone: a figure formed mostly in his imagination and from a fleeting recent memory. From a nearby blanket serving as a rock, two mermaids looked on.

'It's going well then, is it, Gabs?' enquired the blonde one, staying cool beneath her smart boy coiffure.

'Couldn't be better,' replied the brunette, ruffling up her tresses with both hands.

'Who jumped on who first?'

'Don't be rude on a Sunday. But if you must know, no one has jumped on anyone yet. Not *that* sort of "jumped on" anyway.'

'How sweet.'

'We're working up to it slowly.'

'Slowly is good.'

'Oh yes. Phew. Dearie me.'

Gabby wiped away a pretend bead of sweat. Marie, enjoying the new sensation of breeze around her ears, smiled and hugged her knees. Gabby was besotted with a man again but maybe, just maybe, this time it would work out happily. He wasn't her usual type, for sure.

Marie checked the mini-mariner again. 'Any ships ahoy yet, Luke?' He turned with a sombre face and shook his head. Marie checked her watch. It was still only five to three. No need to worry yet.

'So tell me about Big Hands,' said Gabby.

'He wrote to me.'

'Oh yeah? When's the Big Day?'

'Oh, the same day as yours, I expect.'

'Yeah?'

'Yeah, I expect. He's going to carry me away to his castle in the sky.'

'Up there with the birds . . .'

'And all our children will be angels.'

'Like the one you've got now.'

The mermaids laughed.

'Anyway,' said Gabby, 'what did the letter say?'

'Well, it's a bit sad really. Says he's made a mess of everything and that's why he had to go away. And he apologised for dragging me into his difficult lovelife, as he called it.'

'Difficult? I'll say!'

'Anyway, he says he's gonna stay out there for a while until he's better. Apparently the therapy's helping.'

'A brain surgeon who's off his head – that's a good one.'

SINGLE MEN

'And you know his house?'

'Just over there.'

'Well, he says I can move in if I want to!'

'He's after you,' crowed Gabby knowingly. 'It's a certainty.'

'Don't think so. It's only till Mopsy moves up to London – that's what they all do, apparently – or till Guy is ready to come home.'

They were silent for a moment, watching Luke squinting through a toy telescope. Then Gabby said reflectively, 'It is a sad story, isn't it?'

'It is,' Marie agreed. 'First he had a town wife and a country wife, now he's lost them both.'

'Perhaps you should fix him up with Lynda,' said Gabby.

'Don't think so,' said Marie. 'After all, she's got Bobby now.'

Gabby snorted and slapped her thigh. Bobby was a Pekinese puppy. Lynda had bought him – after much consultation with Big and Little Cilla and Luke – from a kennel near Welwyn, and appeared to her daughter to be reconstructing her entire life around him. There were no words to describe Marie's relief. Those thumbnail soap operas that made Amiss household mornings so stressful had had their dramatic sting drawn out of them. They'd turned into a house-pet documentary: Lynda giving Bobby his favourite Cesar dog food on his favourite plate; Lynda tying up Bobby's top knot and brushing Bobby's silky coat; Lynda making Bobby a special bed on her bed, on the sofa, in the kitchen and by the garden shed; Lynda taking Bobby for a morning walk while Luke and Marie used the bathroom. The transformation in Lynda was astounding. Sometimes she went out with no make-up on!

'Is it the menopause?' asked Gabby.

'Could be,' said Marie. In fact, there was a lot more to it than that. Lynda's life had begun to change in a great many ways after Marie had returned home from the graveyard that Sunday. But Marie wasn't ready to Tell All to Gabby yet. It was better keeping mum for the time being.

'And *you*,' said Gabby mock-accusingly, 'are still being mysterious, young lady.'

'Am I?' said Marie. She checked her watch again. It was now just after three. Luke continued to monitor an imaginary seascape. Don't be late, Marie pleaded inwardly.

'Yes, you are,' said Gabby. 'Something's up and you're not saying.'

'Leave me alone! I've just had lots to think about lately . . .'

And this was true. As well as Lynda there had been the realignment of Daniel, Elice and Miss Valencia to adjust to. In theory, this process should have concerned her only marginally: she had prepared the ground for them to start negotiations and so her job had been complete. But each time she had done for Daniel subsequently he had sat her down for ages while his Gaggia fermented, showing her estate agents' hokum and asking her opinion of this maisonette or that loft and the dimensions of the bedrooms and whether the distance of Miss Valencia's prospective dwelling from Marie's home would make travelling there onerous for her.

This mattered because Miss Valencia had insisted – '*Hi* must *hinsist*, *hi have* to, it is *hee-sential* to me!' – that Marie start doing for her too. 'This way, we have connection! This way, we have symbol of unity!' And Daniel was also mindful of Luke. 'He and Elice will still want to be together,' he had assured Marie earnestly, at least seven times an hour.

She was sure he was sincere. She was less sure he was correct. Already she'd noticed Elice relating differently to Luke and herself. The affection was still present but the passion of her interest was waning a little. Elice now had her mother to look after, a more advanced intellectual challenge for a dazzling young woman of the world.

Marie was content to let this happen. Luke too had some new interests, of which Bobby was only one. That said, she was glad of a new client because Marlon no longer needed her. Paradoxically, this had happened because of the good turn she'd done for him.

On the weekend following her momentous trip to Hendon, Marie had been phoned by Elaine Alibhai. The family had done some heart-searching. They had contacted Marlon by phone and convinced him to tell them where he was staying. They'd visited him, full of remorse. The reconciliation had concluded with the parents undertaking to shift the wreckage from the Milman Road flat, preparing the way for Marlon to return. Marie was enlisted to help with the clearance party, and Elaine was there too; also Gabby, who turned up 'just to be nosy'.

It took two hours to empty the living room, leaving only the patisserie-stained pistachio carpet and the videos, DVDs and PlayStation games. They cleaned the flat throughout, except the bedroom which Marie lied about.

'Oh, Marlon must have the key,' she'd said. 'That's a pity.' The truth, of course, was that she had it in her pocket.

She came back and changed the sheets the following morning. The same afternoon, Marlon called her mobile. 'Hello, I am back.'

Marie had leaped on to her bike and cycled straight back to Milman Road to find Marlon sitting cross-legged in the middle of the denuded carpet. He looked morose but calm.

'I am embarrassed by my behaviour,' he told Marie, as if she were his Head Teacher and he had been caught writing on his desk.

'Don't be silly,' she said with feeling.

'And I'm embarrassed by what you know about me.'

'Don't be. It's going to be all right now, honestly.'

'I have a new path to discover,' he'd continued monkishly, 'and many challenges to overcome.'

'You'll do it,' she'd promised him, but her conviction was faltering. The enlightening of his family, the satisfaction had from slinging his ruined furnishings into a skip, had been cathartic for Marie. Yet now she

SINGLE MEN

had seen that what for her was part of a larger ending to a troubled phase of her life was for Marlon a daunting new beginning. Buying a new telly would be the least of it.

He'd looked up at her solemnly and cleared his throat. 'Your new haircut, by the way, is very stylish.'

'Thank you, Marlon. I like it too.' She also liked her new blue top, her new baggy khakis and her new suede shoes. She'd asked Luke's friend Milo's mum for a few tips: it had been time, she'd decided, for her wardrobe to grow up.

'Er, Marie?' Marlon had continued, getting to his feet.

The 'er' had alarmed her slightly, a reminder of the Marlon she'd encountered in the past.

'A friend of yours, I think, helped with the clear-up,' he said.

'Oh. Yes. Gabby. Gabrielle.'

'I feel I ought to thank her. Regrettably, I don't know how to contact her.'

'I'll give you her number,' Marie had said, relieved enough not to have thought twice. 'Here, I'll write it down.'

Back in the present, it was eight minutes past three.

'Where's he got to?' asked Gabby. 'I'm getting twitchy.'

'Me too,' admitted Marie, though she meant it in a different way. Keeping her voice cheery she hailed Luke: 'Anything on the horizon, Cap'n?'

Her levity was not reciprocated. Luke let his shoulders slump theatrically. He shook his head. Climbing to her feet, Marie scanned the human tides: there was the usual weekend mixture of dog-walkers, romancers and sunbathers, half a dozen games of football going on and families carrying on as families do. She had no idea which direction he'd come from – and when, at last, she spotted him, he was already quite near.

'He's coming, Gabs.'

'Where?'

Marie lifted a hand in greeting towards the approaching man. He returned it and Gabby said, 'Time I was leaving.' She adjusted her suntop and got up. 'Good luck,' she told Marie and kissed her on the cheek. Then, pausing only to wave fondly at Luke, she struck out across the grass towards Milman Road where Marlon was ready for her. She wouldn't need to ring the bell. As Marie had noted earlier, she'd only known him a fortnight and already she had her own key – 'almost as quick as me'.

By now, Luke had spotted the man too. He watched him as he joined his mother and they exchanged civilities. It was the man he'd been looking for through his telescope, and now he saw him, he remembered more clearly. Perhaps he'd go and say hello. He carefully dismounted the bandstand steps and walked towards the grown-ups slowly.

'Hello, Luke,' said the man.

'Hello.'

'Come over here then,' said his mother encouragingly. 'Rick hasn't got all day.'

CHAPTER TWENTY-FOUR

Mid-September...

'Do you remember Glen? From our camping holiday?'

'No.'

'He was the football teacher.'

'No.'

'Yes, you do! He took you on the zipline – that scary wire you slid down that went across a lake.'

'No.' Luke put on his 'who, me?' face.

'You're hopeless, Luke!' said Marie. 'Does Big Cilla remember?'

Luke asked her. 'No.'

'Little Cilla?'

This time there was a longer consultation. 'Little Cilla says "woof".'

'I'm sure you'll remember him when you see him.' Marie checked her watch. 'Shall we put your things away, Luke? We're nearly there.'

'Where?'

'At the seaside!'

'Why?'

'Don't start that again, please.'

Luke gave this some thought. A train carriage was quite a good place for being naughty in. Your mummy couldn't get really, really cross with you because of the other people, like in graveyards and shops. On the other hand, being good – which he had been so far – had produced rewards. He'd been allowed to pretend to be a scary tiger – a quiet scary tiger, but you couldn't have everything – and choose a chocolate biscuit from the refreshment trolley. Best of all, Mummy had done his magic trick with him.

'Which cup is the fluffy ball under, Mummy?'

'Let me see . . . the middle one. It must be.'

'Shall we look?'

'Ooh, yes please!'

'It's not the middle one! It's number three!'

And Mummy had shaken her head and looked perplexed and said, 'How *do* you do that? It must be magic!'

She'd got it wrong every time! Poor Mummy. She didn't know it was a trick.

The trick made Luke extremely happy. It had a special name: Rick's Trick. This rhymed! Mummy had said this was a good thing to call it because that way he'd remember who'd given it to him. And Luke did remember. His real name was Richard and he was actually his daddy, though he wasn't married to Mummy and he wasn't going to live in their house. 'Funny!' Luke had said when

Mummy explained this, and he'd frowned and made himself go cross-eyed in the usual way.

But 'Funny!' had been just something to say. Rick was very nice. He'd given Luke the cups-and-fluffy ball trick when he'd met him and Marie in the park. In fact, he'd given him a whole box of conjurer's tricks and said it was his birthday present and he was very sorry it was late. And Rick had shown him how to do the Rick Trick because it was the easiest, and he'd promised to show him how to do the harder ones another day. And they'd played football by the bandstand, and Luke had suspected that Rick had let some of his shots in on purpose, but that was all right because grown-ups sometimes did that to be kind.

Luke decided not to play the 'Why' game any more, as his mother wished. 'OK, Mummy,' he said. It was in his moany voice, but for pretend.

'Thank you, Luke,' said Marie. 'You are being a very good boy.' She blew him a kiss and looked into his eyes.

Was he upset?

Was he confused?

Was she doing the right thing?

Certainly, he seemed to be OK. He'd started in Year One with his brand new teacher Kathy in a class with many children who were new to him too, yet he'd taken the transition in his stride. If anything, he'd seemed calmer lately. Perhaps that was because parents sometimes worried about children unnecessarily. Or perhaps it was because the way they dealt with Luke was one of the things Marie and Lynda had sorted out. There had been no neopets in the Sugar Puffs lately, and a little less of *Cartoon Network* too.

Not that everything was rosy in the garden just yet. But there were buds of encouragement. Marie's decision to reach out to Rick had been made at the graveyard the day she'd forgiven Clay and had been welcomed by her mother as – presumably along with the arrival of Bobby – 'the best thing to come out of all this'. Their subsequent meeting had gone well. In a small Italian restaurant near his office in Holborn, Rick had brought Marie up to date about his management ambitions, his cookery evening classes and the little house he'd bought in Cricklewood where he was happy enough to be a bachelor for the time being. Then he'd got very serious and promised Marie he didn't want to fight her over Luke. But he did want to see him, to help him, to know him, desperately.

Marie had smiled and said, 'OK.'

The carriage tannoy announced that the train would soon be at its destination. Marie helped Luke shove his stuff into his little drawstring bag, insisting that the Cillas went in first: the thought of them falling out and being lost for ever made her shudder at the best of times, and for it to happen on this of all outings would have been too much to bear. Then she gathered up the A-level prospectuses she'd been reading. Outside the window a platform slid by. Marie scanned it but failed to spot the face she longed to see.

The train drew to a halt. Marie climbed down first, then turned to help Luke off. As she took his weight, she felt a presence behind her. She turned with Luke still in her arms.

'Hello, Luke,' said Glen. 'Remember me?'

On Marine Parade Glen gazed out and all around at gardens, funfairs, the far horizon, Great Yarmouth's two famous piers, the two hundred acres of sand. There was a lot to take in. A quick summary wouldn't hurt.

'So the sad one is going to marry your friend Gabby . . .'

'In a couple of weeks, yes.'

'Amazing,' said Glen.

'Isn't it? And just as well 'cos it means she won't be getting her hands on you.'

They laughed and held each other. The more he enfolded her, the less breakable Marie felt.

'And the mad one has run away . . .'

'From his ex-wife and his PA. Still, his kids are hoping that life near Lake Michigan is making him more sane.'

'And the gay one?'

'Doing flamenco dancing.'

'Not bad for a single summer,' concluded Glen.

On the beach Luke was digging with one of the few bucket-and-spade sets still on sale. High season was quickly gone. It was time for the introspection of autumn; for looking back before the winter and then for moving on.

'There's more, though,' said Marie.

'What a life you've been leading while my back's been turned. New haircut and everything!'

'It's about my mum and dad.'

Marie had prepared for this moment: not rehearsed it, exactly, but waited for it steadfastly, knowing she wanted Glen to be the first she told. He sensed something momentous and took her arm. 'Go on.'

'My dad had a secret. He had another wife, and another child.'

'What, before he met your mum?'

'Yes. But also at the same time.'

She watched as the penny dropped in Glen. 'So when he married your mother, he was still married to his first wife?'

'Yes. He was a bigamist.'

'And there was a kid too?'

'A daughter called Stephanie. He ran out on her when she was a baby: left her, left her mum and disappeared to London. They didn't know where he'd gone and maybe no one else did either. Neither of them ever saw him again.'

'And your mum didn't know?'

'Didn't know a thing about it till after he was dead. That's because Stephanie tracked him down – all the way to our house. It was tragic. She found him a bit too late. He'd died four months earlier.'

'That is incredible. So . . .' This was all too . . . big. Glen didn't know where to begin. 'So . . . where's the daughter now?'

'Back in the north-east, where she was born – like him. Her mother's still there too. I've got Stephanie's address.'

The more Glen got to grips, the more questions he

had. Marie did her best for him. First, she took him through how she made the discovery: the sleepless night and the Bonnie Tyler album; the visit to Auntie Barbara; Auntie Barbara's sadness mixed with relief. 'She was ready for it in a way; she'd been ready for eight years. But you could tell it was still a shock. And with me finding out, she was even more worried about my mum. That's even though she'd been getting on at Mum for years to tell me everything. They were always arguing about it.' She laughed. 'I never did understand what all those tiffs were about. She's very laid back, my Auntie Barbara. I don't think I've ever seen her so distressed.'

'So this Stephanie. How did she find your dad?'

'Apparently, it wasn't all that difficult once she got started. It seems like the hardest thing was deciding to do it at all. You'd be nervous, wouldn't you, about what you might find? Anyway, she had a hunch. It was obvious if he wanted to disappear he'd probably be using a false name – surname anyway. She wondered what surname he might be using. Would he pick one at random or would he choose one that had some meaning for him? So, just to see, she tried looking for people called Amiss, 'cos that was his mother's maiden name.'

'And suddenly a light came on?'

'Yes. Under heating engineers. That was the job he had when he was up north. So she found this company in the London *Yellow Pages*. C. Amiss, that's all it said. But it wasn't hard to find out the C was for Clayton. She just rang him up and got his voicemail: "Hello, this is Clayton Amiss, please leave a message" or whatever. He still had a bit of the accent and, you know, you don't get too many Claytons, do you?'

'Very true.'

'So she hired a sort of family history detective. He looked through all the records, all the databases, and he made a few sneaky phone calls pretending to be someone else so he could get more information. Anyway, pretty soon Stephanie was sure it was him – Clayton Daines as he had been. But there was only one way to be certain, and that was to go and see him. So she did. Or tried to.'

'She got your mum instead.'

'Yes. And Auntie Barbara. She'd gone round to see Mum, who was still grieving, of course. I was out – at Gabby's, probably. So the way Barbara tells it they were sitting, talking. It was the November of that year, in the evening, and there was this knock at the door. Barbara says she remembers it vividly. My mum went to answer it, and there's this young woman standing there. She's about the age I am now. She says, "I've come to see Clayton." Well, you can imagine . . .'

'Yeah,' said Glen. 'Clayton's dead. But that's not the end of it.'

'No. It's just the beginning.'

Marie told Glen the story of that evening as Barbara had told it to her: Lynda, on the doorstep, not knowing who this woman was, except there was something about her; Stephanie insisting she had to come in. Then Barbara had gone to the door too, and found Stephanie already in tears and saying, 'I'm sorry, but I'm his daughter.'

SINGLE MEN

'So then they had to let her in,' said Marie. 'And she took them through the whole story, everything.'

The story had gone like this: Clay, a young plumber aged nineteen, had been seeing a local girl called Jean. She'd fallen pregnant by him. It was the mid-1970s, but the old stigmas were still strong, especially outside the cities. Jean hadn't wanted an abortion: she was scared and it had got late. So Clay had done the decent thing, the expected thing, and married Jean before the child was born. But he was restless and he was bitter. He thought she should have got rid of it. He blamed her for getting pregnant in the first place, because he'd thought she'd taken care of everything. He'd bolted when Stephanie was six months old.

'What a terrible shock for your mum,' said Glen. He was holding Marie tight. She was thankful, and also thinking about Luke and Rick.

She said, 'It was a shock all right, but she wouldn't believe all of it. She had to believe Stephanie was who she said she was because the facts were all there – in the papers I found – and Barbara says the more you looked at her, the more she looked like Clay. But, of course, Stephanie had got all this from her mother. And Mum just wouldn't have it that Clay had done such a thing without a good reason. Well, there's always two sides to these stories. But even then it was, like, she couldn't stand to think there was anything bad about him. She told Stephanie where the grave was, but she said she didn't want to talk to her about him. She told her she was sorry but she didn't want to see her again.'

'So Stephanie went back home.'

'That's right. With all her unanswered questions.'

Glen stood up and stretched, and walked around. He spied on Luke, and was extra careful not to let Luke see him doing it. He and Marie needed a few more minutes. He sat back down. 'What about his family, then? Did they know where he'd gone?'

'Well,' said Marie, 'he was an only child, so there was only his parents really. Stephanie told my mum and Barbara that she'd been told they'd moved away about a year after Clay disappeared. I suppose they were under pressure to find him, from Stephanie's mum and her family and everything. If you think about it, that's how it would be, isn't it, especially in a small community.'

'They might not have known anything,' said Glen. 'He could have kept in touch with them without telling them anything, or giving them a way to get in touch with him. I suppose it was easier to hide from people in those days. And he might have been worried that his parents would give him away if they knew anything.'

Marie stroked his cheek and said, 'All I know is they ended up in Brightlingsea. We hardly ever saw them. You can understand it. They were keeping his secret, weren't they? They had to keep on keeping it, even after his funeral. I don't think Lynda's hardly heard from them since. They're quite elderly now. They could have died and us not know it.'

'Crazy, isn't it,' said Glen. 'What must they have been feeling all these years?'

'That's what I said to Auntie Barbara. They had one

SINGLE MEN

granddaughter they hadn't seen since she was tiny, and another one – me – who they were probably half-scared to see. No wonder they didn't spend much time with us. They'd probably have been terrified of saying something. Clay was always on edge with them. Now I can see why.'

It was a bleak thought. Marie went quiet. Glen let her be, then asked, 'Who told your mum that you'd found out about it?'

'I did.'

'How was she?'

'Pretty devastated.' Marie would never forget that Sunday evening, Lynda's shock, sorrow and rage. Suppressed emotions: the full range.

Glen was thoughtful. He said delicately, 'Tell me if I'm being daft, but devastated in what way? I mean, she already knew, didn't she? So . . .'

'It was because she'd have to stop pretending about him – at least to me. She said she'd never told me 'cos she wanted to protect me – and I do believe her. But she was protecting herself too. She didn't want to face the truth about Clay. Think about it: she'd worshipped him and all the time he'd been keeping this big secret. Telling this big lie. It's a hard thing to handle. That's why it's always suited her to keep carrying on as if he was this perfect husband who she'll never get over losing. I think it's been easier for her that way.'

'Not so easy now, though.'

'That's right. But on the other hand, I'd never believed all that Mr Wonderful stuff anyway.'

'You didn't really like him, did you?'

'I did when I was little. He was this fun guy, you see, always laughing and clowning around. But he went off me when I was a teenager.'

Glen laughed. 'A lot of parents go off their kids when they're teenagers!'

'Yes, but I had the definite feeling he really didn't like me any more. He didn't approve of me. I wasn't wild or anything, not a bit. But anything to do with fashion, going out, boys . . . he could get quite nasty.'

'Wonder why that was.'

'I don't know. I don't think he liked the idea of women doing their own thing, being too independent. I think he found it threatening. That's why he liked Lynda.'

'He did like her, did he?'

'Yes, I think he did. And that's the other side of it. For all it got on my nerves how Lynda couldn't get over him, I think he was really good to her in his own way. He used to spoil her. Nice presents. All that D.I.Y. And she did like all that. So they suited each other.'

Glen said, 'Why didn't they have more children?'

'Good question.'

'What's the answer?'

'I don't know.'

They speculated. Was it a biology thing, a Lynda thing or, more likely, a Clay thing? Maybe children spelled trouble to him. Marie knew she'd ask her mother one day. But for now, she thought, Lynda would be keeping that one to herself.

*

SINGLE MEN

Luke continued keeping himself busy on the beach: moats to dig, castles to build, perfectly good socks to fill with sand. The grown-ups, though, were getting cold. The sun was sinking. Night mood was setting in.

'What shall we do now then?' asked Glen. 'Eat, drink, play slot machines, introduce you to my mum and dad again?'

Marie and Glen had lunched with Glen's parents – Mr and Mrs Lawrence – at their café. They were warm, welcoming people and Marie would have been happy to spend more time with them. Glen's big sister had made an appearance too.

'Marie, meet Alexandra.'

'Hello, Marie.'

'Hello.'

'What's he been saying about me?'

'That you tell him everything.'

'Everything but what he needs to know.'

Of course, the thing on both their minds was where they'd share a bed – a *proper* bed – for the first time. The family hotel was one possibility – 'they're very broad-minded,' said Glen – but, by definition, it lacked the perfect privacy they wanted.

'There are other hotels,' said Glen. 'Dozens of them.'

But Marie's mind was working another way. 'We could go back to London and see Marlon and Gabby.'

'Sounds good.'

'And you could meet Lynda tomorrow.'

'An honour!'

'We couldn't stay there, though. Lynda might disapprove. And anyway, it would be too strange.'

'Where could we stay then?'

'Did I tell you that Guy told me I could live in his house if I wanted?'

'Did he?'

'Yes. We could stay there. I've got the key.'

'Forward planning!' said Glen.

'Almost army training! What do you think?'

'What, you and me in a big double bed in an elegant house beside a beautiful park with little Luke asleep in the room next door? Nah, don't fancy it.'

'Me neither.'

'Fair enough. Shall we go by train or car?'

CHAPTER TWENTY-FIVE

Two months later . . .

At the age of five-and-a-quarter Luke Amiss was as eager as ever to learn about his family's life and times.

'Mummy?' he said, yawning.

'Oh Luke, don't you ever get tired?'

'No. I didn't go to sleep last night.'

'You looked asleep to me.'

'I was pretending.'

'Oh I see.'

'Mummy?'

'Yes?'

'Why don't we live with Lynda any more?'

Mid-November and the evenings had closed in. It was eight fifty-three and no light seeped through the curtains of Luke's bedroom in Guy's house. The carousel bedside light projected morphing silhouettes: elephants, dolphins, lions. Big Cilla and Little Cilla snuggled at Luke's side. Little Cilla remained the smaller of the two.

Marie hoped tiredness would finish its work on Luke soon because at this rate it would finish it on her. She could hear Glen pottering downstairs and wanted to sit with him by the fire for a while before getting an early night. Tomorrow, she had work to do. Monday was still Daniel's day.

'Mummy?'

'Yes?'

'Why?'

Marie knew she should be patient. The reason for the move to Kingswood Avenue had been explained to Luke several times, but the fate of his grandmother continued to puzzle him.

'Lynda is my mummy, isn't she?' said Marie. 'It's normal for someone's children to find their own place to live when they're grown up, like me. Especially when they have a boyfriend or girlfriend or a husband or a wife they want to share with, like I have Glen. So Lynda understands. She doesn't mind that we've gone.'

'She misses me, though.'

'I know.'

'She says so.'

'I know.' She says so too often, thought Marie. That's Lynda for you.

'But Luke,' Marie went on, 'we're not far away, are we? What if we'd moved to Scotland?'

'At least it would have been in England,' grumbled Luke. 'Not like here.'

Marie had a short coughing fit. Then she said, 'But it's better for Lynda now in some ways, isn't it?'

'How?'

'Well, she can stay in the bathroom for as long as she wants.'

Luke looked puzzled.

'OK, bad example,' said Marie. 'What I mean is, she can lead her own life more without having us to worry about. And she's got Bobby, hasn't she?'

'Yeah! Bobby!'

'She *loves* Bobby, doesn't she?'

'Yes.' Luke relaxed a bit. Mention of Bobby always had a soothing effect.

Marie waited. She could hear the kettle being filled downstairs.

'Mummy?' said Luke.

'Yes, Luke?'

'Isn't it I've got two daddies?'

'Sort of, yes.'

'Who's my *real* daddy?'

'Well, Rick is your real daddy, I suppose.'

'Why "I suppose".'

'He was the one who helped make you.'

'How?'

'Oh Luke.'

He knew perfectly well how. There again, even Marie still found it a bit unbelievable. Marie said, 'Do you like Rick?'

'Yes.'

He'd seen him five or six times now. One of the times he'd been to the pictures with Rick and no one else. Rick, who was a junior manager now, had opened a savings account for him. Like he'd said, he'd grown up a bit.

'And you like Glen too, don't you?'

'Yeah, *yeah*.' Luke said this in his *bo-ring* voice, meaning isn't it obvious and how many more times and do we *really* have to go through this again? Of *course* he liked Glen: Glen looked after him!

Marie bent to Luke's head and kissed him. 'Time for sleeping. You want to grow up big and strong, don't you?'

Luke said nothing. His eyelids were drooping. But they weren't quite closed.

'And Mummy?'

'Yes, what is it now?'

'Gabby's having a baby.'

'I know she is,' said Marie. It was due in the spring, exactly nine months after the marriage to Marlon: all very Reverend Gary and, in a different way, sort of a virgin birth.

'And Mummy?'

'Yes?'

'Isn't it Marlon goes to Elice's house?'

'One of her houses, yes. Her new one.'

'Why?'

' 'Cos he's making it lovely for her mummy. He and a man called Monty.'

'Why?'

'Because it's a nice house but very old and tatty and Marlon is making it beautiful again. And when he's finished doing that, I'll be going there sometimes. To keep it clean.'

'And Mummy?'

'Luke, this has to be the last question.'

'Who was that lady we went to see?'

It had happened a week ago. They'd driven all the way up on the Saturday morning, arriving late lunchtime. The village was small and out of the way, but not difficult to find. The house was in the little terrace. You couldn't miss it, as Stephanie had said when they'd spoken on the phone. Glen and Luke stayed in the car at first. This was Marie's moment, after all.

It had been a cold, wet day but Stephanie, spotting their arrival from the front window where she'd been sitting waiting, had rushed out and down the path to meet her. Later, after they'd all wrapped up and gone out for a long, windy walk on the beach, she and Marie had sat in the kitchen and studied each other's faces and talked while Luke and Glen had dozed in front of the telly. There had been so much ground to cover, and so much still remained.

There were decisions to be made. What should Stephanie tell her mother, who'd moved to Darlington and knew nothing except that she was a free woman, now that Clayton Daines was dead. She might prefer not knowing the rest. And then there was Lynda, who'd not been very comfortable about this journey into the past up north. Marie hoped she'd warm to meeting Stephanie again. The great irony was that for all she hadn't known about his first daughter and his first wife, Lynda had still known Clay the best of all.

'Mummy?'

'Luke, Luke, Luke . . .'

'What will happen?'

'What do you mean, what will happen?'

'What will happen next?'

He loved the 'what will happen next' story. Marie told it to him again.

'Well, Gabby is going have a baby.'

'I've said that already.'

'And then she's going to work in a hotel.'

'Why?'

'Because it's better than working in a tanning studio. And she's going to learn how a hotel works and be in charge of one, some day.'

'And?'

'And Glen is going to open a café near Elice's school and Elice is going to go there for her fizzy drinks and buns.'

'And?'

'And I'm going to clean Daniel's house and Elice's mum Esmerelda's house. But not this house – that's Glen's job.'

'And?'

'And I'm going to do my A levels and work in the café.'

'And?'

'And Guy is going to come back in the spring.'

'Guy is a big poo.'

'No, he isn't. And we are going to move out of his house.'

'And?'

'Aren't you bored with this yet?'

'No. The best bit's at the end.'

'And after Marlon has finished making Elice's new house beautiful, he's going to do the same for ours. The old house in Kilburn he's helping us to buy.'

'And . . . ?' Luke yawned.

'And Daniel is going to help us find lovely things to go in it. Won't that be great?'

'Yes.'

'Is that the end now, Luke?'

'Not quite.'

'Oh?'

'And will you and Glen get married?'

'Maybe. When we have time.'

'And will you have another baby?'

'Maybe. I hope so. Would that be nice?'

But Luke Amiss didn't answer. A great future awaited him: in football, perhaps, or show business, and he needed his beauty sleep.

You can buy any of these other titles
from your bookshop or *direct from the publisher*.

FREE P&P AND UK DELIVERY
(Overseas and Ireland £3.50 per book)

Sorting out Billy	Jo Brand	£6.99
Man Alive	Dave Hill	£6.99
The Distance Between Us	Maggie O'Farrell	£7.99
The Secret Life of Bees	Sue Monk Kidd	£7.99
Driving Big Davie	Colin Bateman	£6.99
Jenny and the Jaws of Life	Jincy Willett	£7.99
Havoc, in its Third Year	Ronan Bennett	£7.99
Shake	Yvonne Roberts	£7.99
Two of Us	Brendan Halpin	£7.99
The Bad News Bible	Anna Blundy	£6.99
Sitting Practice	Caroline Adderson	£6.99
Small Island	Andrea Levy	£7.99
Dancing in a Distant Place	Isla Dewar	£7.99
Despite the Falling Snow	Shamim Sarif	£6.99
Green Grass	Raffaella Barker	£6.99
The Haven Home for Delinquent Girls	Louise Tondeur	£7.99
The Mountain of Light	Clare Allen	£7.99
Ghost Music	Candida Clark	£7.99

TO ORDER SIMPLY CALL THIS NUMBER

01235 400 414

or visit our website: www.madaboutbooks.com

Prices and availability subject to change without notice.